"[A] dizzying flurry of twists and turns in a plot as intricate as a Swiss watch . . . Ragan's warrior women are on fire, fueled by howling levels of personal pain."

—*Sactown Magazine*

"A heart-stopping read. Ragan's compelling blend of strained family ties and small-town secrets will keep you racing to the end!"

—Lisa Gardner, *New York Times* bestselling author of *When You See Me*

"An exciting start to a new series with a feisty and unforgettable heroine in Sawyer Brooks. Just when you think you've figured out the dark secrets of River Rock, T.R. Ragan hits you with another sucker punch."

—Lisa Gray, bestselling author of *Thin Air*

"Fans of Lizzy Gardner, Faith McMann, and Jessie Cole are in for a real treat with T.R. Ragan's *Don't Make a Sound*, the start of a brand-new series that features tenacious crime reporter Sawyer Brooks, whose own past could be her biggest story yet. Ragan once more delivers on her trademark action, pacing, and twists."

—Loreth Anne White, bestselling author of *In the Dark*

"T.R. Ragan takes the revenge thriller to the next level in the gritty and chillingly realistic *Don't Make a Sound*. Ragan masterfully crafts one unexpected twist after another until the shocking finale."

—Steven Konkoly, bestselling author of *The Rescue*

"T.R. Ragan delivers in her new thrilling series. *Don't Make a Sound* introduces crime reporter Sawyer Brooks, a complex and compelling heroine determined to stop a killer as murders in her past and present collide."

—Melinda Leigh, #1 *Wall Street Journal* bestselling author

Her Last Day

"Intricately plotted . . . The tense plot builds to a startling and satisfying resolution."

—*Publishers Weekly* (starred review)

"Ragan's newest novel is exciting and intriguing from the very beginning . . . Readers will race to finish the book, wanting to know the outcome and see justice served."

—*RT Book Reviews*

"*Her Last Day* is a fast-moving thriller about a woman seeking answers and the man determined to help her find them."

—*New York Journal of Books*

"If you like serial-killer thrillers that genuinely thrill and have plenty of depth, now's the time to discover Jessie Cole and T.R. Ragan. Dare you not to read this one in one sitting!"

—Criminal Element

"T.R. Ragan provides a complicated mystery with plenty of atmosphere, gore, and dead bodies to satisfy readers. This is not a cozy, but a hardcore mystery with a variety of victims, an egotistical killer, and a high-powered ending."

—*Gumshoe Review*

"[*Her Last Day*] hooks you instantaneously; it's fast and furious with a pace that never lets up for one minute."

—*Novelgossip*

"Readers will obsess over T.R. Ragan's new, tenacious heroine. I can't wait for the next in the series!"
—Kendra Elliot, author of *Wall Street Journal* bestsellers *Spiraled* and *Targeted*

"With action-packed twists and turns and a pace that doesn't let up until the thrilling conclusion, *Her Last Day* is a brilliant start to a gripping new series from T.R. Ragan."
—Robert Bryndza, #1 international bestselling author of *The Girl in the Ice*

BEST
HOUSE
ON THE
BLOCK

Other Titles by T.R. Ragan

Stand-Alone Novels

Such a Beautiful Family

Count to Three

Sawyer Brooks Series

Don't Make a Sound

Out of Her Mind

No Going Back

Jessie Cole Series

Her Last Day

Deadly Recall

Deranged

Buried Deep

Faith McMann Trilogy

Furious

Outrage

Wrath

Lizzy Gardner Series

Abducted

Dead Weight

A Dark Mind

Obsessed

Almost Dead

Evil Never Dies

Writing as Theresa Ragan

Return of the Rose

A Knight in Central Park

Taming Mad Max

Finding Kate Huntley

Having My Baby

An Offer He Can't Refuse

Here Comes the Bride

I Will Wait for You (a novella)

Dead Man Running

BEST
HOUSE
ON THE
BLOCK

A THRILLER

T.R. RAGAN

THOMAS & MERCER

Published by Thomas & Mercer, Seattle

www.apub.com

Amazon, the Amazon logo, and Thomas & Mercer are trademarks of Amazon.com, Inc., or its affiliates.

ISBN-13: 9781662517303 (paperback)
ISBN-13: 9781662517310 (digital)

Cover design by Caroline Teagle Johnson
Cover image: © Ali Harper / Stocksy; © Helen King / Getty

Printed in the United States of America

BEST
HOUSE
ON THE
BLOCK

NOTE FROM THE AUTHOR
Don't Ever Give Up on Your Dreams!

When I set out to write my first novel more than thirty years ago, my goal was to someday see my book on the shelves at a brick-and-mortar bookstore. My first novel, *Return of the Rose*, took me five years to research and write. I enrolled in creative writing classes, joined my local chapter of Romance Writers of America, critiqued with other authors, and went to every workshop possible while raising four children. I wrote in the car, in the bedroom, in the dining room, late at night, and early in the morning. I kept a recorder in my nightstand in case I awoke with an idea for a scene. I read every night and I still do. I sent proposals to agents and editors, cried when I read the rejections, and jumped out of my seat every time the phone rang.

I haven't seen one of my books in a bookstore yet. (It still could happen!) But that's okay because bigger dreams awaited me. My stories have allowed me to connect with literary agents, editors, and millions of readers—people who appreciate my vision, understand my characters, and continue to ask for more.

Writing fiction is not for the faint of heart. Dreams take passion, hard work, determination, and an unwavering belief in yourself.

Never stop believing. You can do it!

PROLOGUE

Behind the wheel of his silver Toyota Highlander, he sank into the seat, feeling meh about his job and life in general. The car's brakes squealed as he came to a stop. The glare of the sun piercing through the windshield didn't help his headache, the lingering effect from drinking too much wine last night. He and his wife had often talked about cutting back on their alcohol consumption, even quitting altogether, but it was just that—talk. Even as the rich, oaky flavors swirled around his tongue, he'd known they would never do it. Wine was one of the few things in life that helped to make the world tolerable.

It was lunchtime. Tired of eating at his desk, he had decided to run an errand, one of many on a never-ending list. He would grab a burger and eat in the car. As he drove toward town, he made a sudden right turn, hoping that the brief detour might shake things up enough to jolt him out of the rut it felt he'd been in lately. He inwardly laughed at how stupid the idea was. Basically, his "detour" was the short path to town, taking him through a less than desirable neighborhood. He'd been this way before. The abandoned street was littered with more grocery carts than cars. Nothing moved but a swirl of crumpled papers and plastic.

He blinked twice and nearly slammed on his brakes when he saw a toddler wobble out of a neglected, one-story house—a run-down structure with two broken windows and what looked like a bedsheet serving as a curtain inside. The kid teetered across the weed-choked lawn and headed for the street.

Panicked for the kid's safety, he pulled to the curb before the child reached it. He looked over his shoulder, sure someone would run out their front door at any moment. But nobody came. The toddler had curly hair, was one or two years of age, he guessed. Boy or girl? He wasn't sure. For some reason, he leaned toward boy.

The beat of his heart felt like a drumroll inside his chest as he glanced in the rearview mirror, then left to right. Nobody was around. He kept waiting for a harried parent or babysitter to shout from some distant nook or cranny, but that didn't happen.

What should I do? His hands shook as he opened the center console, reached into one of two brown bags, and grabbed a lollipop, a cherry one. He opened the door right as the kid ran past, climbed out, and said, "Hey there. What are you doing?"

The child looked over his shoulder at him, giggling as if this were a game, and kept moving.

"I have candy! Want a lollipop?"

The kid stopped, looked his way again, his eyes locking on the lollipop.

"It's yours if you want it." His heart was beating so fast he was sure it would explode. If the kid had continued in the direction he'd been going, a car could have hit him. Or worse, someone with bad intentions might have scooped him right up. As he waggled the lollipop, he glanced about at all the houses with windows he couldn't see through. "You don't want it? Should I give it to another kid?"

The child turned away as if going over his options, then pivoted and headed straight for him. The kid was so damn cute. From the looks of things, judging by the hand movements and the trouble he seemed to have with balance and shifting his weight, he had been walking for only a few months. Hardly over a year old? His adrenaline spiked as the toddler wobbled closer, almost within reach.

He didn't think, merely acted. He grabbed the kid and jumped into his car. Snug behind the steering wheel with the kid on his lap, and without another look around, he drove off.

The child squirmed in his arms but hardly made a peep.

Making sure to follow the speed limit, keeping his eyes on the road despite having an awkward hold of the child in his lap, he made a right at the stop sign. A few blocks later, he made a left. Upon reaching a deserted field of dead grass less than a mile from the entrance to the freeway, he pulled to the side, gravel pinging off the undercarriage as he came to a stop. He peered down and to the right as the kid looked up at him. The smile on the child's face made something crack inside him. The corners of his mouth softened. His heart melted. The kid wasn't afraid. Not one bit.

"Let's put you over here, where I can buckle you in safely." He lifted the child and set him gently on the passenger seat. The smell hit him like a tidal wave crashing against the shore—a soggy, poopy diaper. After snapping the child's seat belt in place, he unwrapped the lollipop and handed it over. It was too big for him to choke on. The child was content; no reason to bother with the chloroform hidden away in the center console.

He took a long, deep breath. He'd done it. And yet it wasn't over, not by a long shot. How long until the missing kid was all over the news? *Shit.* He needed to get going. What was he thinking, sitting here for so long? Another quick peek at the child brought a wave of new worries. It was illegal to have a small child in the front seat, wasn't it? And without a safety seat, to boot. He needed to get home. Quickly. The freeway would be faster, but the thought of taking that route frightened him. More cameras. More policemen. Right? All those vehicles with drivers. No, he would avoid the freeway and take the longer route home.

What had he done? He'd been on his way to grab a burger and run a few errands, and now this. Everything was happening too fast.

Fifteen harrowing minutes later, the adrenaline pumping through his veins finally started to slow as the garage door rattled downward and clanked against the ground, shutting out the sunlight and the fear of being caught in the act of wrongdoing. He sat motionless in the semidark, his fingers still clamped tight around the steering wheel. Was what he'd done criminal? No. Whoever was watching over the child, letting the toddler wander off into the unknown . . . *They* were the criminal.

As he worked on convincing himself he'd done nothing wrong, his breathing continued to slow and his palms finally stopped sweating.

The moment felt surreal. It was hard to believe he had done it.

"Gammy?" came a tiny voice from the passenger seat.

He looked at the child with the chubby cheeks covered with sticky goo from the lollipop and found himself mesmerized by how perfect he or she was, horrible poopy smell and all. "You and I," he said to the kid, "are going to have a wonderful life together."

The kid's toothy smile caused his chest to swell with something he hadn't felt in ages: Hope. Happiness. A chance for new beginnings.

As a kaleidoscope of thoughts swirled around inside his head, he zeroed in on the kid's teeth. He had lots of them. At least eight. Maybe more. After Oliver was born, they had spent every day obsessing over firsts: First step. First tooth. First Christmas. Oliver had died from leukemia before his first birthday.

A tear slid down the side of his face at the thought of his baby boy. They'd never ever wanted to replace Oliver. In fact, he was irreplaceable, and yet he and his wife had always planned on having lots of kids. But it wasn't to be. They'd tried everything—OI, IUI, IVF. Nothing had worked. Not even adoption, since their application was denied after discovering he'd failed to list a past bankruptcy. When he tried to explain that it had happened a long time ago and their finances had been healthy for many years, they told him it wasn't about money but about being honest. In the end, he lost the battle. As far as he was concerned, those agencies were depriving parentless children of willing parents. The system was criminal. He'd fallen into a deep depression until one day, while showering, he got an idea. He began thinking—obsessing—over finding a child to bring home.

When he told his wife about his idea, he regretted it instantly. The shame he saw in her eyes was so humiliating he dropped the idea. Months later, unexpectedly, she asked him about his plan to find them a child, only this time she wanted details. Knowing it might be his only chance to sway her, he talked until he was blue in the face, promising her he would find a child in need, convincing her the child would be better off with parents who cared so much. They both knew they would be loving, attentive parents who would be able to give their son or daughter anything he or she needed. And that was that. Her nod spoke louder than words. *Do it.* She was ready.

And so began his search.

Every day he ate his lunch at parks and schools—anywhere small children sometimes wandered off. That was nearly two years ago. Somewhere along the way, his plan took a back seat to his rapidly increasing workload at the office. And thus, finding a child had been the furthest thing from his mind today as he drove to town to pick up the suit his wife had dropped off at the dry cleaner's last week.

"Come on," he said as he unsnapped their seat belts. "Let's get you cleaned up."

"Gammy?"

"Toys," he said happily as if he hadn't heard what the child said. "We have lots of toys inside. You're going to be a very happy kid. I promise. Welcome home."

CHAPTER ONE

Four Years Later

Sixty-five-year-old Rosella Marlow made her way up the long, curved staircase that began in the center of the foyer and ended on the second floor of her stately Victorian home, the most coveted house in the area, winner of the Best House on the Block award in 2018 and again in 2022. Last year, though, the award had gone to Chloe and Wesley Leavitt, whose house was across the street, sending shock waves through the neighborhood. At least, that's how Rosella saw it. The Fabulous Forties district in Sacramento, California, an area so named because of the numbered avenues it occupied—Fortieth through Forty-Ninth, between J Street and Folsom Boulevard—was known for its architecture, an ensemble of Tudor homes with ivy-covered walls, Colonial Revivals, countless Victorians marked by gables and steeply pitched roofs, and charming bungalows.

The Leavitt home was none of those things. It was all stucco and earth tones. No charm or character. Chloe Leavitt defined her residence as having the characteristics of an Arts and Crafts home. But where were the artistic details influenced by nature? There were no stained-glass windows or tile work with fauna motifs. The decorative wood carvings were minimal. Chloe Leavitt and her home were not worthy of such a distinctive award. To make matters worse, Chloe was in charge of judge selection this year. The whole thing was a travesty.

Rosella stopped midway up the stairs to let out a huff at the thought, but also to catch her breath. Although she did her best to eat well and exercise a few times a week, she had recently been diagnosed with osteoporosis. Her daily routine could no longer be executed with the same ease. Aching joints and sore muscles were quickly becoming the norm.

At the landing, she straightened her sore back and took some time collecting herself. A moment later, she was back in motion. The sound of her footfalls bounced off the wood floors and echoed around her as she headed for her office—what used to be her late husband Lance's favorite room, the place he went for privacy and peace of mind. As she stepped through the wide-open double doors, her heels sank into plush carpet. Walking past a long stretch of gleaming dark wood built-in bookshelves, she made her way to the massive antique desk near the fireplace carved out of marble. When Lance was alive, the desk had faced the double doors since he'd preferred to see who came and went, despite few, if any, visitors. After he passed away, Rosella had the furniture rearranged. Now the desk faced the three enormous picture windows looking out over the neighborhood.

Rosella went to the fireplace, opened the gas valve, and lit the bar. Even in the summer months, her bones felt brittle and cold. Once the wood stacked on the grate caught fire, she shut off the starter and took a seat behind the ornate desk her husband had claimed was built sometime in the Napoleonic era and once owned by royalty. Inside the top drawer, she found the mystery letter someone had placed in her mailbox three weeks ago. She unfolded it. No name. No return address. She had received it around the same time she'd first noticed someone was watching her.

On that particular day, she'd been sitting at her desk, distracted by all the commotion going on outside with the annual Fab 40s 5k Run/Walk, which had people passing her house in droves. As she often did when her stack of mail grew too tall, she'd lit the fireplace before sifting through the mail—bills, advertisements, a postcard addressed to someone she'd never heard of—using Lance's sterling silver letter opener, the one with the snake coiled at one end, to unseal the envelopes. In quick, robotic movements, she'd touched each piece, then rolled her chair closer to the fireplace and tossed the advertisements and envelopes into the blazing fire. She'd then sorted the opened mail, unfolded a piece of paper, and read five words handwritten in big red block letters:

I Know What You Did

Perplexed, she'd scanned both sides of the paper for any hint of who the author might be. Realizing she might have tossed a possible clue into the fire, she jumped to her feet, grabbed the iron poker, and scrambled to retrieve the envelope before it went up in flames. Using the tip of the iron to poke and prod, she spotted the envelope right as the heat caused the edges to twist and curl. She reached toward the envelope, but the flames licked her palm, forcing her to draw back and watch it quickly turn to ash.

Every day since, she'd wondered who might have written the note. Was it the same person she had seen watching her from a distance? If they'd set up security cameras outside as Lance had talked about doing when he was alive, she might have caught the person already. She inhaled. She felt threatened and she didn't like it. Who was watching her, and why? Nobody could possibly know what she had done. She was sure of it.

Drawn to the window, she pushed herself from her seat, grabbed her binoculars from the corner of the desk, and went to gaze out at her neighbors' homes, thinking about life and how things tended to change in the blink of an eye.

She had started life off in what she considered to be a house of horrors, running away at sixteen, then lucking out six months later, when she walked into a bank to apply for a job and met the bank's chief financial officer, Lance Marlow. He was ten years older, kindhearted, and smart as a whip with a good business sense. It didn't matter to him that she was inwardly scarred and homeless. He found her a place to stay, became her friend, supporter, and protector. Somewhere between the ages of nineteen and twenty, their friendship became something more, and he proposed on her twenty-first birthday. They married and made their home in this very house.

She and Lance decided not to have children, but a surprise pregnancy when she was forty-five ended up being a godsend. Her son, Daniel, was born happy and healthy. A pudgy little ball of joy. More surprising than the pregnancy was the fact she enjoyed being a mother. She did her best to set a good example for Daniel. Even while working long hours as a journalist, she found time to have fun with her boy.

Fifteen months ago, when she thought life couldn't get any better, Lance and Daniel, nineteen years old at the time, were headed for the mountains when their vehicle hit an icy patch and plummeted down a steep slope, abruptly stopped by a tree. Daniel died instantly. Lance wasn't so lucky. He suffered, lingering in the hospital for days, tortured with pain, until finally he passed, too.

Alone with her dismal thoughts and excruciating grief, Rosella sought help, but therapy felt meaningless. Her beautiful baby boy was dead. She became as hollow as a long-dead tree, the result of physiological stress causing her "heartwood" to be exposed, allowing outside forces to invade like an infection impervious to antibiotics. Bitter and resentful, she turned on coworkers and began to envy people with full, happy lives. Unable to lift herself from despair, she retired earlier than planned and sat alone in her misery until darkness settled comfortably inside her once again.

Fifteen months had passed. And yet her anger and resentment had not. Every morning, she stood by the window and watched the comings and goings of her neighbors, busy people mindlessly going through the motions and getting nowhere. At least, that's how it looked from where she stood.

The occupants of the house to her right were Jason and Dianne Abbott. As if on cue, the garage door rolled upward and a black F-150 pulled out. Rosella took a step back to the right as Jason glanced toward her window. He must have sensed her presence, because his gaze remained, unwavering, for a full fifteen seconds. He was a general contractor. His wife, Dianne, was a part-time intensive care unit nurse at Sutter Hospital. Every so often Rosella heard Dianne and Jason arguing, usually in the backyard, and sometimes right through the walls of their home.

No surprise there.

Jason Abbott was impetuous. Rosella didn't care for him. When Bella, Rosella's Chihuahua, was alive, Jason had complained every time she barked at a squirrel in her own backyard. If Jason wasn't complaining about Bella, he was grumbling incessantly about her hedges, insisting their height prevented sun from reaching the roses in his yard. His latest gripe was over the property line, even though Rosella hired a surveyor and had documented proof of where the property line was located. Jason hired his own surveyor, claimed the property line was at least two inches off, and demanded she relocate her fence. When they convened at the courthouse to meet with a mediator, Jason had been unwilling to reach an amicable agreement.

Jason Abbott had pushed her to her limit.

Bella had passed on, hedges had been trimmed, and now, property line be damned, she would not relocate the fence between their properties. Enough was enough. Jason truly didn't grasp who he was dealing with. Sure, he might know she had been a notable journalist until her sudden retirement after the death of her son. But he couldn't possibly know she was writing a story about secrets—her neighbors' secrets.

With sixty-five years under her belt, she knew a lot about secrets. Common skeletons in the closet included infidelity, abortion, and financial problems. But then there were the deep, dark secrets—knowingly harming another human being, stealing, stalking, and worse. Much worse. Those kinds of hidden truths were often suppressed, corroding the mind, body, and soul of those who held tight to them. They had the potential to ruin lives; the truth didn't always set a person free.

Instead of a famous, award-winning journalist, Rosella now preferred to think of herself as a researcher. She had not only all the important contacts, which were invaluable when it came to making requests, but also the time and resources to dig deep. Once she'd put her sights on Jason Abbott, it hadn't taken long before she struck gold. She was certain the man was embezzling from his company. There were so many warning signs it was hard to believe he had yet to be implicated in any wrongdoing: Vendors she talked to complained they hadn't been paid in full, or even at all. Customers claimed they were repeatedly asked to make payments that had already been paid. And according to an accountant who no longer worked for the company, Jason's project records were filled with odd transactions and duplicate payments.

Rosella had swiftly sent a letter—signed anonymously, of course—to Jason Abbott's company. No need to hire anyone to reposition the fence, as she hadn't heard a peep from Jason since. Which was nice because he wasn't her only subject; she had work to do. Everyone living on her quiet, picturesque block was hiding something. Little secret or big? It didn't matter. She would expose them and make these people suffer, just as she was.

And she would do it with the help of unsuspecting Shannon Gibbons.

Rosella had gone out of her way to find the woman. Convincing Shannon Gibbons to come work with her had been easy: *I'll be your mentor. I'll do whatever I can to help you achieve your dreams of becoming a journalist.*

Shannon had never done anything with her life. She was a wife and a mom, nothing more. An unfair assessment? Possibly. No matter. She was helping Shannon find a new identity outside of family, guiding her toward ambitions that extended beyond the roles of wife and mother, empowering her to embrace her individuality. She was doing Shannon a favor. Rosella planned to use empathy and compassion to pull her in and gain her trust. After that, everything else would fall into place.

Rosella would feel no guilt for uncovering the truth; her neighbors had it coming. Not one person on her block had been there for her when she'd lost her husband and son. Her world had collapsed after Daniel died, but not theirs. Her neighbors had simply moved on, fueling a fire within, a fire that had lain dormant for too long. She could almost taste the bitterness surrounding her.

Was she focused on her neighbors because she no longer had a family of her own? Was she angry with all people, or only the happy ones? Did she want to expose their secrets because her own pain and loss had been laid bare for all to see? Yes, yes, and yes were her answers. She knew better than Dr. Everett Finnigan, the therapist she'd opened up to after losing Daniel, that her obsession with these people was helping her cope. Misery, she realized, truly did love company.

As she stood before the window looking out, she saw Chloe Leavitt head for Kaylynn Alcozar's house. From there, Chloe and Kaylynn met up with Becky Bateman across the street. Their smiles were a cruel reminder of the happiness Rosella had lost. Watching them through narrowed eyes, she clenched her fists tightly at her sides. How dare they be so joyful when her world lay shattered at her feet?

After the women disappeared from sight, Rosella lowered the binoculars. With a heavy sigh, she turned away from the window, retreating deeper into the darkness of her solitude. Most outsiders who strolled down her tree-lined street would believe the inhabitants were living the American dream.

But they would be wrong.

Chapter Two

After dropping her daughter off at her new school, Shannon Gibbons headed for her new home on Forty-Fifth Street. Shannon and her family had moved to Sacramento a week ago. It had been a whirlwind of activity from the moment the moving trucks drove away until now. Today she would meet Rosella Marlow, a celebrity and idol of hers who lived at the end of the block. Rosella was the reason Shannon and her family were living in the Fabulous Forties, one of the most coveted neighborhoods in Sacramento.

Six months ago, Rosella had contacted Shannon via email, explaining how she was looking for an assistant to help with her newest writing project. Shannon's immediate reaction was disbelief. At the time, Shannon had been living in Elk Grove, about twenty minutes away. Rosella Marlow was a renowned journalist, nearly on the same level as Barbara Walters. Why was she calling? Did she have the wrong person?

When Shannon had asked, "Why me?" Rosella had told her Michael J. Barilla, a college professor at California State University, Sacramento, had mentioned her by name and talked about Shannon's investigative nature and relentless pursuit of truth in a world clouded by misinformation.

Rosella Marlow seemed genuine in her desire to help nurture and develop Shannon's talent. Not only did the notion of stepping outside of her daily routine excite Shannon, but the prospect of working with Rosella and learning from the best also filled her with joy and anticipation.

Their first conversation had been followed by a string of emails and a video call, at which time Rosella talked about a story idea having to do with the history of the homes on her street. She spoke passionately about the area known as the Fabulous Forties, how it once had an extensive streetcar network that wound its way through sprawling estates surrounded by manicured lawns and lush landscaping. The opulence and prestige, she'd said, had been unappreciated, but now, decades later, the neighborhood was finally recognized for its spectacular architecture.

The only thing Shannon had found strange was how Rosella seemed to know everything about her. *Everything.* Not only what her favorite restaurant was but also where Shannon had met her husband, as well as her decision to give up her dream of becoming a journalist so she could stay home to raise her daughter. Even more surprising, Rosella knew about Shannon's childhood, her time spent in foster care, the loneliness she'd endured, and how, through it all, she had pined for her biological mother, so much so she used to be all Shannon talked about, thought about, cared about.

Rosella knew she hadn't been adopted until the age of thirteen. The Fergusons, well into their sixties at the time, helped to change Shannon's life. They were patient with her and a kind and loving couple. But all good things come to an end, and when Shannon was sixteen, Mrs. Ferguson was diagnosed with breast cancer and passed away soon after. Two years later, on the anniversary of her death, Mr. Ferguson went to bed and never woke up.

Although Rosella was a great listener, she didn't open up about her own life, except to say they had much in common. When Shannon asked her how so, Rosella told her she had also experienced neglect and abuse as a child and sometimes felt the urge to strike out at those around her.

"I've never felt the urge to strike out at others," Shannon told her.

"Not even after losing Mrs. Ferguson?"

Not even then, she thought. There was no way Rosella could know her inner thoughts or what happened behind closed doors. The truth was, after Mrs. Ferguson's death, Mr. Ferguson had become a broken man. He would come to Shannon's room late at night and want to talk—to cry, mostly. He became a bit touchy-feely: a kiss on the cheek here, an arm around her shoulder there. She began to lock her bedroom door at night. And when he died, instead of grieving, she felt relieved.

"Did you know Mr. Ferguson had a sister whom he talked to nearly every day?"

"Of course. Auntie Jane."

"He told his sister everything, and she, in turn, told her husband, a police officer, about their conversations. His sister and her husband did everything they could to try and talk Mr. Ferguson into handing you back over to the state. They were afraid for his life."

"Why?" Shannon asked, utterly baffled.

"Why do you think?"

"I have no idea. Mr. Ferguson and I always got along. I thought of him as my father."

"Mr. Ferguson told his sister that you were an angry child, but he'd made a promise to his wife to keep you at his side and protect you. And then he died unexpectedly . . ."

"Of a broken heart," Shannon told her.

Rosella sighed as if it were no use trying to explain. "Don't you see?"

Shannon didn't, at all. "See what?"

"Mr. Ferguson's own sister was afraid you might hurt her brother. And when he died unexpectedly, she blamed you."

"No. That's not true," Shannon said, unsure. She thought back to the funeral, how Auntie Jane had been standoffish. Shannon had put it all down to grief. Everyone processed death differently. Shannon hadn't spoken to Auntie Jane in years. The woman had to be in her late eighties. "Did you speak to Auntie Jane?"

"Of course. That's what the best journalists do: they search for the facts, make phone calls, perform in-person interviews, visit libraries, and even pound the streets if they want to talk with hard-to-reach people."

"You did all that before contacting me?"

"Yes," Rosella said with a wistful sigh. "It's what I do, what I've always done. The point is, you and I were made from the same cloth. Wrongfully treated. Misunderstood. We both harbor a darkness within."

Shannon didn't agree, but she kept quiet. Yes, she thought the world was harsh. And yes, she felt misunderstood, but she wasn't angry. She didn't blame the couples who declined to adopt her, because the first thing she always asked them was if they would help her find her real mother. But a darkness within? Most likely, Rosella was talking about "dark" emotions: sadness, loss, and even shame.

Relieved when Rosella moved on to something else, Shannon figured it was the woman's unique background as a journalist with a sea of contacts that made her privy to so many details. A few months after her first conversation with Rosella, Shannon's husband was offered a job as a surgeon at Sutter Hospital in Sacramento. Days after he was hired, Rosella called Shannon to let her know there was a house on Rosella's block that would soon be listed and gave her the name of the agent to call. The house would be going for a spectacular price, and if they were interested, they needed to act fast.

It all seemed too good to be true. And yet that didn't stop Shannon and Trey from pouncing on the opportunity. The icing on the cake, in Shannon's view, was the prospect of working closely with Rosella. The woman might be a bit eccentric, but she was an extraordinary journalist who wanted to pass on her knowledge, skills, and experience to the next generation.

Shannon's job would entail providing notes, ideas, and detailed supporting material on Rosella's work in progress, *The History of Homes on My Block*. The project itself sounded boring. But there was no way Shannon would dare pass up the chance to work with someone of

Rosella's stature. The timing couldn't be better. Shannon's daughter was a sophomore in high school. It was time to think about what she wanted to do with the rest of her life.

She turned onto Forty-Fifth Street and was greeted by a breathtaking sight of towering oaks that provided a sturdy framework for the vibrant maples, sycamores, and elms stretching above and gracefully shading the entire block. The garage door rolled open and Shannon pulled inside. When she stepped out of the car and shut the door, she was surprised to see four women standing in her driveway. They were all smiling. The woman in the center of the group waved. She wore a colorful, knee-length sundress and bright-white sneakers, and exuded grace and style. Her blond hair was thick and shiny, cut bluntly an inch above her shoulders. Shannon walked toward them.

"Hello," the woman said. "My name is Chloe Leavitt." She turned to her left. "This is Becky Bateman, and"—pivoting to her right—"this is Kaylynn Alcozar and Dianne Abbott."

"So nice to meet you," Kaylynn said. "I live right next door to you."

Dianne lifted one hand. "Hi. Welcome to the neighborhood."

"I live across the street," Becky said, pointing to the house behind them, the house Shannon saw through her living room windows. The house reminded her of something you might find in a fairy tale. It was painted in soft pastels. A turret with gingerbread trim crowned the structure, and its conical roof was covered in copper patina. She'd been admiring the house since she'd moved onto the block.

Shannon looked at her watch. She was running short of time. She didn't want to be late for her meeting with Rosella Marlow, but she also didn't want to come across as rude. Surely, Rosella would understand if she was a few minutes late. "I'm Shannon Gibbons," she said as she reached them, offering her hand to each in turn. "So nice to meet you all."

"Becky mentioned you had a daughter," Chloe said.

"Yes. MacKenzie. We call her Mac. I just returned from taking her to Saint Francis. Her first day as a sophomore in high school."

Chloe's face lit up. "Saint Francis? My daughter, Ridley, goes there. She's in her third year. We must introduce them. In fact, Ridley has a twin brother. They both drive, but Blake drops his sister off at school on his way to Jesuit High School every morning. If you would like, Blake would be happy to take your daughter to school and back."

"Oh, I don't know."

"He's responsible," Kaylynn chimed in. "He's even watched my little one a few times."

Becky nodded her agreement. "He's babysat my kids, too. They love Blake."

Dianne nodded along.

"You can think about it," Chloe said. "The reason we popped over is because we walk two or three times a week, or whenever the stars align, and when we saw you pull in, we thought we would introduce ourselves and invite you to join us."

"I would love to, but I have a meeting with Rosella Marlow this morning."

Dianne's eyes grew wide, while Becky's eyebrows pulled together in worry.

"A meeting with Rosella Marlow?" Chloe asked. "Whatever for?"

"That's none of our business," Kaylynn said. "We can all walk another time."

"I don't mind sharing," Shannon said. "The truth is, Rosella Marlow is a big part of why we moved here."

Dianne's eyes grew even larger.

Kaylynn simply smiled. She looked like a younger, but shorter, version of Nicole Kidman with her red hair, flawless alabaster skin, and blue eyes. Shannon's gaze shifted from one woman to another while she explained. "Rosella emailed me months ago about needing an assistant to help her with a writing project. Everything after that sort of fell into place. My husband was offered a job at Sutter Hospital, and then this beautiful house we've moved into came onto the market." Shannon exhaled. "We feel so lucky to be here."

"Did you ever meet the last owner, Caroline Baxter?" Becky asked.

Shannon shook her head. "We never got the chance."

"She used to walk with us," Kaylynn said.

"And she always said this was her forever home, so when she up and moved without saying goodbye to any of us, it was a bit shocking," Dianne said.

"Definitely," Chloe said. "We do miss her." Her frown quickly turned to a smile. "But now we have you . . ." Chloe's expression changed from happy to excited, and she reached out and grabbed hold of Shannon's forearm. Her grasp was gentle but firm. "If you don't mind, I'm going to stop by later—before school is out, of course—and make you a proposition I hope you can't refuse."

"Lucky you," Dianne said with a laugh.

"When is your appointment with Rosella?" Becky asked. "The last thing you want to be is late."

Shannon glanced at the Apple Watch with the beaded band her daughter had made for her. The beads tended to pull on the little hairs on her arms, but every time she took it off, Mac noticed. "I was supposed to be there five minutes ago."

A couple of the women jumped in unison, as if a car had backfired. They all shared worried looks.

"We'll leave you to it," Kaylynn said. "Good luck!"

"Good luck?" Shannon asked with a smile. "Is there something I should know?"

Becky winced. "Let's just say Rosella is a woman of contradictions. Her personality walks a tightrope between overbearing and genial."

"I don't know about *genial*," Dianne said. "Doesn't that mean friendly or cheerful?"

"I think of *genial* as pleasantly warm at times," Becky said. "But yeah, she is also known to be stubborn and sort of scary."

Chloe sighed. "I think what Becky means to say is that her assertiveness can be intimidating at times."

"I have a voice," Becky told Chloe. "What I mean to say is what I've already said, but I would add that Rosella has a no-nonsense approach to life. Her opinions are shared freely . . ."

"A little too freely, if you ask me," Dianne said.

"We need to let Shannon form her own opinion regarding Rosella," Kaylynn said before heading off with Becky and Dianne.

"You'll be fine," Chloe assured Shannon. "I'll see you later, okay?"

"Sounds good," Shannon replied.

Chloe quickened her pace to catch up with the others.

Shannon liked Chloe Leavitt, who seemed kind and full of energy. In fact, Shannon liked them all. They were a nice change from her old neighborhood, where everyone stayed to themselves. After eight years, Shannon had never felt connected to the people who lived on her street. Trey had suggested she brought it on herself because she was inwardly afraid of rejection, which could be true, but Shannon didn't believe that had anything to do with her feelings about the people in their old neighborhood.

The thought of Rosella waiting flashed through her brain. She ran back into the garage and hit the button. The door rolled down as she entered the kitchen through the side door. She glanced at the time. If she left now, she would be fifteen minutes late. She was still in her sweatpants and tee. She needed to change her clothes and brush her hair.

Shannon rushed up a flight of stairs and hurriedly made her way into her cluttered bedroom. Boxes and plastic bins lay scattered about, a reminder of the unfinished task of settling into her new home. She plunked her hands on her hips. Time was not on her side. Amid the chaos, she caught sight of a yellow summer dress through one of the bins. She swiftly pulled it out and slipped it on, the soft fabric hugging her around the hips. In the bathroom, she gathered her hair into a ponytail and secured it with an elastic band.

A glance at her watch prompted her to hastily apply a dash of lipstick to brighten her features, then scan the bedroom and the walk-in closet for her sandals. Frantically, she riffled through a jumble of shoes. No such luck. Finally, she slipped on a pair of ugly clogs and darted out of the room.

Outside, she took in a deep breath, hoping the fresh air would calm her nerves. When Shannon had last spoken with Rosella on the video call, she had been warm and friendly. Although she felt bad about keeping her waiting, she was certain Rosella would understand.

Her toes curled, gripping the clogs as she walked. She would have been better off wearing her old sneakers. Sweat gathered under her arms. If she weren't so flustered, she might have been completely awe-struck by the beauty of Rosella's Victorian house, with its wraparound porch, ornate trimmings, and countless columns. Gabled dormers peeked out from the steeply pitched roof. No wonder the home had won Best House on the Block more than once. As she drew closer to the main entry, her heart began to thud against her chest. Afraid she might chicken out, she quickly rang the doorbell.

CHAPTER THREE

Standing at the front entrance, before long, Shannon heard footsteps—not the soft footfalls she would have expected but more like marching-style thuds.

Every nerve tingled with anticipation.

Meeting Rosella Marlow in person was a dream come true. The door swung open with an air of impatience, revealing a tall woman with silver hair bluntly cut between shoulder and ear and clear blue eyes filled with what could be concern, or maybe frustration. The creases on Rosella's forehead deepened, and her voice trembled with barely contained anger. "You're late."

It took Shannon a moment to collect herself. "I-I'm sorry. Some women in the neighborhood stopped by to introduce themselves, and I couldn't find my shoes—"

Rosella waved a hand between them, as if shooing away a fly. "Excuses merely serve to reveal a certain feebleness and, most likely, a lack of confidence."

Stunned, Shannon said, "But it's not an excuse. It's the God's honest truth."

Rosella shook her head as if talking to a petulant young child. "Excuses expose mediocrity. They are a tool used by the weak-minded. Had you broken your leg on your way here, maybe that would be different. But you didn't. Using your inability to find a pair of shoes as the cause of your tardiness shows an intent to absolve yourself of accountability."

Shannon struggled to swallow the gigantic lump in her throat as she wondered whether she should turn around and walk away. She seldom cried, but she felt the urge to do so now. Dissolving into tears would most likely spark another lecture, so she swallowed, blinked, and didn't dare say a word.

Rosella's disappointment hung in the air like a bad smell as Shannon awaited instructions on where they might go from here. She had planned to express her amazement over Rosella's immaculate gardens, but all sense of cordiality had left her completely.

Rosella exhaled. "My time is valuable. In the future, I expect you to be punctual. Do we understand one another?"

Shannon had never been great at sticking up for herself, and this moment was no exception. She deserved respect and told herself she wouldn't tolerate being spoken to in such a demeaning manner. But she didn't say a word. Trey called her a big softy. He was right. She stood there stiffly, lips sealed tight, and nodded.

"Wonderful," Rosella said. "Perhaps we should start over."

"That would be amaz—"

The door shut in Shannon's face before she could finish her sentence. *What the hell?* The woman was a—

No sooner had the door closed than it came open with a flourish, yanking Shannon from her thoughts, which were far from gracious.

Rosella's smile, the one Shannon had observed during their internet call, suddenly materialized. Her expression was now warm and friendly, appearing so genuine it caused the corners of her bright-blue eyes to crinkle. "Shannon Gibbons. So nice to finally meet you."

Rosella offered a hand, and Shannon took it in hers. "Nice to meet you, too," she answered with as much enthusiasm as she could muster, telling herself Rosella's initial coldness likely stemmed from a personal difficulty, maybe due to lack of sleep, a health issue, or one of myriad other possible concerns.

"Come inside so we can get started." After waving Shannon through, Rosella shut the door. "Follow me upstairs and perhaps we can attempt to make up for all the time lost due to your lack of punctuality."

Climbing the steps on the woman's heels, Shannon felt her insides squeeze together. She opened her mouth, ready to attempt a more detailed explanation involving being new to the area and taking a few wrong turns while driving her daughter to school, but quickly thought better of it. *Let it go.*

Issues or not, Rosella Marlow didn't appear to be the kindhearted individual she'd expected. But she had been warned. Becky had compared Rosella's personality to walking a tightrope between overbearing and genial. Shannon's description of Rosella might lean toward something more like Jekyll and Hyde. For now, Shannon thought, if she could ignore a few jabs here and there, she might be able to learn from one of the best.

As they made their way through the house, the sheer scale of the residence became apparent. The exterior had been impressive, but the interior was a sight to behold. Rich wood paneling adorned the walls, exuding a timeless elegance that whispered of a bygone era. Crystal chandeliers hung from the high ceilings, casting a warm glow throughout. Every detail, from the ornate crown moldings to the elaborate banisters of the grand staircase, was meticulously crafted and uniquely charming.

Despite the remarkable beauty at every turn, including the massive office soaked in natural light and filled with antiques suitable for a museum, a sense of unease hung heavy in the air the moment they stepped inside. Rosella gestured toward the sturdy wooden chair in front of her desk. A solid chunk of wood without cushions or armrests, the chair looked out of place, causing Shannon to wonder whether it had been pulled from the basement. With her back to the windows overlooking the neighborhood, Shannon clung to a spark of hope that Rosella would stop, blink, and return to the friendly person she'd been during their chat months ago. If Shannon weren't ridiculously fearful of the woman's reaction, she might consider asking her if something was wrong. Instead, feeling her confidence dwindling fast, she sat with her back uncomfortably straight and didn't say a word. She felt like a teenager sitting in front of the principal.

It wasn't until Rosella took a seat at her desk that Shannon noticed a hint of desperation etched across her face. "I should have called you weeks ago, but I was afraid you might not come." Rosella's voice was no longer stern. "Everything has changed since we last spoke."

Shannon nodded and listened closely.

"Someone has been following me, lurking in the shadows, watching me from a distance."

"That's so frightening," Shannon said, believing that must be the reason Rosella was acting so erratically. "Do you have any idea why someone might be following you?"

"I think whoever it is, they wish me harm," Rosella said in a hushed tone. Her gaze scanned the room, as if for any signs of lurking danger. "I'm certain it's one of our neighbors, but the question is who."

Of all the reasons that had swept through Shannon's mind as to what might be causing Rosella's perplexing behavior, this was not one of them. "You think someone in this neighborhood wishes to do you harm?"

"Without a doubt."

Shannon didn't know what to do, afraid of exacerbating the situation or causing Rosella further distress. "Why? What happened?"

Rosella pulled open a desk drawer and withdrew a piece of folded paper. "Here," she said, reaching forward. "Read it for yourself." Her arm brushed against the letter opener on her desk, sending it toppling to the floor. Shannon stood and reached for it, then set it back on the desk. Rosella impatiently waggled the note again.

Shannon grabbed hold of it and returned to her seat. The second she unfolded the paper and read the five simple words—I KNOW WHAT YOU DID—handwritten in red capital letters, goose bumps formed on her forearms. Shannon flipped the paper over. No name, address, or signature. No date, either. She handed the note back to Rosella. "Do you have any idea *what* the sender might be referring to?"

Rosella pushed herself to her feet and went to one of three enormous windows. "Come."

Obediently, Shannon went to stand by her side.

"The house there," Rosella said, pointing, "separated from mine only by a fence, belongs to Jason Abbott, his wife, and their son, Finn. Jason is embezzling from the company he works for."

Rosella hadn't answered her question. Shannon wondered where the woman was going with that bit of gossip. "Is he in jail?"

"He should be. He's been a thorn in my side for a while now." Rosella rambled on for a few minutes about Jason's string of complaints about her noisy dog, tall hedges, and most recently, a property-line dispute. "Dealing with him has been stressful," she said. "I have tried to be civil, but Jason Abbott is impossible." Rosella lifted her chin. "He has forced me to do what I've done with anyone who pokes me too many times."

Shannon's eyebrows curved upward. "What did you do?"

"I sent an anonymous letter addressed to Jason at his workplace, letting him know I was onto him."

"Do you think he knows you were the one who sent the letter?" Shannon asked. "That *could* explain the cryptic note you received."

"He might suspect it was me, but he can't know for sure," Rosella stated matter-of-factly. "The truth is, anyone on the block could have left me that note."

"Anyone on the block?" Shannon asked. "But why?"

Wagging her finger toward the window again, Rosella said, "Next to Jason, living in the pastel-colored house with that god-awful turret, are Becky and Holly Bateman."

Another beautiful house, Shannon thought.

"The women used a surrogate and now have two small children. A five-year-old boy and a three-year-old girl." She released a heavy sigh. "I'm fairly certain Jason turned them against me, whispering lies about me in their ears, making mountains out of molehills, no doubt, after I told his wife, Dianne, what I thought about them."

"What did you say to his wife?"

Rosella stiffened as if her hackles were rising just thinking about it. "I told her the truth . . . that those women have nothing to talk about except their bratty kids. *Ethan did this and Charley did that. Ethan is so smart and clever for his age—he's going to be president of the United States someday.*" Rosella rolled her eyes. "They are so busy hovering over their children, as if they think someone might snatch them if they blink, they have no time to watch the news or read about world events. They didn't even know who I was!"

Shannon held in a groan.

"And that's not all. Fundraising. You can't go near Becky or Holly without one of them asking for money for one organization or another. It never stops. They held a fundraiser for the American Cancer Society three weeks ago, and they're throwing another one in the next week or two."

A minute ago, Shannon had felt a bit sorry for the woman. But now she felt only pity. "You don't like these women, but you still attend the events they put on?"

"Of course. It's expected of me. I have a reputation to withhold." Rosella huffed as if she didn't like being questioned. "Across the street from the women, the house next to yours, are the Alcozars, Kaylynn and Nicolas."

Shannon held her breath, waiting for the ball to drop. What was it about the Alcozars Rosella didn't like?

"Like everyone else on the block, they have children." Rosella released a pitiful groan. "It won't be long before the whole neighborhood is overrun with disrespectful teenagers who take everything for granted, use *like* way too much, and are glued to their cell phones."

As Rosella rambled, Shannon noticed a pair of binoculars sitting on an antique, birch empire table set against a wall and found herself wondering how often Rosella used them. And if she did use them, what did she use them for? When Rosella paused, Shannon asked, "So you're good with the Alcozar family?"

"Oh, no. The entire family is afraid of their own shadows. Kaylynn is skittish and meek, and Nicolas can't maintain eye contact."

Shannon kept quiet.

"He can't be trusted," Rosella went on. "And Kaylynn is such a frail, weak little thing. She's afraid of her own shadow and too friendly for her own good." Her eyes narrowed. "I think there's a good chance they might be hiding something."

She shifted her gaze so she was looking directly into Shannon's eyes. "I spent decades interviewing people, important people. Doing so was never easy. It not only involved preparation and homework but also required discipline and hard work. Learning how to read body language became my forte. I was quite adept at observing facial expressions, gestures, and posture." Rosella drew her brows together. "A furrowed brow might indicate defensiveness, while a relaxed posture often signals quite the opposite."

"And that's how you've determined the Alcozars might be hiding something?"

"Exactly. Are you doubting me, Shannon Gibbons?"

"No. Of course not." But that wasn't true. Rosella was being unreasonable, but how could she argue with the woman? She was Rosella Marlow—a superstar. And besides, Shannon hardly knew her.

Rosella turned back toward the window. "Their attempts to avoid me are blatantly rude at times. If I dare approach them, it seems they're always making some absurd excuse before rushing back to the safety of their home."

"Avoiding someone is one thing, but why would they, or anyone in the neighborhood, want to hurt you?"

"Because they must know I'm onto them."

"The Alcozars?" Shannon asked.

Arms flailing, she said, "All of them."

Shannon thought about what Chloe and Becky had already told her about Rosella. They were right; Rosella appeared to be making assumptions about the neighbors based on body language, such as eye contact and personality. Everything Rosella had said so far made Shannon wonder whether Rosella suffered from paranoia, which would explain her unrelenting mistrust and suspicions when there was no reason to be suspicious.

Shannon was trying her best to lend an empathetic ear, but it wasn't easy. It made sense that Rosella's neighbors would run whenever they saw her coming their way; Shannon wanted to run away, too. Before she could think of an excuse, Rosella found a new victim to talk about: Chloe Leavitt, whom Shannon had just met and who lived in the house directly across the street from Rosella's. According to Rosella, Chloe was fifty-five years of age and lived with her husband, Wesley, and three children.

"Does the name Chloe Leavitt ring a bell with you?" Rosella asked.

Shannon shook her head. "Should it?"

"Well, she has been in the local paper a few times for her *goodwill and generous character*," Rosella said, her tone laced with sarcasm. "Not many people like her."

"Why not?"

Rosella shrugged. "Despite the facade—meaningless fundraisers and such—she's selfish, the kind of person who puts her own needs above all else, often at the expense of her family. No need to go on about her. You'll see for yourself."

But Rosella did go on about Chloe Leavitt . . . and on and on. Apparently, Rosella and Chloe had become fast friends after Chloe and her husband moved into the beautiful house, with its charming mixture of brick, shingles, and siding, directly across the street. According to Rosella, it wasn't long before Chloe set her sights on Rosella's husband, Lance. Their friendship went south and had been tumbling downhill ever since.

Rosella perceived Chloe Leavitt as conniving. She also had a lot to say about Chloe's apparent lack of control over her unruly children, who Rosella said ran amok without consequence. Rosella's dislike of the woman was much more extreme than her animosity toward the others living in the neighborhood. Her resentment was apparent in the icy edge of her voice and the subtle tightening of her facial muscles as she talked about Chloe. *Talk about body language,* Shannon thought. Rosella was not difficult to read.

"Her husband is oftentimes away on business," Rosella went on. "And I have no doubt that man of hers has wandering eyes, which more times than not leads to wandering hands . . . like most men . . . even yours. I mean, let's be real . . . a young Brad Pitt look-alike who happens to be a doctor. Keep an eye on him, my friend."

"Excuse me?"

"Oh, please. Don't act as if you've never once suspected your husband of cheating on you."

She never had, but Shannon saw no reason to bother disagreeing. The statement was ridiculous and didn't warrant a reaction. If anything, it only fueled Shannon's desire to cut their meeting short and leave. There was no point in staying; Shannon no longer had any desire to work with Rosella. Mustering a halfhearted smile, she reached out and gently touched Rosella's arm, ready to announce her need to get home and unpack some boxes. But apparently nothing short of a bomb going off would stop Rosella's long-winded diatribe.

"Chloe Leavitt's relentless pursuit of the coveted Best House award, a title I've claimed twice, was the last straw." Rosella's face contorted into a mix of disapproval and contempt as she swept her hand toward Chloe's house. "Look at that place! It's an eyesore."

Far from it, Shannon thought as she followed Rosella's gaze. The Arts and Crafts–style house was extraordinary. Exposed roof rafters added a touch of rustic elegance, while tapered columns gracefully supported a large, covered porch. The patterned windowpanes were works of art. And that was all from a distance. "I think it's beautiful."

"Don't be ridiculous." Rosella turned her way, arms crossed tightly over her chest, her elbows sticking out like sharp sticks. "You think my distrust of these people is misplaced, don't you?"

Yes. Yes, I do. "I don't know them, so it's impossible for me to have an opinion one way or another. But I do find it easier to be kind than cruel."

Rosella scoffed. "My last encounter with Chloe Leavitt," she said, as if there had never been an interruption in her story, "ended in a heated exchange where I boldly declared that Chloe's only chance of winning another Best House award would be over my dead body."

And there it was: the reason, no doubt, Rosella thought Chloe wanted to cause her harm. The woman seemed out of sync with reality. Her contempt for her neighbors seemed to emanate from her core, and yet her reasoning had no substance. Clearly, it wouldn't be long before Rosella was spreading rumors about Shannon, too.

"Please take a seat," Rosella said. "We need to get down to business and talk about my project."

Reluctantly, Shannon returned to the hard wooden chair and plopped down. She had no spine. Her husband knew it, her daughter knew it, and now she knew it.

Back at her desk, Rosella said, "As you've probably guessed, I am no longer interested in writing about the history of the homes in the area."

Exactly what Shannon was afraid of. And not a big surprise.

"But I do need your assistance in helping me figure out who sent the note I showed you."

"But—"

Rosella didn't care to hear what she had to say. "The spotlight will shift away from the homes on my block. We will be delving instead into the lives of its residents and their deepest, darkest secrets."

The idea of her first journalistic endeavor involving observing her neighbors made Shannon's stomach fill with dread. "You would need their permission—"

"Don't be silly. I wouldn't use their real names, dear." Rosella made a *tsk*ing noise before continuing with her plan. "This will be an exposé. I will need to personalize the story and include investigative information."

Shannon entwined her fingers in her lap. "I was taught that an exposé had to do with a social issue or problem, concluding with a possible solution."

"Oh my. Don't you see? This *is* a social problem, dear. People all over the world are living among strangers. Their neighbors could be absolutely anyone. Take Jeffrey Dahmer, for example. He fed his neighbor human meat."

"Are you comparing your neighbors to a serial killer? A little far-fetched, don't you think?"

Rosella shrugged.

Shannon had no further words.

"Call our little project whatever you want, but let's be clear . . . I want to know everything about these people—their likes and dislikes, but more importantly, their inner feelings and thoughts."

Their inner feelings and thoughts?

"I need your help unearthing the truths that lie hidden behind every closed door and hushed conversation on this block."

Shannon had no words. This was madness. Rosella's desire to know everything about these people appeared to have more to do with control than anything else. What else could it be? Knowing their vulnerabilities might allow Rosella to hold power over them, just as she was doing with Jason Abbott to get him to back off about the issue he had with property lines and whatnot.

If Shannon had to guess, she would say Rosella wasn't interested in idle curiosity or gossip. Maybe she wanted to gather information so she could use it to manipulate people. If so, it was Rosella's motive that remained unclear. Maybe she got some sort of weird satisfaction from the knowledge she collected, fueling her sense of superiority, empowering her to shape lives according to her whims?

Rosella smiled. "Don't look so worried. You'll have fun getting to know the neighbors! We'll meet every day, which will allow me to shape and guide you." She leaned forward. "Nobody will be the wiser, because of *course* you would be curious to know what your neighbors are up to. And when you're not out and about, you can use your journalistic skills to learn more about their backgrounds, where they came from, what their childhoods were like. I think it best if you start with Chloe Leavitt."

Shannon swallowed. She didn't bother telling Rosella she'd met Chloe Leavitt before coming here and liked the woman straightaway. "I can't possibly spy on my new neighbors."

Rosella's eyes gleamed with a renewed urgency. "I don't think you understand. I'm giving you a chance to show the world you're more than a stay-at-home mom. I'm asking you to help me. My life is in danger."

A bit dramatic, Shannon thought. Keeping eye contact wasn't easy, but she held strong as she told Rosella how she felt about the matter. "To be honest, from what you've told me so far, there doesn't seem to be any reason for you to believe anyone is out to get you. Do you think it's possible your fears and anxieties have gotten the best of you?" When Rosella said nothing, Shannon added, "Maybe you need to take a break, go somewhere, and get away from it all."

"I have no one else to turn to," Rosella said. "Did I mention someone attempted to break into the house recently?"

"When?"

"Two days ago. The police arrived before the intruder was able to enter, but what will happen to me if they try again and succeed?"

If the story was true, it did worry Shannon. What if crime was a problem in the area? "Did they break a lock?"

"No. I happened to be looking out the window when I saw someone fiddling around below. The next day I discovered footprints in the dirt outside the basement window. I took a picture. I have proof."

"Could the footprints be from a landscaper?"

Deep lines of worry cut into Rosella's face. "Somebody is after me. I know it, and any true journalist worth a grain of salt would gratefully help me gather information and prove me wrong if they thought I was crazy."

"I never said you were crazy."

"But you thought it."

Shannon couldn't deny it, so she remained silent. Every time Shannon blinked, Rosella went from borderline bully to desperately frightened woman. *Is it all an act?*

"I need your assistance in unraveling this mystery. We must figure out who sent me the note, who is watching me, and why."

Rosella's fear hung heavy in the air, carrying the weight of the vulnerability she seemed to be trying to hide beneath a wall of dominance and authority. It was clear she yearned for someone to validate her fears, take her concerns seriously, and join her in uncovering the truth.

"I've done my research," Rosella said. "You have a keen eye for detail and an uncanny ability to connect with people."

"I don't know about—"

"You spend a lot of time online, trying to solve cases, don't you?"

Shivers coursed through Shannon. "How do you know that?"

Rosella no longer seemed fearful for her life; she looked smug. "I know people who know people who also know people." She exhaled. "Something is bothering you. Talk to me."

"I don't understand why you went to all that trouble to know so much about me."

It was true. Shannon had always possessed a fascination with true crime. By the time Mac had reached the age of three, Shannon had joined a couple of online sleuthing groups in order to stay sane. She considered it a form of self-care. Her favorite online group was Sleuthsolvers, a gathering of amateur dicks who required members to put in a few hours a week. If Rosella had originally contacted her to help write a story about the homes in the neighborhood, why would she have dug so deep into Shannon's personal life?

Rosella's eyes bored into hers. "Maybe I was wrong about you. Maybe you're not ready to work with someone of my caliber. Maybe being a mother is all you were ever meant to be."

Her words caused heat to rise to Shannon's cheeks, a flush of embarrassment mixed with irritation. Shannon loved being a mother to Mac, and yet she would be lying if she didn't admit to having moments when she didn't feel fulfilled, when she thought being a mother wasn't enough. She wanted more.

And yet, for all she knew, Rosella Marlow could be deliberately trying to needle her. Shannon straightened her spine. "I don't think you know me well enough to make any sort of judgment about me."

Rosella placed a hand on her chest. "Okay," she said. "Fair enough. But you agree you're a true-crime fanatic, wouldn't you say?"

Fanatic? Shannon thought about all the hours she'd been spending on her computer lately, looking through digitized phone books and yearbooks, scouring the internet for clues. "Sure. I guess . . ."

"Then help me."

The thought of this being Rosella's plan all along—to get Shannon to relocate so she could spy on the neighbors—popped into her head. Ridiculous. There was no possible way she could have arranged for Shannon to come here. There were too many moving pieces: her husband's job, the house, the timing. But what if Rosella could and had? If that was the case, who was Shannon dealing with?

Shannon had to stop her active imagination from getting the best of her. Although Rosella Marlow was proving to be an oddball, that didn't mean she'd spent months plotting some sort of wacky plan to get Shannon to move to the neighborhood. "I know I've asked before, but tell me the truth," Shannon said. "I'm sure anyone you asked would have been thrilled to work with you. Why me?"

One side of Rosella's mouth lifted. "As I mentioned before," she said, "when we spoke months ago, I told you I believe we both possess a darkness within. It's what drives us. And it's one of the reasons I was drawn to you."

Shannon had assumed Rosella was talking about all the emotions that came with having a troubled childhood. "What sort of darkness are you referring to?"

"The vindictive kind," she said matter-of-factly. "We both have a history of being betrayed, which might fuel our desire for revenge, wouldn't you agree?"

Shannon didn't have a vindictive bone in her body. But no sooner had the thought sprung to mind than she remembered her foster mom Mrs. Bickford kicking the family dog, Lucy, a golden retriever, in the ribs. Not once but twice, yelling at the dog until she peed right there on the kitchen floor, setting the woman off again. Ten-year-old Shannon had screamed, begged her to stop hurting Lucy. Finally, she picked up her water glass and threw it at the woman, barely missing her head. The glass hit a cupboard and shattered.

Red in the face and angrier than Shannon had ever seen her, Mrs. Bickford told her it was no wonder her mother had given her away. Who would want a ferocious child with evil eyes? As she grew older, Shannon knew it would serve her well to come to terms with the fact that her mother had given her away, but it was a constant struggle. "It's not true," she told Rosella now. "I'm not vindictive or spiteful."

A subtle shrug of Rosella's shoulders made her appear doubtful, which caused Shannon to question her own character. She was afraid of making mistakes and letting people down. Oftentimes she felt inadequate, incompetent, and even unloved.

A swirl of emotions swept through her, taking her back to sixth grade. In her mind's eye, she saw Alex, a redheaded boy who was fond of tripping her at school. She had spent the entire school year wishing him dead. And what about the mean girls in high school? And the night she forgot to lock her bedroom door and Mr. Ferguson, the only man she'd ever called Dad, climbed into bed with her, his breath reeking of liquor.

Maybe she *was* resentful. And vindictive and spiteful, too. Her head fell forward. She listened to her breathing, thought of Trey and Mac and all the love the three of them had for one another. *No,* she inwardly scolded. *Rosella is wrong.* Shannon was a good mother and wife. She was a good person. She raised her head and met Rosella's gaze. "All I ever wished for when I was young was for my mother to find me and take me home. That's all I ever wanted."

Rosella's eyebrows pulled together. "I'm prepared to offer you triple the pay we discussed over the phone."

Shannon frowned. Had Rosella even heard what she'd said? Shannon rarely talked about her deepest feelings. The woman was completely absorbed in herself.

Rosella took the skeleton key that dangled from a miniature bronze statue of a small boy pointing at the sky and fiddled with her desk drawer. After a moment, she lifted her head and asked Shannon to look away.

"Lance loved his antiques," Rosella said, still talking after Shannon turned away, her view now of floor-to-ceiling bookshelves lined with Rosella's extensive collection of biographies and history books.

"My husband never allowed anyone to touch his seventeenth-century desk with all these silly doodads and secret compartments. 'If they can't find it, they can't steal it,' he was fond of saying."

Shannon heard a drawer somewhere within the desk being opened. From the sounds of it, Rosella was struggling. "Damn lever," Rosella muttered right before what sounded like a compartment popping open. Thinking it was over, Shannon turned around in time to see Rosella jabbing her finger at something, maybe a button. A whir and a click sounded, followed by another pop.

"There we go!" Rosella produced a large manila envelope. "Here's some information to help you get started."

"But—"

Rosella held her arm straight out, the manila envelope grasped tightly in her hand. "No buts. I'm being followed. Everywhere I go, I feel their eyes burning into the back of my skull. A chilling note was left in my mailbox. Someone tried to break into my home. They are taunting me, and I'm convinced danger lurks in the shadows. Prove me wrong, dear. If you have the courage."

Rosella had lost her mind. Shannon's wish to decline working with the journalist sat firmly on the tip of her tongue, but the words refused to take the jump. Instead, a reluctant sigh escaped as she took hold of the offered envelope. She wasn't vindictive or spiteful. She was weak. And Rosella knew it.

Rosella's hands came together in one resounding clap. "We'll meet again tomorrow. Same time. Don't be late."

CHAPTER FOUR

The minute Shannon returned home, she headed for the guest room, where she promptly tossed the manila envelope into the trash can next to her desk. She sat down and logged on to her computer. Her heart was beating fast, and her jaw hurt from gritting her teeth for more than an hour. There was no possible way she was going to work for the woman. If she wanted to be an investigative journalist, she would do it without Rosella Marlow's help.

But first, before she could put it all behind her, she wanted to find out more about Rosella. Because not only did it bother Shannon that Rosella knew so much about her, it also annoyed her to realize she hadn't done her homework. She'd thought she knew Rosella, but in reality, she was only familiar with what the media world put out there for all to see. Rosella's words continuously poked and prodded, egging her on: *Any true journalist worth a grain of salt would gratefully help me gather information and prove me wrong if they thought I was crazy.*

Okay. I will. She clicked on the link to the site. Searchvio was a platform she sometimes used when helping with online investigations. Ones Rosella apparently knew about. Why the hell would she have bothered to dig so deep? The question boggled the mind.

Stop, Shannon told herself. *You need to focus.*

For a fee, Searchvio provided a variety of services and features that helped organize billions of records and paint a picture of the person behind a name. It was a remarkable service, but she didn't use it often because it was ridiculously expensive.

As she typed in information about Rosella—her full name, address, details about her husband and son, her property, and even her eye and hair color—Shannon kept thinking about her meeting with Rosella and how unpleasant, conniving, and paranoid the woman had been.

Once she initiated the search, Shannon cradled her face with her hands, her fingers pressing against her skull as she stared at the computer screen. Five minutes passed before information regarding her inquiry popped up on the screen. References and links emerged, one after another, mostly for projects Rosella had been involved with over the years. Included were facts Shannon probably could have found on Wikipedia. But as she read through the list, one particular reference stood out from the rest.

Marlow, Rosella (1974), Rolling Greens Psychiatric Hospital

Shannon clicked on the link. Despite Rosella's strange behavior this morning, she was surprised to see what turned out to be three pages of handwritten notes in hard-to-read cursive by a Dr. Lee Baker. Medical records, under the Health Insurance Portability and Accountability Act (HIPAA), were supposed to be private. Based on experience, though, Shannon knew that wasn't always true. Most people would be surprised to learn that health care organizations attracted hackers due to the large amount of patient data they stored. Patient records were easy to monetize. All the hacker needed was to find an organization that used an older version of Windows, which allowed them to create a backdoor access to the system so they could walk right in and take any information they wanted.

Shannon read every word. Apparently, Rosella and her parents never got along. There were multiple stories about Rosella lashing out, kicking doors and walls whenever she didn't get her way. After an incident with a shovel, the girl's parents brought her to Rolling Greens Psychiatric Hospital because, they claimed, they were afraid of her. One year later, she was released. She ran away and met Lance Marlow, a wealthy banker, ten years her senior. On the last page was an update, along with a reference to an arrest. Rosella had been jailed for attacking a woman she claimed was flirting with Lance. Her life changed for the better, Dr. Baker wrote, after her husband convinced her to enroll in school. She got her master's in journalism, and the rest was history.

Or was it?

Shannon took a few minutes to let what she'd read sink in. Apparently, Rosella hadn't been exaggerating when she'd talked about having a darkness within. Her actions today, her mistrust of others, and her mood swings prompted Shannon to google the symptoms of paranoid personality disorder: People with the disorder tend to believe others are trying to demean, harm, or threaten them. They can be hostile and argumentative and cannot see their role in problems or conflicts.

Shannon knew about the tragic car accident that had occurred fifteen months earlier, in which Rosella had lost her husband and son. Had the event triggered something within? Made a borderline PPD disorder unmanageable?

Feeling restless, Shannon tapped the tips of her short nails on her desk. The tiny wheel on the upper right corner of her computer screen spun as content continued to download. She clicked on links referencing articles Rosella had written. There was the one titled "A Day in the Life of a Journalist," another called "Femininity," and a popular story about AIDS. Rosella had covered a diverse range of subjects, and Shannon was familiar with almost everything the woman had ever written. Just when it seemed her search had nothing more to reveal about Rosella, a new link appeared.

Marlow, Rosella (2023), article, Sierra Adoption Agency

Shannon's heart accelerated. She clicked on the link. Rosella had written an article about biological parents and adoptees trying to connect. It just so happened Sierra Adoption Agency was the same place

Shannon had been left as an infant. The same place she'd reached out to at the age of twenty, asking if they would contact her biological mother to let her know she would like to meet. The reply from the agency came weeks later—her mother had declined her request.

For a few seconds, Shannon simply sat there and breathed. Not once had Rosella mentioned the agency or Shannon's connection to it. That in itself would not have been strange, had she not mentioned all the other random and obscure snippets she knew about Shannon's life.

Shannon printed the article and read it twice. Rosella had written it six months ago, and it wasn't her best work: wordy, confusing sentence constructions, overuse of figures of speech, and so on. There was no emotion. The reason Rosella's work stood out among all the other journalists, at least in Shannon's opinion, was because of her ability to focus on details. She was observant and possessed the analytical skills needed to clearly assess a situation. She not only relied on facts and evidence but also knew how to put emotion into a story.

But this story about the adoption agency was flawed. Boring. Emotionless. No focus. Rosella Marlow didn't appear to truly care about the agency or any of the people involved, so why had she taken the time to do a write-up about the agency?

Shannon stared at the article, the words blurring. Her fingers drummed against the top of the desk for another five seconds before she broke out of her trance and began searching for the agency's number. She gave them a call. Maybe someone there would know why or what had prompted Rosella to do a story about them. Nobody answered. She left a message asking someone to call her.

After she hung up, she noticed the manila envelope Rosella had handed to her sticking out of the garbage. Curiosity got the better of her, and she pulled it out and dumped its contents onto her desk. Notes and unorganized lists spilled out. Some had been typed on a computer and printed out; others were handwritten. As she skimmed through the pages, she noticed that most of Rosella's scribbles were about the neighbors:

Dianne Abbott

- Nurse at Sutter Hospital (part-time). Works in the ICU.
- Graduated from nursing school in 1995.
- Strong-minded. Athletic. Independent.
- Parents live in Florida.
- Son, Finn, five and a half years old.

A lot of pages had been torn from a yellow-lined notepad. She squinted as she read scribbles written in the margins: *Kaylynn Alcozar and her husband can't afford to live here. So why did they purchase a home in one of the most exclusive areas in East Sacramento?* The observations about Jason Abbott filled at least three pages, every margin crammed with hard-to-read writing. There were notes about Becky and Holly Bateman, including how they both identified as straight when they first met at UC Davis. Why in the world did Rosella care about any of this? Another scribble caught her attention. It had been lined through, but she could still make out the word *Trey*. And beneath his name was *Tori Hudson* with a question mark. And also a one-word question: *Affair?*

Shannon felt a tightening in her chest. This was insane. There was no other word for it. Why would Rosella have bothered researching Shannon's husband? And even crazier, why would Rosella give Shannon these papers, knowing she'd made these disturbing observations? Tori Hudson had been their neighbor in Elk Grove. Trey used to golf with her husband, Josh. And Mac had been friends with her daughter, Amelia.

Annoyed with herself for looking inside the envelope to begin with, Shannon scooped up the papers and shoved them back inside. She had a good mind to take it all straight back to Rosella's house right now and ask her point blank what she hoped to prove with all her silly remarks and annotations. She also wanted to ask Rosella about the story she'd written concerning the Sierra Adoption Agency. Did Rosella know of Shannon's connection to the place? No way. She would have said something.

All Rosella's erratic behavior made her think about the professor at California State University, Sacramento. Michael Barilla had been passionate and dedicated to helping students develop their skills. That's why she remembered him. But something niggled, prompting her to look up the primary number for CSU. Once she connected with someone at the front desk, she told them it was important she talk to the professor about Rosella Marlow. She hung up. All she could do now, she figured, was hope that he called her back.

CHAPTER FIVE

Chloe Leavitt strolled through the neighborhood, relishing the sights and scents around her as she made her way to Shannon Gibbons's home. She had seen Shannon leaving Rosella's house a while ago. Chloe enjoyed developing new relationships and expanding her social circle whenever possible; many considered her a one-woman welcoming committee.

The sun was shining and the birds were chirping, making it the perfect day to not only get to know Shannon but also show her around the area before pouncing. She hoped it wasn't too soon, but she had no choice in the matter. Time was running out, and she needed to ask Shannon Gibbons a very important question: Would she be interested in being a judge for the Best House on the Block competition? Shannon was new to the area and would offer a fresh perspective.

Feeling optimistic, Chloe followed the pathway to the front door and rang the doorbell. As she waited, she thought about what her kids often said about her tendency to be "too much" at times. When Chloe had asked for clarification, they said she was "too intense," "too dramatic," "too talkative," and "too enthusiastic." She smiled, thinking how her kids, all three of them, were too serious and way too judgmental.

When the door came open, Chloe tossed all thoughts of her kids' opinions aside. "Come on!" she said. "I'm taking you on a drive."

"A drive?" Shannon asked. "Where to?"

"You'll see," Chloe said. "It'll be fun. We have lots to talk about."

"I need to grab a few things first," Shannon said. She glanced downward at her feet and winced. "I also need to change shoes. My feet are killing me."

From the looks of it, the woman either hadn't had time to unpack her clothes or needed to go shopping. "Not a problem," Chloe said, stepping inside and shooing her away. Shannon ran off, and Chloe closed the door behind her. "Get your sunglasses!" she said in her loud voice, the one she used for her kids every morning when she was downstairs and they were upstairs. "We might have time to grab a bite to eat or a cup of coffee before school ends, too."

Never one to stand still for long, Chloe walked around the kitchen and adjoining rooms, surprised to see so many unopened boxes in the living and dining rooms. She grabbed one labeled KITCHEN SUPPLIES and brought it to the center island. It was a beautiful kitchen with marble countertops, custom cabinets, a porcelain farmhouse sink with Brizo faucets and Thermador appliances. She searched through the drawers for a pair of scissors, grabbed a steak knife instead, and used it to slice through the tape and open the cardboard flaps. By the time Shannon returned, she had emptied two boxes.

"There," she said. "Two down and only a dozen more to go!" Chloe laughed, but Shannon didn't appear to be laughing with her. "Oh no. I've done it again, haven't I? Overstepped my boundaries." She rested a hand on her chest over her heart. Despite her best intentions, her tendency to offer unsolicited help and advice had garnered mixed reactions over the years. "I'm so sorry."

"No," Shannon said as she walked into the kitchen. "It's fine."

"I see it written all over your face. You're too nice to tell me to mind my own business. It won't happen again. But," she added, "if you ever want help unpacking these boxes and assisting you with getting organized, I'm your gal!"

Shannon smiled. "Thank you. I'll take it from here, but I do appreciate what you've done, and I'll let you know if I need help."

"It's a deal," Chloe said. "Ready to go?"

———

Shannon had no idea what Chloe had meant when she'd said they had lots to talk about, but it didn't take long for the tension to leave her shoulders as they drove down Forty-Third Street to Forty-Second, and finally to Fortieth, all lovely. Chloe was everything Shannon wasn't—talkative, outgoing, and opinionated, for starters—and Shannon enjoyed her company.

Chloe pointed at various homes and went into great detail about defining characteristics of certain architectural styles. "There's a perfect example of an Arts and Crafts home," she said, slowing before she pulled to the curb. She pointed at one of the more earthy and subdued homes on the street, the exterior a combination of wood and stone. "Notice the broad, overhanging eaves that provide shelter and contribute to the horizontal emphasis of the design," she said. "The roofs, like this one, are typically low pitched and often feature exposed rafters." Chloe sighed. "Beautiful, isn't it?"

"It is. I love the simplicity and its overall connection to nature."

Chloe pulled her black BMW back onto the street. After a few more turns and a couple of stops, she pulled to the curb again, this time stopping in front of a charming Tudor home on Fortieth Street. She shut off the engine, unbuckled her seat belt, and turned toward Shannon. "If it's okay with you, I'd like to take a walk and show you one of my favorite houses."

"Great. I could use some fresh air."

They hadn't walked far before a white Range Rover stopped in the middle of the road. The window came down. A woman with dark, curly hair and dangling earrings that glittered in the sunlight stuck an arm out of the window and waved. "Hello! Book club is at my house next week. Don't forget!" Her eyes swept over Shannon. "Hello. I don't believe we've met."

"Shannon Gibbons."

"Janelle McKinnon," the woman offered cheerfully. "Nice to meet you."

"Nice to meet you, too," Shannon said.

"Shannon recently moved into the Craftsman across from Holly and Becky," Chloe informed Janelle.

"Caroline Baxter's place?" Janelle asked.

"Yes. That's the one," Chloe said.

"I heard from Peggy that Rosella offered Caroline a hefty sum to sell her house at a ridiculous price. That's why she moved so quickly."

Shannon's jaw dropped. "We used a respectable title company. There was nothing in the disclosures about a payment being made."

"Don't you worry. Sounds like gossip to me," Chloe said. "Peggy is a bit of a know-it-all who likes to make up stories."

"I know, I know," Janelle said. "But Sophie Pushkin, three doors down, confirmed the story when I asked her about it." She glanced at her rearview mirror and saw a car approaching. "I better go. I'll see you at book club!"

"Janelle is married to the head coach of the Sacramento Kings," Chloe explained to Shannon, then frowned. "Hey, what's wrong?"

"That's the second time I've heard Caroline Baxter's name," Shannon said. "Becky and Dianne seemed surprised by Caroline's quick move. And now this."

"There's something else on your mind, isn't there?" Chloe asked, her voice softening. "I dragged you out of your house and never stopped to ask whether you were interested in taking a short tour of the neighborhood."

"It's okay. I needed to get my mind off my conversation with Rosella, and I guess the thing about Caroline Baxter brought it all back. I'll be fine."

"I take it your meeting with Rosella didn't go well?"

Shannon exhaled. "You could say that."

"Want to talk about it?"

"I do have a question."

"Okay," Chloe said, waiting.

"Rosella was definitely acting strange. I don't know her, but I thought I did, and she was nothing like the person I had conjured in my mind." Shannon tried to sort through all the questions Rosella's behavior had raised before she said more.

"She was cruel? Unsettling? Outlandish? All the above? Sorry," Chloe added. "I don't mean to be flippant."

"Yes," Shannon said. "I would say she was all of those things. After I met with Rosella, before you knocked on the door, I did some research and found out she had been in a psychiatric hospital when she was a teenager."

"That's a new one," Chloe said.

"According to the doctor who wrote the report, Rosella was violent, and her parents were afraid of her." Shannon winced. "God, what am I doing? I shouldn't be sharing this with anyone. This sort of information could do a lot of damage to someone's reputation."

Chloe placed a hand on her arm. "I won't tell a soul. I promise. We used to be friends, Rosella and I. Sometimes, I actually miss the conversations we used to have. We would delve deep, beyond surface-level topics, often in ways that were meaningful and thought-provoking."

Chloe appeared wistful until another car drove by, the woman in the driver's seat honking and waving as she passed. "Maybe we should finish our tour and talk about Rosella later," Chloe suggested.

"Good idea." Shannon was glad to move on. She had mixed feelings about discussing Rosella, especially so soon after meeting her. As they continued on, walking beneath the canopy of trees lining both sides of the street, she thought it was a wonder Chloe could fit in a breath between sentences. She had a flair for verbal expression, and Shannon found herself thoroughly entertained as Chloe spoke about each stunning residence they passed.

"Every house," she said, "is a masterpiece in its own right, proudly displaying a unique blend of architectural styles." She raised her arms in awe. "Where else would you see such majestic Tudor homes with steeply pitched roofs, half-timbered facades, and leaded glass windows standing shoulder to shoulder with stately Colonial Revival residences, their symmetrical, white-painted exteriors and imposing porticoes speaking to a regal and timeless era?"

Chloe was right; Shannon had never seen anything like the Fabulous Forties—or "Fab Forties," as those living in the area called it. When Shannon had thought she would be working with Rosella on a story about homes in the area, she'd done a fair amount of research on some of the grander estates. "It does seem as if each home tells a different chapter of architectural history," she said.

Chloe stopped in her tracks. Her eyes brightened. "Yes! You get it, don't you?"

Shannon smiled. "This place. The trees. These amazing homes. It does feel magical."

They stood silently on the sidewalk, side by side. There was no awkwardness between them, only serenity. Shannon listened to the quiet murmur of leaves rustling in the breeze, and somewhere in the treetops, she heard birdsong. She felt as if she were listening to a symphony of nature when the front door of a two-story home across the street came open. A woman and her children made their way to the SUV parked at the curb. The woman ushered her children into the vehicle, waved, and said, "Hello, Chloe! Any luck finding a judge yet?"

"Not yet," Chloe said. "I'm working on it." She rested a hand on Shannon's shoulder. "Emily Carter, I'd like you to meet my new neighbor, Shannon Gibbons."

"Nice to meet you," Emily said. "I do have to go, but we'll all have to get together sometime."

Shannon and Chloe waved as the woman drove off.

"A judge?" Shannon asked.

Chloe nodded. "That's what I need to talk to you about."

Shannon waited for her to explain.

"You might have heard about the Best House on the Block award held in the Fab Forties each year."

"Yes, I have." In her mind's eye, Shannon saw the sneer on Rosella's face when she talked about the notion of Chloe Leavitt ever winning the award again. She heard the disgust in Rosella's voice when she'd said, *Over my dead body.*

Chloe pointed. "Do you see the home there, the one next to Emily's?"

"The Colonial with the gorgeous pillars," Shannon said. "It's the first house I noticed when I stepped onto the sidewalk."

"The house belongs to Greta and Henry Knightley. I am happy to report it will be part of the tour this year. Wait until you see the inside. There's a gourmet kitchen with a delightful butler's pantry, and a kitchen nook, and oh my goodness, a sophisticated fireplace with french doors leading to a music room—"

Chloe stopped midsentence, prompting Shannon to follow her upward gaze to a floor-to-ceiling window on the top floor. There was someone near the window. A man.

"Is he practicing yoga?" Shannon asked.

"I believe so," Chloe said.

The man pivoted so he was facing the window straight on.

"He's in the Tree Pose," Shannon said. "Is he naked?"

"Yes. Yes, he is."

"Oh no," Shannon whispered.

"Yessiree. He's doing the Downward-Facing Dog." Chloe grabbed hold of Shannon's arm and dragged her back toward the car. They both started laughing as Chloe fumbled to unlock the car so they could get away as fast as possible.

They buckled up and Chloe started the engine and took off.

Shannon couldn't stop giggling like a twelve-year-old schoolgirl.

Chloe was smiling from ear to ear. "I don't think I've ever seen that side of Mr. Knightley."

"I would hope not. Does this mean Mr. Knightley's odds of winning the BHOTB award are even better?"

Chloe glanced her way. "Are you serious? Absolutely!"

They both burst out laughing again.

"Thanks for taking me on a drive," Shannon said once she got control of herself. "I needed a good laugh."

"Don't thank me," Chloe said. "Thank Mr. Knightley. Hey, do you want to go to Temple and grab some coffee?"

"I'd love to."

Fifteen minutes later, they had their lattes and were sitting at a table outside Temple Coffee Roasters on H Street. The day was bright and clear, not a cloud in sight. People were coming and going, some with dogs, others with strollers. "What was it you were going to tell me about needing a judge?"

Chloe set her latte on the table. "Well, I do realize I am asking a lot from you. You're new to the neighborhood, we only met today, and here I am asking for a favor—"

"Spit it out," Shannon said with a laugh. "The suspense is killing me."

"I was hoping you would consider being a judge for the Best House on the Block award."

Silence.

Shannon thought of Rosella and how much the award meant to her. How could she tell Rosella she wasn't going to work with her and then judge her house? "I can't . . . I couldn't. Rosella is one of the reasons why we moved here. I couldn't do that to her."

"Rosella wouldn't mind at all."

"Oh, no, I disagree," Shannon said.

Chloe's brow shot up. "Please tell me she didn't mention the Best House on the Block award when you met with her."

"She did. She said she told you the only way you would receive the award would be over her dead body."

Chloe snorted. "She might have said those words. Who cares?"

"I do. Becky said Rosella was scary, stubborn, and overbearing. She wasn't wrong."

"I don't want to pry," Chloe said, "but I will tell you it would be unwise for you to make any decisions based on fear over what Rosella Marlow may or may not think."

"I'm just not sure being a judge would be a good idea."

"Think on it before you give me an answer."

"How much time do I have?" Shannon asked.

"Twenty-four hours."

Shannon laughed.

"I'm serious," Chloe said. "Scheduling begins in a few days. All volunteers and judges will be meeting later this week to talk about the duration of the tour and how much time participants will be allowed to spend inside each home. We have to decide whether it will be a single-day event or span an entire weekend. Please consider helping a girl out. While we drove around, I saw how much you appreciated the architecture and history of the area."

"Yes, but—"

"No buts." Chloe extended her right arm like a traffic cop. "Sleep on it. Okay? And we'll talk tomorrow."

After spending only a few hours with Chloe, Shannon realized she hadn't laughed this much in a very long time. Chloe was charismatic and fun to be around. "Okay," she finally said. "We'll talk again tomorrow."

"And no pressure," Chloe added before sipping her latte. "No matter what you decide, we're good."

CHAPTER SIX

At not yet seven thirty the next morning, Shannon set about washing strawberries and cutting into a pineapple, her daughter scrambling eggs on the stovetop while they discussed her teachers at her new school. Mac's youthful chatter filled the air, making Shannon smile, despite her eagerness to go see Rosella and confront her about what she'd learned.

"We all had to reach into a hat and pull out a piece of paper," Mac said. "Guess what fictional character I picked?"

Mac's excitement made Shannon think it might be a character from one of her favorite series. "Katniss Everdeen from *The Hunger Games.*"

"Nope."

Shannon tried again. "Jace Lightwood from Mortal Objects."

"Mortal *Instruments*," Mac corrected.

"Is that the name you picked?" They had forty minutes to eat and get out the door. Trey had left for work while it was still dark. When Shannon reached for the plates in the cupboard, she noticed Mac had grown another inch, surpassing her own height.

"Nope."

"I give up. Tell me."

"Sherlock Holmes. Pretty cool, right? I figured you could help me, since I'm supposed to write about him as if he's a real person. What's he doing now? That sort of thing. We could make up a case he's working on—"

Their conversation was interrupted by a ding of Mac's phone. She slid the frying pan off the burner and pulled her cell phone from her back pocket. "It's a text from Blake Leavitt from our block. He takes his sister, Ridley, to my school every day and said he could pick me up on the way, if that's okay with you?"

Although she liked Chloe, the thought of her daughter being in a car with a teenager she didn't know didn't sit well with her. "Since I haven't met him, I'm going to have to say no."

"Please, Mom. You told me a thousand times before we moved that I would meet new friends. I like Ridley, and it's not that long of a drive from here to Saint Francis."

"How old is Blake?"

"He's seventeen. He goes to Jesuit."

Mac stood there making puppy-dog eyes. The expression always worked on her dad and sometimes, like now, on Shannon. "Ask him if he can get here a few minutes early so I can meet him."

Mac didn't protest. She sent him a text.

No problem was the reply that came back within seconds.

By the time Mac finished eating her eggs and rinsing her plate, a black Mercedes had pulled up in front of the house. She grabbed her backpack, and Shannon followed her out the door. Blake and his sister, Ridley, leaned against the car, waiting. Blake straightened when he saw them exit the house. He and his sister were both tall with wavy brown hair, oval faces, and mischievous green eyes that tilted at the corners.

Mac's cheeks flushed when her gaze fell on Blake. "This is my mom, Shannon Gibbons."

"Hi, Mrs. Gibbons. I'm Blake, and this is my sister, Ridley."

Ridley looked bored, but she managed a nod. It wasn't until the girl set her attention on Mac that a smile broke out. When Mac walked over to her, Ridley talked to her in low whispers.

"Mom told me she met you," Blake said.

"Yes," Shannon said. "We had fun together."

"She wanted you to know I'm a responsible driver."

"So I've heard. You're seventeen?"

"Yes," he said. "I've been driving for a while now. I'm a careful driver. I follow the rules."

Shannon smiled. He seemed like a sweet kid.

"Time to go!" his sister called out before she climbed into the front seat and shut the door. Mac looked at Shannon as if waiting for her approval.

Shannon nodded, then watched Mac climb into the back of the car and dutifully put on her seat belt.

"Is there anything else you want to know?" Blake asked. "My dad is a workaholic, my mom is a talker who tends to worry too much, and my little brother is even more annoying than my sister."

"No," Shannon said with a laugh. "I don't have any further questions. I'm going to take your word for it that you'll drive with extreme care."

"I have to pick up my sister after school, so I can bring Mac home, too."

Shannon hesitated before saying, "Sure. We'll give it a try."

"Okay. Time to get going." As they drove off, he gave a little wave. Shannon crossed her arms. The boy was too charming for his own good. He probably had dozens of girls swooning at his feet. Mac didn't stand a chance of resisting his charms.

Shannon knocked again. *I'm here, Rosella,* she thought. *On time. Five minutes early, in fact. I have a few questions for you.* The door creaked open, and Shannon jumped. She hadn't even touched the door handle. Through the opening, she saw the gleaming wood floor in the entryway. Using two fingers, she pushed the door open another three inches and called out, "Rosella! Are you there?"

Nothing.

Shannon waited.

There was a squeak. Someone stepping on loose flooring? A cabinet door?

Chills crawled up her arms, prompting her to glance over her shoulder. If not for the magnolia trees in front of Chloe Leavitt's house, she might have been able to see whether anyone was outside and ask whether they had seen Rosella this morning.

Instead, she turned back toward Rosella's front entry and lectured herself for getting worked up over nothing. Rosella could be in the shower or hard at work in her office. Time had probably slipped away from her. Maybe she'd forgotten Shannon was coming.

Though worried she might get her head bitten off if she entered without permission, Shannon did it anyway. She'd hardly slept last night, thinking about all the questions she had for Rosella, starting with, *What prompted you to do a story about the Sierra Adoption Agency? And what's the deal with those random notes suggesting my husband is having an affair?* Shannon had left a message at the agency but had yet to receive a call back.

With those questions swirling inside her head, she stepped into Rosella's house and walked quietly toward the kitchen, not wanting to startle her if she caught her unaware. The bottom floor of the house had a wide-open concept. The kitchen was massive, with lots of natural light and a twelve-foot white marble island and leather stools. Nobody was there.

Shannon continued through the house, peeked into the laundry room, and made her way down a long, narrow hallway. The walls were lined with framed pictures of Rosella hanging out with famous people: Anderson Cooper, Martha Stewart, and Maria Shriver, to name a few. There was a closed door at the end of the hallway. Resting her hand on the doorknob, Shannon considered turning around and leaving. Instead, she took a breath and opened the door wide.

What on earth?

Every wall in the small, square room was plastered with a collage of pictures of Rosella's son. Dozens of cutouts of the name Daniel had been taken from newspapers and magazines and taped, glued, or stapled to the wall. Baby photos were mixed in with older pictures of her son. Many of the photos had his age written on the photo with a thick black Sharpie. Also fastened to the wall were wilted flowers, a key, and a child-size green-and-gold jersey with Daniel's name on it. A long rectangular table had been pushed against the wall and was adorned with an eleven-by-fourteen-inch, framed picture of Daniel and surrounded by thick, cream-colored candles covered with wax drippings. School papers and drawings of stick people were taped to the windows, along with report cards and certificates. Every trophy Daniel had ever received appeared to be lined up neatly on the floor.

Transfixed by what she was seeing, Shannon opened the closet. Her eyes widened as she took it all in. The inside of the closet was covered with red hearts. The space appeared to be a canvas of love and longing, with hearts of all shapes and sizes pinned directly onto the walls. Some had been meticulously crafted from paper, others cut from fabric. Hearts encapsulated within shadow boxes and picture frames also clung to the wall, one with broken glass. The space was hauntingly beautiful yet achingly poignant. Bankers Boxes covered the floor. She lifted the lid from one of them. It was filled with pictures and memorabilia.

A wave of compassion washed over her. She couldn't even try to put herself in Rosella's shoes. If something ever happened to Mac, how in the world would she ever find a way to move on? Rosella's mean and erratic behavior could be a manifestation of her grief. It shamed her to think of how she'd struggled to sympathize with the woman's distress. She needed to apologize.

Footfalls on the floor above alerted Shannon. Rosella was here! She exited the room, shutting the door behind her before rushing to the bottom of the stairs. "Rosella! I'm here. It's Shannon."

Still no answer.

Despite wanting to talk to Rosella, she again considered leaving. But then what? Call the police in hopes they'd come check the house?

If she told them about Rosella's worry she was being watched, maybe they would come pronto. Or maybe they wouldn't.

Damn. She felt as if she were left with no choice but to head upstairs. Her stomach curdled at the thought of interrupting Rosella while she was working. Most likely she was using her binoculars to watch the neighbors. People she disliked and apparently wanted to destroy.

At the top landing, she called out again and headed for Rosella's office. The wide, heavy double doors were shut. Frustrated it had come to this, she knocked twice before pushing open the doors, ready to lecture Rosella for leaving her front door open, especially when she was so certain someone was watching her.

A knot of worry tightened in her chest when she spotted Rosella slumped over her desk. "Rosella?" She stepped closer. Her breath caught in her throat as her gaze landed on the letter opener sticking out of Rosella's pale neck. A stream of blood flowed like lava from the wound. There was blood splattered across the desk. Her desk calendar was soaked crimson. Reaching for Rosella's hand, Shannon wrapped her fingers around her wrist to see whether there was a pulse. "Rosella," she said, her voice quivering.

No. Please. She can't be dead.

A grunt, followed by the rhythmic thuds of feet hitting the hallway floor, caught her attention. She looked in the direction of the noise in time to see a shadow sweep past.

"Wait! What are you doing?" Shannon dropped Rosella's hand and ran down the hallway toward the landing. When she reached the stairs and saw the entry door slam shut, she stopped, realizing it would be foolish to give chase—they could be a killer. She rushed back to the office and pulled out her phone and called 911. After giving the operator her name and Rosella's address, she noticed one of Rosella's fingers moving.

Oh my God! She's alive. She hung up over the 911 operator's objections and reached for Rosella's hand.

"Rosella! Can you hear me? The police are on their way." Shannon looked around for something, anything, to use to try to stop the bleeding, but there was nothing. If she pulled out the weapon, which she could now see was a letter opener, Rosella would die almost instantly. Rosella's lips moved, prompting Shannon to lean close, her ear hovering over Rosella's mouth.

"Will-i-sss," Rosella said in a breathy whisper, ending with a wet, crackling moan.

"Willis?" Shannon asked, trying to understand.

"Son," Rosella said next, the word long and drawn out, followed by a gurgly cough.

Whatever she was trying to say made no sense to Shannon.

Rosella's breath rattled. "He's here." Her head rolled to the side, and her body went limp.

"Who is here, Rosella? Please. Hang on. Help will be here soon."

Shannon put two fingers to the inside of Rosella's wrist, pressing lightly, feeling for a pulse. There was none. She felt queasy. This couldn't be happening. Every part of her trembled.

He's here, Rosella had said.

"The killer is here?" Shannon asked aloud. Was that what Rosella was trying to tell her?

Sirens sounded in the distance. *Thank God.* Running to the window, she was relieved to see a police vehicle approaching the house. She made a mad dash out of the office and held tight to the railing as she hurried down the stairs, opening the door as two police cars and an ambulance lined up at the curb.

She waved her arms above her head. "She's upstairs," she called out to the officer. "You need to hurry."

Before entering the house, he said to his partner, "Frank, take her somewhere private and stay with her until Detective Seicinski gets here."

"I need to return home and call my husband," Shannon said, wishing Trey were here with her now.

He shook his head as he headed upstairs. "Stay put for now, ma'am."

Looking as if he'd picked the short straw, Frank ushered Shannon to the living room. Teetering slightly, afraid she might faint, she plopped down on a white linen couch and drew in a breath.

Two EMTs entered the house, and Officer Frank directed them to the upper floor. He then pulled a notebook and pen from his shirt pocket, flipped the page, and said, "Name, address, and phone number?"

"Shannon Gibbons." She rambled off her cell phone number. "I live two houses down. We haven't been there long. It's, um, 4520 Forty-Fifth Street. The gray house with white trim."

"One *b* or two?"

"What?"

"Gibbons. One *b* or two?"

"Oh. Yes. Two."

"Address?"

Hadn't she just told him? "4520 Forty-Fifth Street."

"What's going on?"

At the sound of a familiar voice, Shannon turned and was glad to see Chloe standing inside near the door.

"Ma'am," the officer said, his voice stern. "I'm going to have to ask you to leave the premises."

"Why? Where's Rosella? Is she okay?"

Frank rubbed the back of his neck as he went to talk to Chloe.

"Rosella's one of my best friends," Chloe told the officer. "I need to talk to her."

Officer Frank took hold of Chloe's upper arm and showed her the way out. Back inside, he remained in the entryway for a moment, looking toward the street, no doubt making sure she left. Then he turned back to Shannon, he pointed a finger. "Stay put. Detective Seicinski will be here soon." He headed upstairs, leaving her alone.

The house was eerily quiet. The thought Rosella might really be gone had not yet sunk in. To think Rosella's fears had not been caused by paranoia at all made Shannon's stomach roll. How could she have been so insensitive to the woman's concerns?

"Is he gone?"

Shannon turned toward the door. It was Chloe. She tiptoed through the entry and into the living room. "What's going on?"

"I think Rosella Marlow is dead," Shannon said, relieved to share the burden of knowing with someone.

Chloe sank onto the couch next to Shannon. "What happened?"

Visions of finding Rosella filled her head. Shannon covered her face and began to sob, then pulled her hands away when she noticed the blood on them. It was all too much. She felt a hand on her back. Chloe was trying to comfort her, rubbing her back, saying nothing.

"It was awful," Shannon said when she found her voice. She filled Chloe in, shaking her head as her gaze focused on the splintered trim on the archway leading to and from the entry. Something was stuck on the wood.

"Are you okay?" Chloe asked.

"A little dizzy. I'll be fine." She recalled what Chloe had said to Officer Frank. "I overheard you tell the officer you and Rosella were close friends."

Chloe scrunched her nose. "I only said it in hopes he would tell me what was going on. I didn't say anything yesterday because I wanted you to form your own opinions. But the truth is, Rosella despised me. And to be honest, I didn't like her much, either."

"Oh."

Chloe patted her on the knee. "I am sorry this happened, though." She exhaled. "We had our differences, but I never wished her dead."

The clunking of shoes coming down the stairs prompted Chloe to jump to her feet. It was Officer Frank. His eyes met Chloe's at the same time his feet hit the landing. "Lady, I told you to stay out. This is a crime scene."

Chloe gestured toward Shannon. "She's new to the neighborhood. I was only trying to help." The officer shook his head, and both of Chloe's hands rose in a sign of compliance. "I'm leaving. For good this time."

No sooner had Chloe walked out the door than another woman entered. Shannon assumed it was Detective Seicinski, since Frank had mentioned the detective was on her way. She was five three, maybe five two. The dark suit she wore was a size too big and hung on her small frame. Her shiny black hair was rolled at the back of her head and clipped. In the middle of her conversation with Officer Frank, she glanced Shannon's way. She had an oval-shaped face and a youthful jawline. The sunlight coming through the door highlighted the shadows under her eyes, reminding Shannon of her husband after a long stretch at the hospital. The detective was fatigued. Either Detective Seicinski had a house filled with small children or she worked too long and too hard at her job. Maybe both.

"She's dead," Officer Frank said. "Attacked while she worked at her desk, from the looks of it."

It was true. Rosella was dead. Murdered. As she stared in the woman's direction, Shannon couldn't help but feel as if she'd stepped into a nightmare. Just yesterday, she had been inside her beautiful new home, in a beautiful neighborhood, with her beautiful family. And now, in the blink of an eye, her life had been turned upside down. Rosella was dead, murdered—possibly by someone Shannon had met. Someone on this block?

CHAPTER SEVEN

Officer Frank and Detective Seicinski had asked Shannon to stay seated. The medical examiner had arrived, and they would be back soon. Alone with her thoughts, Shannon was drawn to whatever was stuck to the splintered wood. She walked that way. It was a piece of fabric, soft flannel with jagged edges. No bigger than a nickel. When her fingers brushed over the small bit of cloth, it dropped to the floor as she heard someone descending the stairs.

It was Detective Seicinski. Her suspicious eyes bored into Shannon's. "Why don't we take a seat?"

"Can I wash my hands?" Shannon asked.

Detective Seicinski took note of the blood. "Not yet. We'll need photographs."

Another man walked through the front door. He stood well over six feet tall, broad-shouldered with a thick neck. "I came as soon as I could." His voice sounded scratchy and rough.

"This is Detective Toye. He'll be working the case with me."

Shannon set her gaze on Detective Toye and said hello. He didn't respond in kind, hardly sparing her a glance. The man appeared surly, bordering on hostile. In contrast, he made Detective Seicinski look approachable and pleasant. Shannon took a seat on the couch.

Detective Seicinski didn't waste any time getting down to business. She pulled out her phone, jabbed her finger at it, and scrolled. "I'm Detective Seicinski."

"Officer Frank told me you were coming."

"Your name is Shannon Gibbons, and you live a few doors away. Is that correct?"

"Yes."

"If you don't mind, it would be helpful if you could tell me what happened this morning."

Shannon's heart was beating fast. Too fast. She had done nothing wrong. "Um, after my daughter left for school this morning, I came to see Rosella as planned."

"What time was that?"

"Our meeting was set for eight. Rosella was upset when I arrived late yesterday, so I made sure to be at least five minutes early. When I knocked, I noticed the door was ajar, which surprised me."

"Why would that surprise you?"

"When I met with Rosella yesterday, she was worried someone was watching her. She thought everyone in the neighborhood was out to get her. That's why my first thought was, Why would she not lock her door?"

"I see." Unlike Officer Frank, who had used paper and pen, the detective took notes directly on her cell phone. When she was done, she raised her gaze to meet Shannon's. "And what did you do after you noticed the door was open?"

"I pushed the door wide enough to see inside and call out to Rosella. She didn't answer."

"And you entered the home anyway?"

"I thought I heard something," Shannon said in her defense.

"And what was it you thought you heard?"

"I'm not sure. A squeaky noise. The creak of a floor, maybe."

"Go on," the detective prompted.

"I stepped inside. It was quiet, and I was at a loss of what to do. On one hand, I didn't want to interrupt Rosella if she was working, but on the other, I didn't think it was right to leave without letting her know I had arrived as scheduled."

"What did you do next?"

Shannon skipped the part about seeing pictures of Rosella hanging out with high-profile celebrities and the bizarre room paying homage to her dead son. "I went upstairs and noticed the office doors were shut. I didn't want to enter, but—"

"Why would you hesitate at that point?"

Shannon sighed. "Because I thought I would find Rosella standing at the window overlooking the neighborhood with a pair of binoculars in hand."

The detective's hand grasping the iPhone dropped to her side. "Maybe we should start from the beginning."

"The beginning?"

Detective Seicinski nodded. "How long have you known Rosella Marlow?"

"She first emailed me to see if I would be interested in working with her six months ago."

Detective Seicinski made a note before saying, "Officer Frank said you were new to the area."

"Yes. We've only been here for a week. My house is a mess. Boxes everywhere. We—"

"Let's back up," Detective Seicinski said. "What do you do for a living?"

"I'm a stay-at-home mom," Shannon answered.

"Do you have any experience in journalism?"

"I have a degree in journalism."

"Six months ago, when Rosella Marlow emailed you out of the blue, you had never met her before?"

"Correct."

Detective Toye frowned. "Hold on a minute," he said. "One of the premier journalists in the country reached out to *you* to see if you would be interested in working with her? Don't you find that a little odd?"

"I did," Shannon said. "I mean, I still do."

Detective Seicinski said, "Why don't you tell us more about what the email said?"

Shannon spent the next twenty minutes telling the detectives everything. About her desire to become a journalist, and how she'd always idolized Rosella, and how shocked she was when she received Rosella's email, thinking it had to be a mistake. She told the detectives about her husband landing a job at Sutter Hospital, and the house coming up for sale, and Rosella's job offer. The story ended with finding Rosella slumped over her desk, soaked in blood, and the loud thumping of footfalls as someone ran past Rosella's office, down the stairs, and out the door.

Detective Seicinski appeared skeptical. "Was it a man or a woman you saw leave the house?" she asked.

"I don't know," Shannon said. "The person rushed by in a blur. It all happened so fast. I was holding on to Rosella's wrist, trying to get a pulse, when they ran past. By the time I got to the top of the stairs, they were gone."

"And after that?"

Shannon put a hand to her forehead, tried to think. "I called 911, then I saw Rosella move and told her help was on the way." She put a hand to her stomach. "There was so much blood, the raspy voice . . . I feel sick."

"Lower your head to your knees," Seicinski told her. "Now take a couple of breaths."

Shannon did as she said. After a minute passed, she lifted her head and inhaled.

"We're almost done, okay?"

Shannon nodded.

"After you called 911, you saw Rosella move, and she spoke to you?"

"I think she was trying to tell me something, but I couldn't understand what she was saying."

"Take your time."

"It sounded like she said *Willis*, but then she started coughing. It was awful."

"Did she say anything else?"

"I thought she said the word *son* and *He's here*. Do you think it's possible she was dying and she thought she saw Daniel?"

They didn't answer.

"After she spoke," Shannon went on, "I felt for a pulse, but there wasn't one." In the entryway, Shannon heard two men talking about the primary bedroom being a mess, drawers open, items tossed about, and how jewelry appeared to have been stolen.

"It could be a burglary gone bad," one of the men said. "Whoever it was snuck inside, pocketed some jewelry, found the lady in the other room, and quickly plunged the letter opener into her neck before the victim had time to scream."

Detective Seicinski cleared her throat, prompting Officer Frank to peek inside the living room. "You're needed upstairs, Detective."

"Can I go home now?" Shannon asked.

Detective Seicinski held up a finger to stop Officer Frank from running off. "I need the photographer to take pictures of Mrs. Gibbons's hands."

Officer Frank headed off to do her bidding.

"You look pale," Detective Seicinski said. "Do you need help getting home?"

"No. I just need to go home and lie down for a minute. I'll be okay."

"I may need to speak with you again."

"I have all her personal information," Office Frank said as he walked back into the room with a tall, lanky man holding a camera.

Detective Seicinski slipped her phone into her coat pocket. "We're done here. After pictures have been taken, Mrs. Gibbons, you can go."

Behind the detective, two EMTs rolled out a gurney with Rosella zipped up in a body bag.

"You're not planning on leaving town?" the detective asked. "No vacations scheduled?"

"No," Shannon said, feeling jittery and uncomfortable, as if she had done something wrong. "I have no plans to go anywhere."

CHAPTER EIGHT

Shannon's knees felt like jelly as she walked home. Her hands shook as she opened her front door, then locked it behind her. She went upstairs to her bedroom, looked around as she thought about going through the pile of clothes on the floor in hopes of finding a pair of sweats. But then she saw her bloodied hands and thought of Rosella lying on the gurney beneath a heavy sheet. She made a mad dash to the toilet, where she heaved and retched, then clung to the porcelain bowl, beads of sweat forming on her forehead, her breathing erratic. She felt weak and shaky.

When she could move again, she got up to wash her hands and brush her teeth. She changed into loose jeans and a T-shirt before walking to the kitchen to make tea, hoping it would help calm her nerves.

The sound of the doorbell startled her. Figuring Detective Seicinski had further questions, she opened the door. It wasn't the detective after all, but a man she'd never seen before—a large man. Not as tall and broad-shouldered as Detective Toye, but muscular and intimidating. He stood on her welcome mat, his brow furrowed, his eyes narrowed. "Shannon Gibbons?"

"Yes," she said. "And you are?"

"Sorry." He wiped his right hand on the front of his Levi's and offered it to her. "Jason Abbott. I live next door to Rosella."

Jason Abbott. She knew the name well. Every horrible thing Rosella had said about him played through her mind as she shook his hand and hoped he wouldn't notice her apprehension.

"Mind if I come in for a minute?"

"Oh. Now is not a good time. I've had a rough morning. Maybe another—"

"It's important," he said.

"I'm sorry. I'm expecting a call at any moment, and—"

His eyes darkened. "Fine," he said, although clearly, it wasn't fine at all. "I was only hoping you could tell me what's going on. My wife told me a body was taken from Rosella's home, and after the ambulance drove off, she saw you exit the house and head this way."

"Rosella was murdered this morning."

"She's dead?" he asked.

Maybe Rosella had been right about Jason Abbott. He showed no emotion whatsoever. The furrow in his brow deepened, making him appear cold and calculating. "I'm afraid so."

"I heard you were working for Rosella."

How would he know anything about it? she wondered but didn't ask.

Jason's Adam's apple bobbed. "Did she mention me, by any chance?"

Why does he care? Shannon felt uncomfortable and wanted him to leave. "I hadn't agreed to work with Rosella," she told him. "We were still figuring things out."

His jaw twitched. "May I ask what she was working on that would prompt her to seek your help?"

"I really can't say."

"You can't? Or you won't?"

A dull pain started at the back of Shannon's head, and behind her eyes, right before she recalled seeing a dark figure run past when she was inside Rosella's office. *Was it him?* "I need to go." She tried to shut the door, but his foot shot out, preventing her from closing the door.

"You didn't answer my question," he said. "What did the two of you talk about yesterday? Did it have anything to do with me?"

Her heart was racing. Before she could think of what to do next, Chloe appeared at the end of the walkway. She marched right up to the door and plunked her hands on her hips. "What are you doing, Jason Abbott?"

He glanced over his shoulder at her. "It's no business of yours."

Chloe's gaze locked on his foot wedged in the doorway. "Yes, it is. The police are right down the street. If you don't remove your foot, I'm going to scream."

"For Christ's sake," he said, twisting his foot loose and pulling it back. "Rosella has been telling lies about me for months now." He gestured toward the police vehicles. "And after finding out you were at the house talking to the police, I assumed the worst." He raked a hand through his salt-and-pepper hair, his face lined with frustration.

Chloe nudged her way past him and stood side by side with Shannon. "Nothing you said makes coming to Shannon's house and trying to force your way inside okay. You've got to get control of your temper."

"What sort of lies?" Shannon asked, still wary but also curious about what he had to say about Rosella.

"The list is long." He shifted his weight from one foot to the other. "Rosella was not fond of me. She told anyone who would listen that I yell at my wife, my kids, and even her dog. She sent a letter to my boss at work, telling him I've been stealing from the company."

"Embezzlement?" Shannon tried to sound surprised, which in a way, she was. Because Rosella told her she'd sent the letter to Jason. Also, the man appeared to be genuine.

He nodded. "My boss hired an outside company to do an audit. The whole thing was humiliating, but I was able to prove my innocence."

"What about a property-line dispute?" Shannon asked.

He sighed. "I took her to court to show her what it felt like to be constantly badgered. I'm not proud of it. In fact, I wish I could have ignored the woman."

"Did Rosella's actions make you want to retaliate in some way?"

His gaze met hers, his dark eyes boring into hers. It was as if he were trying to figure out what she was thinking. "She *did* tell you things about me, didn't she?"

Shannon didn't answer. She didn't have to. He said, "I'm not a violent person. The thought of doing Rosella harm never crossed my mind. The only thing I wanted to do after the letter incident was move away from here. I'd had enough. But my wife refused. She's convinced Rosella went off the deep end after losing her son."

Shannon let that soak in. "So you never sent Rosella a note in retaliation?"

"Is that what she said?"

Shannon said nothing.

"No. I never sent her anything. I steered clear of the woman. Never said a word to her about the hell she'd caused me at work." He sighed. "And in case you're wondering, I had nothing to do with her death."

"You need to go," Chloe said. "Can't you see Shannon has dealt with enough trauma for one morning?"

"Sure. Whatever." He raised a hand in surrender. "I've said what I needed to say."

Chloe shut and locked the door, then escorted Shannon to the living room and told her to sit down. Shannon was too worn out to argue. Chloe headed for the kitchen and returned with a damp cloth. "Here. Lean back and put this on your forehead."

Shannon had to admit the cool cloth felt nice.

"I found some tea and put the kettle on the stove." Chloe took a seat on the couch beside her. "Are you going to be okay?"

"I'm fine, but I can't believe Rosella is gone. Forever. Who would do such a thing?"

"I don't know. It could have been anyone. She wasn't well liked, but still, the thought of someone hating her enough to kill her is beyond my imagination."

"You don't think anyone in the neighborhood killed her, do you?"

"No. Of course not. Jason has always been a hothead. It doesn't take much to set him off, but I don't think he would hurt anyone."

"What about everyone else on the block?"

Chloe's eyes widened. "You mean Becky and Holly? Jason's wife, Dianne? Kaylynn and Nicolas?" There was a long pause before she said, "Me?" She shook her head. "No way." The kettle began to whistle. Chloe went to the kitchen, returning a few minutes later with steaming mugs of tea. "Do you need sugar? I put a slice of lemon in your cup."

Shannon removed the cloth and sat up. "It's perfect. Thank you." After a moment of silence, she said, "I don't know Jason like you do, but he really did scare me."

"I promise you, cross my heart and hope to die, that Jason Abbott is all bark and no bite."

"I'm not convinced. His clenched jaw and the way his eyes darkened . . ." Shannon shivered. "Rosella was afraid of him, too. In fact, she was afraid of everyone in the neighborhood."

Chloe set her mug on the coffee table. "She said that?"

"Yes. I know we talked a little about my meeting with Rosella yesterday, but all I can say is that it was strange. For starters, she was upset with me for being late. And she couldn't let it go, went on and on about it."

"That sounds like Rosella."

"The entire conversation was strange. One moment she was trying to convince me she was frightened, telling me she was being watched from afar, and in the next moment, she was expressing her dislike for Jason Abbott."

"So she did talk about Jason."

"Yes. She talked about everyone," Shannon said. "She wasn't fond of Becky or Holly, either."

Chloe's eyebrows shot upward. "Those ladies are angels from heaven. They organize cleanup activities and all sorts of neighborhood projects."

"Rosella said they are always asking for money for one fundraiser or another."

"Go on," Chloe urged. "Did she say anything about the Alcozars?"

"Only that she thought they might be hiding something."

"Hiding what?"

"Rosella didn't know, but she was confident in her ability to recognize those kinds of things."

"Nonsensical chatter," Chloe said.

Shannon sighed, feeling uneasy, as if she were betraying Rosella's confidence, which was absurd. The woman was dead.

"I have to admit," Chloe said as she rubbed her chin in thought, "Rosella has been acting stranger than usual of late."

"The truth is, Rosella not only thought everyone was hiding something but also thought everyone in the neighborhood was out to get her."

Chloe pulled a face. "Out to get her?"

"Yes. Rosella was certain somebody meant to cause her harm."

"Very strange," Chloe said. "And what about me? Did she say anything about me?"

Shannon nodded. "She said the two of you had been close friends until you set your sights on her husband."

"It's true." Her gaze met Shannon's. "Not the part about me setting my sights on Lance, but the part about us being close friends. In the beginning, at least." She shrugged. "I treated Lance like anyone else. I was friendly. I thought he was a nice guy. But I'm sorry, never mind that he looked like a frog, he had the personality of faded wallpaper."

Shannon sipped her tea, thankful to have Chloe here with her. She was a good distraction after what had happened.

"What did the detectives want? You were there for a long time."

"I think I'm a suspect."

"Seriously?"

"I not only found her but tried to feel for a pulse, and so I had blood on my hands."

"I guess that sounds like a reasonable assumption under the circumstances. I mean, you were the last person to see Rosella alive. But you didn't kill her, did you?"

Offended, Shannon said, "Of course not!"

"Then you have nothing to worry about. The police always look at the husband first. But since—you know—Lance is no longer with us, the person who *found* the victim is going to be under the most scrutiny. Don't you worry, though. Once they make the rounds and talk to the people living on the block, I'm sure we'll all be suspects."

"Why does that make me feel better?" Shannon said with a meek smile.

"Because you're human."

Shannon swallowed. "Can I tell you something?"

"Of course. Anything at all. I'm all ears."

"Granted, Rosella said some bizarre things, but she talked about most men, in her opinion, having wandering eyes, which usually leads to wandering hands, including my husband, Trey. She looked me straight on and told me to 'keep an eye on him.' Trey's not like that, but still, hearing it from Rosella, a woman who has gone out of her way to know everything about me . . . Well, it rattled me."

Chloe made a face, of which she had many. She was like Mac in that way. Expressive. Animated. "Try to put it out of your head," Chloe told her. "Rosella believed the worst of everyone, whether she knew them or not. I don't know how well you knew Rosella before you moved here, but she had issues. Number one being jealousy."

Shannon thought about the research she had done yesterday and about the mental ward where Rosella had been and what the doctor had written. She nodded. "I have always been a huge fan of Rosella Marlow," she said. "She was a trailblazer . . . a legend, an inspiration to people like me." Shannon exhaled. "But meeting her face-to-face for the first time was shocking. She was nothing like the person I imagined her to be. She was cruel. All I could think about while she was talking was how I could end our conversation and escape without causing offense."

"I've been there," Chloe said. "Believe me. I once ran into her while shopping at a department store. I was with a friend from college. Rosella stopped to say hello, examined my friend, and said, 'My God, you are ugly.' Can you imagine? If I was ever called down to the police station and told them half the things Rosella has said and done to me and my family over the years, they would put me at the top of their list of suspects. The woman was shameful."

"But not always, right?" Shannon asked. "I mean, if you were once friends with her, there must have been a time when she was normal, maybe even nice?"

Chloe gave the question some thought. "When I first met Rosella, she could be pleasant at times. But it always seemed forced. If we were in the same room, I could feel her watching me. I used to tell Wesley how I thought she seemed a little off. And then she lost her son, and I think she lost her grip on reality."

"In what way?" Shannon asked, curious, hoping for details.

Again, Chloe appeared to collect her thoughts before speaking. "Rosella had changed. After the accident, any warmth was replaced with an icy reserve. This might sound a little over the top, but I swear the loss of her son triggered her disordered thinking. She became much more reclusive, and her behavior grew erratic."

"She did seem paranoid, and her rapid mood swings were alarming," Shannon said.

Chloe nodded. "It was sad to see. Any of us who dared approach her were sometimes met with a storm of unpredictable emotions. The last time I spoke to her, she seemed on the fringe of sanity." There was a pause before Chloe said, "Daniel was her only child, and he meant the world to her. Everyone on the block tried their best to be there for her . . . Becky, Holly, Dianne, Kaylynn. But Rosella made it clear she no longer wanted anything to do with any of us."

Shannon began putting a timeline together in her head, speaking her thoughts aloud. "When I first spoke with Rosella, she wanted my help with writing a story about the homes in the area, but by the time I met with her, everything had changed. And now hearing what you think happened to Rosella makes my meeting with her much more understandable."

"If you don't mind my asking, what changed?"

"Instead of having me assist her with a story about the Fabulous Forties, she decided to write about the people living in the neighborhood. More specifically, on this block. She wanted me to get to know all of you, find out what made you all tick, learn your every secret."

Chloe's eyes widened. "What in the world?"

"Right? The whole thing—the entire conversation—was not only unexpected but also outlandish. I told her I didn't want to spy on my new neighbors."

"But she wouldn't take no for an answer," Chloe said, as if she'd been right there in the office with Shannon.

"Exactly. She was convinced everyone on the block had secrets, the kind of secrets that could destroy lives, and she was adamant about finding out what they were."

"But why would she care?" Chloe asked.

"Control? Manipulation? Rosella told me Jason had embezzled, which he told us was a lie. Even so, instead of going to the police, Rosella used the information she had to scare him and get him to back off when it came to the property dispute they were having."

"Do you really think Rosella wanted to find dirt on each of us and use it to blackmail us in some way?"

"I thought the idea was absurd, but after what you just told me, it seems logical. I did picture her wanting to use information she gathered to scare someone, to hold whatever she'd found in her back pocket until a time when it might be useful." Shannon sighed. "You know, by the end of our conversation, I wondered if Rosella wanted her neighbors to suffer as she was suffering. I figured it wouldn't be long before I was on her enemy list, too."

Chloe's head bobbed up and down. "Your logic is sound. She wanted everyone around her to feel her pain."

"Yes."

Chloe plopped both hands on her lap. "I should go now. Let you get some rest. I wrote my cell number on the pad of paper in the kitchen. Call me if you need anything. Anything at all."

"I will," Shannon said. "Thank you." She lifted herself from the couch and walked Chloe to the door. With Mac back in school and Trey working long hours, it was comforting to have someone to talk to, and yet her heart felt heavy with the weight of shattered admiration for Rosella, the woman she'd held in high esteem for so long.

Chapter Nine

After Chloe left, Shannon tried to eat something, but she wasn't hungry, so she took a nap instead. She was awakened an hour later by the sound of the door opening and closing.

"Mom! Are you here?" Mac stood at the bottom of the stairs. "Is Rosella really dead?"

Shannon plowed her fingers through her hair, pushing it away from her eyes. She felt as if she could use a few more hours in bed. "Who told you?"

Mac followed her to the kitchen. "Mrs. Leavitt called Ridley on our way home. She said you were the one who found Rosella and that you had to talk to the detectives on the case and everything. Are you okay?"

"I'm fine."

"You don't look fine." Mac wrapped her long arms around Shannon and squeezed. After she let go, she went straight to the refrigerator and grabbed a handful of green grapes. She popped a couple into her mouth, chewed, and swallowed. "Do you think someone in the neighborhood could have killed Rosella?"

Shannon sat on one of the stools pushed under the kitchen island. "Is that what Chloe said?"

"No. It's what Ridley and Blake said. They told me a bunch of stories about Rosella and how nobody liked her."

"What stories did you hear about Rosella?" Shannon asked.

Mac took a seat on the stool next to her. "After Ridley got off the phone with her mom, she and her brother started talking about how cruel Rosella was. They had so many stories, there's no way I can remember them all. Like how Rosella called the pound to have them come pick up a 'stray' dog. Rosella knew the Frenchie belonged to the Leavitts, but she took off the dog collar with all the tags before the animal service truck arrived. The only reason the Leavitts found Carlin—that's the dog's name—was because he had a microchip."

"That is horrible."

"It gets worse," Mac said after eating another handful of grapes. "Whenever their dog poops on Rosella's lawn, she scoops it up and leaves it on their welcome mat."

"How would she know it belonged to their dog?"

"That's what I wanted to know," Mac said. "Rosella told them she had a video of it on her phone. One time she even called the cops on Blake and Ridley when their parents were out to dinner. Rosella told the police they were having a party and doing drugs. Two uniformed officers insisted on entering the house and having a look around. They even went upstairs and put a bottle of pills for anxiety into a paper bag and took it with them."

Shannon had no words.

"Rosella even hit Blake with a broom once," Mac went on. "Ridley said he had bruises all over his chest and neck, but I guess it turned into a 'he said, she said' argument, and the police told Mrs. Leavitt there was nothing they could do about it. Pretty wild, don't you think?"

"I agree," Shannon said, her thoughts drifting back to the day before, when Rosella had rambled on about the horrible people in the neighborhood. "I don't think Rosella was ever the same after losing her son and her husband in a tragic car accident."

"Yeah, I heard about that."

"No matter how awful Rosella was at times, it's sad, and something for us to keep in mind when we hear these stories."

"Yeah. You're right." Mac got up and went to the refrigerator again. "Mind if I eat the rest of this spaghetti?"

"It's all yours."

Mac pulled two glasses from the cupboard, filled them with filtered water from the fridge and handed one to Shannon.

"Thanks." Shannon took a gulp as her daughter emptied every last noodle from the plastic container into a bowl before placing it in the microwave.

"I also heard about Jason Abbott coming to the house," Mac said.

"It wasn't a big deal."

Mac tilted her head. "Mrs. Leavitt said he tried to push his way inside, but she stopped him and sent him packing."

Shannon nodded. "Mr. Abbott left. No harm, no foul. Let's keep this between you and me. Dad has been putting in long hours and doesn't need anything else to worry about." It wasn't the whole truth, but the last thing Shannon wanted was for Trey to confront Jason Abbott and cause a scene. There was enough chaos in the neighborhood right now as it was. She would talk to him about it another time.

The microwave beeped. Mac returned to the stool next to Shannon with her spaghetti and dug right in. "I am sorry about what happened, Mom," she said after a few bites. "I know you were excited about working with Rosella."

"Thanks." Guilt crept over her at the thought that she'd had no intention of taking the job.

"I was so distracted by my new school, making new friends, and all those papers I brought home last night I forgot to ask you about your meeting with Rosella. Did you like her?"

"Not really."

Mac dropped her fork into her dish, wiped her mouth with a napkin, and said, "Seriously?"

Shannon nodded. "She wasn't nice, and meeting her face-to-face was disheartening." Even now it made Shannon sad to think of the Rosella Marlow she had idolized for decades. She'd been an outstanding writer and journalist. And yet the person she'd met yesterday wasn't anything like the woman Shannon had built up in her mind.

"She was still going to mentor you, though, right?"

"I'm not sure." Shannon shrugged, remembering Rosella's taunting words. *Maybe I was wrong about you. Maybe you're not ready to work with someone of my caliber. Maybe being a mother is all you were ever meant to be.* Rosella wasn't the only one with good instincts. Shannon had left their meeting yesterday knowing in her heart of hearts she'd been duped. Rosella Marlow had only intended to use Shannon as her minion to do her bidding. She'd had no intention of passing on her knowledge and skills. But why had she dug so deep into Shannon's life and gone out of her way to find her?

"Earth to Mom!"

Shannon broke out of her thoughts and noticed her daughter staring at her.

"This is your chance, you know, to write your own story about what happened," Mac said. "Whether Rosella was naughty or nice, people are going to want to know what happened to her."

Shannon reached over, grabbed Mac's fork, and took a bite. She chewed as she thought it over. After swallowing she said, "I don't know if we should be having this conversation. She hasn't even been dead for twelve hours."

"If you were found murdered, wouldn't you want someone to figure out who did it?"

"There are detectives working the case."

"Mom. Listen to yourself. What are you afraid of? You have nothing to lose. All my life, I've watched you sit in front of your computer and help people, strangers you've never met, figure out who committed a crime. Think about it. A story of a lifetime just fell from the sky, right into your lap!"

Shannon saw the wheels inside her daughter's head spinning. She didn't want to scare Mac, but neither did she want her walking blindly into danger. "This isn't a Lois Duncan novel we're talking about, Mac.

With everything that's going on, you need to always, and I mean *always*, be aware of your surroundings. You need to be careful."

"You *are* afraid someone in the neighborhood killed her, aren't you?"

Shannon let out a heavy breath. "I didn't say that. I have no idea who might have done such a thing. And until we do know who was responsible, we need to be careful."

"I get it, okay? I'll be careful. But this is what you do, Mom. You always wanted to be a reporter, right?"

"A journalist," Shannon corrected.

Mac snorted. "Reporter, journalist, whatever. My point is, this is your chance to do your thing."

More exasperated than annoyed, Shannon asked, "And what's my thing?"

"Exactly what you've been doing forever. Following your instincts. Using Sherlock Holmes's methods of observation and deduction. He's able to gather small details and draw conclusions from them."

"He's a fictional character," Shannon reminded her daughter.

"You can do it, Mom. Uncover the truth. Figure out who killed Rosella so you can tell the world in your own words what happened."

"Don't you have homework to do?"

Mac gave Shannon a hug. "I am sad about what happened to Rosella. I'm also sad she wasn't the person you thought she was."

"Thanks, honey. I'll think about everything you said, okay?"

Mac was at the sink now, rinsing her bowl and putting it in the dishwasher. She looked over at Shannon and said in a motherly tone, "That's all I ask."

A stream of gratefulness passed through Shannon as her daughter disappeared upstairs. Despite everything going on, she felt thankful to have her daughter. Mac was growing fast. It was hard to imagine her daughter going off to college, so she swept the thought away.

Mac was right. Shannon had hoped to work with Rosella so she could learn and grow and challenge herself. Rosella may have discovered many things about Shannon, but she didn't know everything. She had no idea how much Shannon resented being played for a fool. Shannon would do whatever it took to figure out who had sent Rosella that note, and she wouldn't stop searching for clues until she knew whether someone in the neighborhood had hated Rosella enough to kill her.

It was past eight o'clock when Shannon heard keys rattling outside the front door. Trey walked in, and their eyes met. He shut the door and rushed toward her, wrapping his arms around her and holding her tight. "I'm sorry I wasn't here for you," he said. When he pulled away, he asked, "Did you get my message?"

"I did. Thank you."

"I swear it's never been so busy at the hospital. Are you okay?"

Even in his blue scrubs, Trey looked more like a surfer than a surgeon. His light-brown hair with natural blond highlights was wavy, thick, and hard to tame. His eyes were a dark bluish green, like the Atlantic Ocean. The dark circles hinted at the long hours he'd been putting in at Sutter Hospital. "Today has been beyond belief, but I'm fine," she told him.

Mac appeared seemingly out of nowhere. "She's not fine, Dad." She opened the refrigerator, scavenging for a snack before she stopped to add, "Did she tell you about the neighbor, Jason Abbott, the guy who drives the black truck?" Mac didn't wait for an answer. "He tried to barge into our house, put his foot in the doorway so Mom couldn't close the door!"

"What?" Trey looked from his daughter to Shannon.

"It was no big deal," Shannon told him, shooting a look Mac's way. "Jason Abbott lives next door to Rosella. He wanted to know if Rosella had said anything about him yesterday."

Trey's face reddened. "I'm sorry, but when someone—anyone—attempts to come into our house uninvited, that's a big deal."

Shannon sighed. Besides telling Trey she found Rosella to be a little strange and a lot paranoid, she hadn't gone into much more detail than that.

Trey headed back for the door. "I'm going to go have a talk with him."

"No," Shannon said. "Please don't. Once Chloe showed up and told him to knock it off, he removed his foot and we talked."

"About?"

"Rosella. He wanted me to know she had a tendency to lie."

Trey crossed his arms. "Why would it matter to him—on the day Rosella was murdered, no less—that you be aware of such a thing?"

"Let it go. I'm the one who has to deal with these people while you're at the hospital. I can handle Jason Abbott."

"You were here alone," Trey reminded her. "What if he *had* forced his way inside? What then?"

"But he didn't. He has a wife and two children. From what I've already gathered, Rosella hated everybody on this block and was out for revenge."

"Oh, that makes me feel better. And now she's dead." Trey rubbed his face as if he hoped to scrub away all the tension away. He dropped his hands. "Jason Abbott could be dangerous. In fact, maybe he killed the woman. I'm going to talk to him."

Mac's eyes widened. "Wait until this weekend, Dad. Ridley told me Becky and Holly were putting on a fundraiser this Saturday. Mom RSVP'd to let them know we were all going. Everyone in the area will be there. Talk to him then."

"That's a fine idea," Shannon said.

"There's no way I'll be able to go to work tomorrow without imagining Jason Abbott returning and kicking the door down." Trey headed for the door. "Don't worry," he said. "I'll be civil."

The door shut behind him.

Shannon plunked her hands on her hips.

"Sorry," Mac said. "I didn't know Dad had turned into such a hothead."

"He's frustrated. He's been working long hours. It bothers him that he wasn't here to protect me."

"Oh, please. Outside of a Liam Neeson movie, when does a woman need a man to protect her?" Mac shook her head in teenage disgust. "I mean, really. What's Dad going to do if someone comes to the door with a gun? Drop-kick him?"

Shannon sighed. "It's how he was raised."

Mac rolled her eyes, and the door came open, making them both jump.

"That was quick," Mac said.

"Nobody was home. I'll have to talk to him later, but in the meantime, I want you"—he directed his gaze at Mac—"to come straight home every day after school until an arrest has been made for Rosella Marlow's murder. Understand?"

Mac saluted. "Yes, sir."

"Dinner is in the fridge, if you're hungry," Shannon told Trey. "Would you like me to warm it up?"

"I'm going to take a shower first." He left the kitchen and headed upstairs.

Shannon turned to Mac, her eyes narrowed.

"What?" Mac asked. "I thought wives weren't supposed to keep things from their husbands?"

Shannon made a face. "Is that right? Maybe I should go tell your dad about the call I got from Mrs. Baumgarten before we moved."

"I told you, it wasn't me. I had nothing to do with TPing her house."

"You and your friends set off her security camera. I saw the whole thing."

"Wow. You can't get away with anything these days."

Shannon pointed toward the stairs. "Go finish your homework." Once Mac was upstairs, Shannon went straight to the living room and ungracefully plopped down onto the couch. Visions of Rosella slumped over her desk, two suspicious detectives looming over her, and Jason Abbott's dark and foreboding eyes swirled around like a twister inside her head while the conversation she had overheard played in the background: *It could be a burglary gone bad.*

Shannon bolted upright. That wasn't what had happened. Maybe Mac was right. In a way, Shannon had been training her whole life for this. As an online sleuth, she critically evaluated information and made connections between people, places, and events.

Rosella Marlow was dead.

Shannon needed to do what she'd always done: Observe and gather information. Talk to people. Search for motives and use logic and deduction to piece together the puzzle.

CHAPTER TEN

Wednesday morning, as Kaylynn Alcozar rinsed off the dishes left in the sink by their son, Holiday, she saw two people, a man and a woman, exit their car and walk toward Rosella's house. At first, she thought it might be a religious group spreading the word. Their shoulders were slumped, and their suits were wrinkled as if they had slept in their clothes, slipped on their shoes, and popped out the door.

Rosella's not there, Kaylynn thought sadly. *Rosella is gone forever.*

She wondered if she should call Chloe Leavitt. Chloe tended to be nosy, which came in handy whenever Kaylynn wanted to know what was going on in the neighborhood. Chloe had a cheerful demeanor, and she loved to gossip. Kaylynn had to admit she was envious of her at times. The woman had everything: a hardworking husband, three beautiful children, the nicest house Kaylynn had ever set foot in, and no outside job. Kaylynn had the smallest house on the block, which was fine, except it was old and needed a few updates. The roof was leaking and the dishwasher needed to be replaced. The house was either ridiculously hot or freezing cold—there was no in-between. Her husband, Nicolas, was a lawyer, and after he'd been promoted four years ago, they had moved to the Fabulous Forties. The area, and the house, was way out of their league, but they were good at budgeting, and they knew if they refrained from taking vacations and going out to eat, they could make it work.

Kaylynn worked at a local grocery outlet. She was the assistant manager, coordinating operations and training and supervising employees. Every once in a while, if an employee called in sick, she would find herself at the cash register checking out customers.

Kaylynn liked her job; she'd been working since she was sixteen years old. Though occasionally, she couldn't help but think about how nice it would be not to have to work so she could stay home with Archer. He would be six years old soon. The world revolved around her little boy.

Their older child, Holiday, was Nicolas's son from his first marriage. Holiday was quiet, spent most of his time playing videos on his computer upstairs in his room. He had politely informed Kaylynn early on in her marriage to his dad that he would not be calling her Mom. He had a mom, and although he rarely saw her, he thought about her often. Kaylynn knew this because he kept a journal. She would never have thought of snooping through his things, but on one particular day, when she and Nicolas were still newlyweds and she was collecting dirty clothes, she saw a notebook sticking out from beneath Holiday's pillow. Even now, it broke her heart to think of what he'd written.

The first entry she'd read ended up being a good representation of many of the others she had skimmed that day: *I spent all night crying, wondering why Mom never showed up.* Another entry read, *I called her five times. I told her I missed her. Two weeks later, she called to apologize. I could hear someone in the background, and I asked her who was there, but she lied and said she was alone; I asked her if I could live with her, but she told me she was super busy and it wouldn't work.* And so on.

Kaylynn sighed, her thoughts drifting to Rosella when she noticed that the man and the woman had disappeared inside Rosella's home. It dawned on her then that they must be detectives working the case.

It saddened her to think of Rosella.

Who would do such a thing? She understood why her neighbors had problems with Rosella and why they didn't care for her. But murder? Sure, Jason Abbott could stand to attend a few anger management courses, but he would never have killed Rosella. And not because he wouldn't want to risk going to jail, either. He was the one who had cared for the squirrel that had fallen from a tree and hurt its leg a few months ago. For over a week, Jason had kept the squirrel in a box in the basement and spent hours giving the animal food and water through a dropper until it was time to set it free.

Nicolas accused her of liking everyone. He always said she didn't have a mean bone in her body. Which was why she would make a horrible law enforcement officer, because she would set everyone free, and a horrible teacher, because all the kids would get straight As.

If Nicolas knew what she and Archer did every Thursday on her day off, when he was at work and Holiday was at school, he would go apeshit. He wasn't a violent man, but if she did something he didn't like, he would stomp around the house, slam doors, and lecture her for days. That's why Nicolas could never know she and Archer went to Rosella's house every week to keep her company for an hour or two.

The social calls had been awkward at first. Mostly it seemed Rosella was trying hard not to like her or Archer, pushing them away at every turn, telling them not to bother coming. Rosella told anyone she met that she didn't like kids. But it wasn't true; she liked Archer. Sometimes, Kaylynn thought maybe Rosella was fond of her, too. Despite Rosella's constant scowl and bitter words, whenever Kaylynn left the room for a minute, she would hear warmth in the woman's voice as she tried to teach Archer a new game or song. Nobody would believe Kaylynn if she told them, but Rosella looked forward to their visits. And so did Kaylynn and Archer.

Nicolas didn't trust Rosella, said he thought she was always judging them, which she most certainly was. She and her husband didn't argue much, except when it came to Rosella. Sure, Rosella was a bit eccentric, but she was also lonely. Kaylynn was confident Rosella would never tell any of the neighbors about their visits because she enjoyed being loathed. She seemed to revel in the hatred directed toward her, wearing it like a badge of honor. If only, Kaylynn thought, Rosella hadn't started asking so many questions, crossing a line from curious to downright intrusive. *What are you so afraid of, Kaylynn? Are you worried about Holiday? He did try to break into my house, you know. Tried to pry open the basement window. I took pictures of the footprints outside the window. He wears a size ten, doesn't he? You can tell me—everyone has secrets.*

Holiday did wear a size ten. That's when Kaylynn decided to stop visiting.

And then Rosella was killed.

The man and the woman, Kaylynn noticed, were knocking on Becky and Holly's front door. They must be detectives. They probably had questions. They probably had questions for everyone living on the block. Yes. That made sense. It was a homicide after all. It was logical they would talk to people in the neighborhood.

She put the dishes in the dishwasher and hurried to the living room, where Archer was coloring. Paper and crayons were scattered about the coffee table and floor. She glanced at her watch. She had nearly an hour before she needed to pack everything up and take Archer to Mrs. Whitlock's house over on T Street in the Newton Booth area.

She thought about leaving a little earlier in case the detectives decided to pay her a visit. She wasn't in the mood to talk to them. What if they asked her about Rosella? She would freeze up like she always did when someone asked her about something she didn't want to talk about. The idea of interacting with them filled her with apprehension. What if her reluctance to engage made her appear guilty?

CHAPTER ELEVEN

Chloe's thoughts were running wild, making her head spin. Horrible thoughts about the neighborhood. About her husband. About the kids. Even their Frenchie, Carlin, had somehow gotten thrown into the mix.

What had happened to Rosella had rocked the neighborhood like a comet crashing right into the street. From where she stood, even she could throw a Frisbee to Rosella's house. She had to get her mind off it. And there was only one thing that would help.

Cleaning.

The NPR podcast blared from her iPad in the background as she worked, organizing the random crap inside her junk drawers. She'd already taken care of the larger drawers holding the pots and pans. Wesley and the kids stayed out of her way when she got on a cleaning spree like this. Nothing could stop her.

She walked over to the iPad she kept on the kitchen counter and cranked the volume even louder. An elephant in India had learned how to help schoolkids cross the street, and now the local authorities were trying to put a stop to it.

After the junk drawers were sorted, she headed for the pantry to grab a bottle of Windex and the step stool so she could clean the window above her sink. She started scrubbing. The voices blasting from her iPad had become white noise.

Rosella was dead.

The bottle of Windex fell from her hand and spilled all over the floor.

Half a roll of paper towels later, she found herself back on the stool, staring out the window. She could see four or five houses down in each direction. She was like the warden of some neighborhood prison, with a view of the whole yard.

It wasn't her place to be worried, she knew that. But deep down, she didn't care. Every neighborhood had a cop. Not a real cop, but the neighbor who knew if one of your mailboxes had been hit by a car. Or saw the plumber earlier and wondered whether everything was all right. Every neighborhood needed that cop.

Chloe fancied herself as the cop for Forty-Fifth Street. She was okay with it. Hell, if she was being honest, she couldn't help it. Her daughter had once accused her of being nosy and fearful of strangers. But it wasn't that at all; it was the neighborhood itself. She felt a sense of responsibility toward its well-being. And to be perfectly honest, watching over the neighborhood gave her purpose.

Movement down the street caught her attention. Holly Bateman stepped out of her and Becky's Victorian rose cottage. At least that's what Chloe called it—the Victorian rose cottage, with its stained-glass windows depicting vibrant roses. Holly appeared to be fidgeting around with the unfinished, decorative front yard fence, a cute picket fence she worked on whenever she wasn't being a nurse over at Sutter Hospital. Holly turned, and for a moment there, Chloe thought she might have to duck out of view. But Holly wasn't looking her way. She was staring at Rosella's place. A whole minute passed. Holly still stared, and not any normal kind of stare.

Chloe nearly fell off the step stool when her phone buzzed. She pulled her cell from her back pocket. It was some random number, so she muted the call. By the time she looked back at the Bateman house, Holly was gone, leaving Chloe to wonder what was going on with her.

Maybe it's time I pay them a visit and check in? Before she could inwardly tell herself to *mind your own business*, she was out the door, heading toward the Bateman house. A flash of yellow captured her attention—the caution tape still wrapped around Rosella's veranda.

It took her only a hundred steps before she was knocking on the door. "Hi, sweetheart," said Chloe warmly to the little girl in Becky's arms. "Is this a bad time?"

"No," Becky said. "Come on in."

"I was taking a stroll and thought I'd stop by and check in to see how y'all were doing with everything going on." Chloe brushed a finger over Charley's pudgy cheek. The little girl smiled shyly at her. Her five-year-old brother, Ethan, was sitting on the floor in front of the television. "Hi, Ethan."

No response.

Becky shut the front door, locked it, then put the chain lock on the bolt. Even tested the door to make sure it was shut tight. "What happened to Rosella is just so scary," Becky said. "Holly and I have been shaking our heads all morning. We can't believe it. We feel like we're in a Netflix crime documentary right now. Only, you know. It's happening right here. And it's real."

"I know," Chloe said. "I feel horrible for everyone. Imagine being brand new to the area, like Shannon Gibbons."

Becky winced. "Oh, I hadn't even considered that . . . moving into a new house on the block and then, wham, someone is murdered. That would be frightening."

Chloe looked around the room. "Where's Holly? How's she doing?"

"Holly, are you coming down? Chloe's here." Becky set Charley down.

"Hey, Chloe," Holly said as she made her way down the stairs. Her hair was all over the place. She looked as if she hadn't slept in days.

"Hi," Chloe said, giving her a hug when she reached the landing.

"I'm sorry about Rosella," Holly said. "I know you two were close. Or you used to be close."

That was a long time ago, Chloe thought but didn't say. "Thanks. Like I was telling Becky, I'm sorry for the whole neighborhood. It's weird, you know—not normal to have someone murdered right next door."

Becky nodded along.

"Yeah," Holly said. "Now we're gonna be known as the murder block, or something like that. Kids are going to avoid biking past this street."

Becky peered through the blinds. "This whole thing scares me to death."

"She's having a tough time with it," Holly said, gesturing toward Becky. "I'm trying to tell her it was probably a break-in. They were probably looking for cash or jewelry, saw Rosella, and panicked."

"That doesn't make me feel any better," Becky said. "That's just as scary."

Chloe wondered how much she should prod. Nobody in the neighborhood had a good relationship with Rosella. And because of that, she figured she was safe to ask. Besides, she'd come all this way. "What did you guys think about Rosella?"

Holly and Becky shot looks at each other. One grunted. The other seethed.

"You want to take this one, or do you want me to?" Becky asked.

Holly plopped onto the couch and curled up next to Charley. She ran her fingers through her dirty hair. "I mean, it's nothing."

"Tell me." Chloe pushed Holly to speak.

Holly sighed. "I've had this weird thing going on with the CDPH. I wanted to confront Rosella about it. I needed to know if she was the one sending complaints to them."

Chloe frowned. She wanted to play it cool, act as if she weren't being nosy, just curious. But who was she kidding? "What's the CDPH?"

Holly said, "The California Department of Public Health is like the oversight board for nurses. If you complain about the hospital staff, they're the people you talk to. I got a complaint recently, saying I'd been unprofessional and that the patient could smell alcohol on my breath." Holly shook her head. "I was finally able to talk to the director. He said an internal investigation was being done and I just needed to be patient and focus on doing my job."

Becky folded her arms. "Holly doesn't even drink."

"Right," said Chloe. "You always have soda or whatever when we get together."

"Yeah, Cactus Cooler if I can find it. Anyway, we both think Rosella could have been the one sending the complaints."

Nothing Rosella might have done should surprise Chloe, but this did. Holly was one of the nicest people on the block. "Why would she do that?"

"Because," said Becky. "Because of what happened with Rosella's husband at Holly's hospital. Holly works in ICU. Lance was one of four patients she had to tend to, and Rosella blames her for him dying there."

"Yep," Holly said. "She told me exactly that at my last fundraiser."

"No!"

Charley was now sitting next to her brother on the floor, watching a *Magic School Bus* episode. The little girl cast a sideways look at Chloe when her voice escalated. "Sorry, sweetheart. Go back to your show."

"Yeah, so yesterday I went over to Rosella's house," Holly said.

Becky snapped her head around so fast it reminded Chloe of a scene from *The Exorcist*. "I'm sorry. You did *what*?"

"I thought I would be able to peer into Rosella's eyes and know whether or not she was lying." Holly glanced at Becky. "Stop looking at me like that."

"Like what? Like you're an idiot? Why didn't you listen to the director? Even if it was Rosella who filed a complaint, did you really think she would admit to any wrongdoing?"

Chloe was caught in the middle, like a spectator watching a tennis match where one of the opponents wanted to maul the other. If Rosella had been the one sending the complaints about Holly, she could understand her frustration. The complaints would be enough to not only lose a job but also lose a house, ruin a family.

Holly rubbed the back of her head. "Well, you probably won't like the next part, either. When Rosella didn't answer the door, I went inside."

Becky's eye twitched. "When were you going to tell me this?" She glanced at Chloe, who suddenly felt like she'd overstayed her welcome. "You should have called the police, like any normal person would have done under those circumstances."

"I was worried about Rosella."

"You couldn't stand that woman."

"True, but I never wished her harm. I just wanted her to leave me alone," Holly said. "I called her name, and when no one answered, I walked out the door and left for work."

Chloe wondered whether Holly was telling the whole truth. Her foot wouldn't stop shaking, as if nerves were getting the best of her.

There was a knock on the door. They all froze. Becky was the first to make a move. She took a breath before walking to the door. Chloe peeked through the blinds. "It's the detectives working Rosella's case."

"Why are they here?" Becky wanted to know.

"Don't worry," Chloe said. "I'm sure it's standard procedure and they're simply making the rounds. They'll probably come to my house next."

Becky exhaled and set about opening the door, which took a minute since the woman kept the house locked down. After introductions were made, Detective Seicinski asked if they could speak with Holly Bateman.

The house was small, making it easy for Chloe to listen as she quickly gathered the kids.

"Who is it?" Holly asked.

Becky turned to face Holly. "Detective Seicinski and Detective Toye with the Sacramento Police Department would like to speak with you."

CHAPTER TWELVE

Chloe had to act fast. "Do you want me to take the kids upstairs? I can watch them while you guys talk." She shot Ethan a big smile. "We can play with your toys!"

Becky and Holly both waved their hands. "No," Holly said. "Go on with your walk."

"We don't want to keep you," Becky agreed.

Chloe wagged her finger. "My walk can wait." She wasn't kidding. No way was she leaving now, right when things had a decent chance of getting interesting.

"If you're sure," Becky said.

Ethan jumped up. Excited. "I just got the *Ultimate Protectors Pack*! You can be Hulk."

"Wonderful." Chloe took Charley's hand and they followed Ethan up the stairs, one step at a time.

"Have fun, you guys!" Becky said in an overly cheerful, high-pitched voice.

Chloe glanced back at her, right as Detective Seicinski stuck her head through the door. For a flash of a second, she and Chloe locked eyes before she continued upstairs. The detective knew who she was because after Chloe saw Shannon leave Rosella's house yesterday, she'd gone back over there, to Officer Frank's dismay, and introduced herself, even gave the detective her cell number in case she had questions. Wesley had been furious when she'd told him that part. But she didn't care. What was the big deal? She didn't kill Rosella, but she sure as heck wanted to know who did.

At the top of the stairs was the loft with a couple of toys scattered about. That is, if *a couple* meant a hundred. Judging by the mats and dumbbells in the corner, the space had been a workout room at one time. Now it was filled with toys, including a miniature ice cream stand and a metric ton of colorful plastic blocks. Chloe smiled as she ordered a strawberry ice cream from Charley. She was promptly given a tiny spoon. Downstairs she heard them talking and strained to make out every word of the conversation.

Detective Seicinski said, "Your name is Holly Bateman?"

"Correct."

"You're married?"

"Yes. Becky and I married last year."

"You're an ICU nurse at Sutter Hospital?"

"Yes. For nine years now."

"Did you know Rosella Marlow?"

Holly nodded. "We were acquaintances, certainly not friends."

"Why 'certainly not' friends?"

Holly's tone was callous. "Because the woman was never nice to me."

"How so?"

"Oh gosh. The woman never smiled. Her expression was like your partner's—gruff and unwelcoming." Chloe heard nothing, which must have meant things were getting uncomfortable.

Holly finally said, "Rosella made it clear she didn't like children, backing away if they crossed her path. She was critical of the fundraisers we held here at the house. I can't remember a time when she had anything even semipleasant to say to me or Becky."

"And yet you invited her to your house, and she supported your charity work with her checkbook."

"True. Yes. She could be generous at times."

Chloe was impressed by how much these detectives already knew.

"But you didn't like her," Detective Toye interjected.

She paused. "No. I didn't like her."

Detective Seicinski spoke next. "Can you tell us where you were between Monday evening and eight a.m. on Tuesday?"

Becky said, "Weren't you at—"

Detective Seicinski cut her off. "If you don't mind, I'd like Holly to answer."

"Yes, um, of course," Holly said, stumbling. "I woke up around five and made coffee. The kids were awake by six thirty, maybe earlier. Becky had been out late, so she was still asleep. I made the kids breakfast, and I got dressed for work."

"What are you doing?" Charley asked, holding a stuffed pony. Chloe's ear was flat against the floor.

Ethan had handed Chloe the Hulk figure, and he kept bashing her figurine with the Black Panther in one hand and Captain America in the other. "Shouldn't they be fighting the bad guys instead of each other?" Chloe asked.

"If you want to see those police people," Ethan told her matter-of-factly, "you can look down the hole."

"What hole?"

Ethan ran to his room.

"Grab some toys and let's go," Chloe told Charley.

The little girl actually did as she asked. She dropped her ice cream cone, swept up an armful of Barbies, and excitedly followed Chloe to Ethan's room. The kid had already laid out the protectors in a perfect line and now dug through a bin filled with plastic toys.

"What time did you start work?" asked Detective Seicinski.

"On Tuesdays I don't have to be to the hospital until eight thirty."

Chloe's eyes widened. The voices were clear as day. She followed the sound to the floor vent, took a seat on the ground, and got comfortable.

"You were ready for work early that day?"

Holly stuttered before saying, "Yes."

"And you went straight there . . . to work?"

"Well, um . . . yes. I went early."

"I want to show you something we found inside Rosella's house," Detective Seicinski said.

"Okay."

This was too good! Chloe lay flat on her stomach and peeked through the decorative iron vent cover. Ethan was a genius. She could literally see Detective Seicinski retrieve a plastic evidence bag from her carrying case and place it in front of Holly, who gasped. "That's frightening. Why are you showing me this?"

"Because it seems to me whoever left this for Rosella obviously didn't like her."

Holly said nothing.

Chloe squinted. *Oh my God.* The detective wasn't kidding— Seicinski had placed some sort of weird-looking stick figure in front of Holly. A nail dripping with a gooey bloody substance protruded from the head. *Didn't like Rosella?* Understatement of the year! Chloe puffed her cheeks and blew out air. Whoever had left that thing for Rosella *despised* her.

"And as you can see," the detective continued, "it appears to have been made from the branches of a weeping willow."

Chloe couldn't see Holly's face, but she might as well have been sitting at the table with all of them, because she could feel the tension in the air. Holly was probably even more nervous because she had two weeping willows in her backyard. She had planted the trees herself because they reminded her of her childhood. Unfortunately for Holly, there were no other weeping willows on the block.

Detective Seicinski picked up the bag, let it dangle in front of Holly's face. "Have you seen this before?"

"No. It's disgusting."

She's right, Chloe thought. The doll was disgusting, but there was something familiar about it, and that worried her. Was she experiencing déjà vu? Whatever she was feeling, she didn't like it. It was confusing. She pushed all those weird feelings aside when she saw Holly's hands shaking. Panic was setting in. The poor girl.

"Were you at Rosella Marlow's house Tuesday morning?"

Holly didn't hesitate. "No."

Well, that was a lie. Charley picked that moment to sit on Chloe's back, her little legs straddling Chloe's waist while she played with her Barbies. She tried to hand Chloe a headless doll, but Chloe had her standards and quietly asked Charley to find her one with a full head of hair and a cute outfit. It worked, too. Charley ran off.

Through the vent she saw another evidence bag placed in front of Holly. Inside the bag was a mask. Through the entire Covid fiasco, no one ever saw Holly without a mask. She still wore them to the grocery store.

"Is this your mask?" Detective Toye asked.

Holly's voice sounded strained. "No. Uh, I don't think so."

He pointed at the mask. "That's a Sutter Hospital logo, isn't it?"

"A few of us living on the block work at Sutter," Holly told him. "It could be anyone's."

"Anyone's?" He flipped the bag over and jabbed his finger at something. "Looks like your name was stamped right here in black ink."

Everyone knew Holly stamped everything: books, notepads, shoes, even the brown paper lunch bags she took to work. Chloe knew because she found a baseball hat once and thought it belonged to her youngest child, Rowan, until he showed her the HOLLY BATEMAN stamp.

"Any idea what your mask might have been doing in the hedge plant outside Rosella Marlow's house?" Detective Toye asked next.

"I have no idea," Holly said. "I often have a mask hanging from my wrist. Maybe I lost it in my driveway and it ended up wherever you found it."

Charley was back. She plopped down on Chloe's back again, pushing the breath right out of her, and shoved another Barbie in her face, covering her view of what was going on downstairs. But she had to admit, cute little Charley had done a good job of picking out the right Barbie doll. Sequined dress, diamond earrings, matching heels. "Nice job," she whispered.

"Does she need to get a lawyer?"

That was Becky's voice. Chloe couldn't see her, but she imagined her standing there, arms folded and her face as forbidding as Detective Toye's.

"No," Holly said. "I don't need a lawyer. I did nothing wrong."

"We'll need you to come to the station today to be fingerprinted."

"Why?"

"Anyone who's been to Rosella's house will need to be fingerprinted."

"But I wasn't there," Holly said.

"There were fingerprints on the murder weapon," Detective Seicinski said. "Fingerprints we already know do not belong to the house cleaner or Rosella Marlow."

"Okay," Holly said.

Her voice sounded shaky and small. Chloe's heart raced. She felt sick for her friend. She had a strong desire to take action and support Holly in some way, but she was powerless, and it was not a good feeling.

"Okay, what?" Detective Toye asked.

"Becky's right. I want to get a lawyer."

Shit! This was not good. Holly had done nothing wrong. Why would she need a lawyer? Chloe refused to doubt Holly's innocence, and yet she knew her conviction went beyond logic or evidence. The loyalty she felt toward Holly was rooted in their history together, experiences shared, and the trust they had built over time.

Charley climbed off her, praise the Lord, prompting Chloe to push herself to her feet, which wasn't easy. Every joint creaked. She needed to get back to the gym. Right when she thought things couldn't get any worse, she saw a Channel 10 News van pull up in front of Shannon's house. "I think the visitors are leaving," Chloe told Ethan.

He frowned. "We didn't even beat the bad guys yet."

She heard the door downstairs open and close. Holding Barbie with her beautiful sequin dress in the air, Chloe used her ventriloquist voice to say, "I'll be back. I promise. And me and my friends are going to take you out!" She used Barbie's head to bop one of his figurines in the head.

Charley giggled, but Ethan crossed his arms and stared her down.

"Come on, kids. Let's go."

Chapter Thirteen

Shannon had walked to the mailbox and was heading up the brick steps leading to her front door when she heard an engine and turned toward the street. A Channel 10 News van pulled up to the curb in front of her house. The driver's door swung open. A young man with wavy brown hair and long, gangly limbs came around the front of the van and opened the side door. Two more people emerged, everyone concentrating on sorting wires and cameras. The woman sitting in the passenger seat jumped out, too.

Shannon recognized her as a reporter on the Channel 10 News. Dark hair, blue eyes, slender build. After brushing invisible wrinkles from her beige pencil skirt, she tucked in her white button-down blouse and grabbed a mic from the seat. She turned Shannon's way as something caught Shannon's attention, a movement to her right—a shadowy figure half-hidden behind a California bay laurel with a thick trunk. Whoever it was wore dark clothing and a hoodie pulled low over their face.

"Hello," the woman said, mic held firmly in front of her chest as she approached. "Devin Hawke with Channel 10 News."

It took longer than it should have for Shannon to realize why they were here. Rosella. Of course. When she glanced back at the spot where she'd seen the shadowy figure, nobody was there. Feeling off balance, Shannon hoped to escape before the woman cornered her. But Devin Hawke had a lot of experience, and the look of determination on her face said she was here to get what she came for. In the time it took Shannon to glance the other way, Devin had moved fast and was now standing less than a foot away, holding the mic in Shannon's face. The cameraman stood behind Devin, a heavy-looking piece of equipment settled on his shoulders, his legs set wide as if he were a human tripod.

"We're here on Forty-Fifth Street in Sacramento with Shannon Gibbons, who lives only a couple of houses away from Rosella Marlow. Is it true you were the last person to see Rosella Marlow alive?"

Shannon's feet felt like cement blocks. She couldn't move. And all she could think about was the dark figure she'd spotted up the street. Was it the same person Rosella had said was watching her?

"I-I—"

"She can't talk right now. You all need to leave."

Chloe Leavitt to the rescue again, Shannon thought when she spotted her.

Chloe swept past the cameraman and jumped over all the wires. After squeezing her way between Devin and Shannon, Chloe grabbed Shannon's hand and ushered her up the brick steps and straight through Shannon's front door. She let Shannon loose and turned back to Devin Hawke. "You should all be ashamed of yourselves. This woman is not only new to the area but also has been through a traumatic experience. Please respect her privacy."

"And who are you?" Devin asked.

Chloe smacked the door shut and locked it.

Shannon sat on the couch in her living room and let her head fall back on the cushioned seat. "Thank you. I didn't know what to do. I froze."

"Understandable." Chloe was already in her kitchen. She grabbed the teakettle sitting on the stove, filled it with water, put it on a burner, and fired it up.

"You know my kitchen better than me," Shannon said. "You have saved me twice in two days."

"It's what I do," Chloe said. "I was worried about the local news station coming around and making a nuisance of themselves. I just didn't think they would show up this quickly."

The thought of Devin Hawke popping out of a van this morning had never dawned on Shannon. But it should have. Rosella Marlow had been murdered. Of course Channel 10 News would race to the scene of the crime first thing.

Chloe ran around the kitchen like a woman on a mission, grabbing mugs from a cabinet and a spoon from the drawer as she talked. "Everyone in the neighborhood is freaking out, wondering if someone we all know might be capable of murder."

"I don't blame them. Who have you talked to?"

Chloe swished a hand through the air. "I talked to Kaylynn last night. She's worried about her boys. Holiday is sixteen and Archer is almost six. I spoke to Dianne, too. That's Jason's wife. She wasn't happy with him after she found out he came to your house. And I was at Holly and Becky's house across the street when I saw the news van pull up outside. You're never going to believe who showed up at their door."

"Who?"

"The detectives working Rosella's case."

"They let you stay?"

Chloe shrugged. "I quickly ushered the kids upstairs and they didn't try to stop me."

Shannon walked into the kitchen and sat on a stool. "I wonder why they started with Holly and Becky?"

Chloe placed a mug of tea in front of her. "I know why."

"You do?" Shannon blew on the tea and took a sip.

"Yep." Chloe stood on the other side of the island and drank from her own cup. "Guess who was at Rosella's house Tuesday morning before you got there?"

"Becky?"

"No. Holly." Chloe set her mug on the counter and filled her in, the words rushing out like water after a dam burst. She talked about the stick doll, the mask with Holly's name on it, the multiple fingerprints on the murder weapon, and how Holly needed to get fingerprinted, ending with Holly telling the detectives she wanted a lawyer.

"Holly didn't mind telling you everything?"

A sheepish smile played on Chloe's lips. "Holly told me she had gone to Rosella's house the morning of the murder. But when the detectives asked her if she'd been there, she said no."

"She lied?"

Chloe nodded.

"I thought you said you weren't in the same room as everyone else?"

"I wasn't."

"How—"

"Through the floor vent in Ethan's room. I could hear the tension in Holly's and Becky's voices and see the kitchen table where they were all sitting, including the evidence bags as they were presented to Holly."

Shannon shook her head in wonder. Was Holly the person she had seen run past Rosella's office? Could she be the killer? The image of the person she saw in her mind's eye was at least five-eight. "How tall is Holly?"

"Hmm. Five-three at most," Chloe said. "I hate to change the subject, but I need to know if you can come over tonight to discuss the Best House on the Block competition. I've invited all the women in the neighborhood. Some you know, some you don't. It will give us a chance to do a quick debrief about the murder."

"A debrief?"

"Yes. I don't know about you, but I'd like to know if anyone in the neighborhood might know something about what happened to Rosella." She anchored her hair behind her ear. "There are multiple fingerprints on the murder weapon. Fingerprints that don't belong to Rosella or her house cleaner." Chloe blew out a stream of pent-up air. "There's no way I'm going to be able to go about my business while waiting for two overworked detectives to figure out who the killer might be. What if I'm next?"

"Why would anyone want to kill you?" Shannon asked.

Chloe waved a hand through the air. "I was kidding. That was a joke."

"Oh." Shannon managed a weak smile.

"My point is, I refuse to sit still while a murderer walks around free. I get chills thinking about it."

"What about Holly?" Shannon asked.

"What about her?"

"She was at the house."

"So were you." Chloe's brow furrowed. "I think it's too soon to speculate."

Shannon wanted to ask Chloe about Holly—what she was like and how she felt about Rosella. But she decided it would be best if she went to the meeting at Chloe's and met Holly in person. "I agree. Patience is key."

"So you'll come, right?"

"I don't want to leave Mac home alone."

"Bring her, of course. Everyone brings their kids to these things. There will be appetizers and wine, too." She stood and headed for the door. "Oh. One more thing before I leave."

Shannon waited.

"Have you made your decision about whether or not you'll be a judge for the BHOTB award?" Before Shannon could answer she added, "It will give you a chance to meet everyone in the neighborhood. Even Mr. Knightley."

Shannon chuckled. "Sure. I'll do it." She had already been leaning toward saying yes. Mostly because she couldn't get Rosella's words out of her head: *They are taunting me, and I'm convinced danger lurks in the shadows. Prove me wrong, dear. If you have the courage.* Being involved with the Best House competition might be the lead-in she needed to get to know the neighbors. She just needed to ask the right questions. Intuition was a powerful tool, but it wasn't enough. She needed to respect her neighbors' privacy and not push too hard. Simply talking and observing them might offer insights into their behavior and maybe lead her to the answers she was seeking.

Chapter Fourteen

Out of the corner of her eye, Kaylynn saw the detectives exit Becky and Holly's home. She was in the driveway loading her car, getting ready to take her son to the babysitter. Were they walking her way? She stood tall and brushed the wrinkles out of her pants as they drew near, hoping to find a way to shoo them off until another time. Or never, which would be even better.

"Hello," the female detective said, holding up a badge. She was at least five inches shorter than Kaylynn, who was five foot eight. Her eyes were dark brown, her hair pulled back into a tight bun. "I'm Detective Seicinski, and this is my partner, Detective Toye, of the Sacramento Police Department. We're investigating the murder of Rosella Marlow."

Other than a quick nod, Kaylynn remained silent. They were detectives, just as she'd thought. She had nothing to say to them. She should have left earlier, when she'd spotted them through the window.

"I can see you're getting ready to go somewhere," Detective Seicinski said, "but we have a few questions, and it won't take any time at all."

Kaylynn glanced at her watch. "I only have a few minutes."

"Your name?"

"Kaylynn Abbott. Truthfully, I can't even recall the last time I saw Rosella, let alone talked to her."

"Did you attend the fundraiser last month?" Detective Toye asked. "The one held at Becky and Holly's house across the street?"

Kaylynn lifted her gaze heavenward, as if trying to recall. But she already knew the answer, and she was pretty sure he knew it, too. She didn't like Detective Toye. "Oh. Yes, I was there. Was that only a month ago?"

"Closer to three weeks," he said.

Smartass, Kaylynn thought.

"Have you noticed anything unusual in the week leading up to Rosella's murder?"

"No. Nothing that I can recall."

"Go ahead and think about it for a moment," Detective Toye said.

She glanced at her watch again before shrugging. "I can't think of anything. And I do need to get going. My son is inside alone. I need to check on him."

"When will you be back?" Detective Seicinski asked before she could escape.

"I work at the Grocery Outlet in Midtown. By the time I finish work and pick up my son, it will be dinnertime."

"If you're certain you cannot spare a few minutes now, perhaps you can come down to the police station during your lunch break. It's not far from here."

When she failed to answer right away, Detective Toye interjected, "It's against the law for your workplace not to provide breaks for its employees."

"Okay," Kaylynn said between tight lips. *Let's get this over with,* she wanted to say. Instead, she softened her expression and said, "What else do you need to know?"

"Did you see anyone go in or out of Rosella Marlow's house in the past week?"

"I see landscapers and the housekeeper coming and going once a week. Every Thursday, I believe." She knew it was Thursday because that was when she and Archer spent time with Rosella. No way was she going to tell them everything, though. What if they talked to her husband and told him?

"And no one else?"

This time she did concentrate, since she didn't want them to return, and she certainly had no intention of going to police headquarters. Her lips pressed together as she lifted her head toward the sky before settling her gaze on Detective Seicinski again. "I was walking with some other ladies who live on the street when I met Shannon Gibbons. She's the new gal on the block. She was in a hurry because she was to meet with Rosella."

"What day was that?" Detective Seicinski asked.

"Monday."

"Did she say why she was meeting with Rosella Marlow?"

"No. She only said Rosella was the reason they had moved to the area."

"You don't work on Mondays?" Detective Seicinski asked.

"No. I don't work on Mondays or Thursdays."

Detective Seicinski tilted her head. "Is that the only time you saw Shannon Gibbons at Rosella's house?"

"No. As I was driving off for work yesterday morning, before eight, I saw her walking toward Rosella's again."

"And what about Holly Bateman? Did you see her at Rosella's house yesterday morning?"

That little tidbit took Kaylynn by surprise. "No. Why? Was she there?"

Neither detective answered her question, but something else came to mind, and Kaylynn said, "I did see a flash of light the other night."

"Monday night?" Detective Seicinski asked.

"Yes."

Detective Seicinski had her notebook open. She'd been jotting things down the entire time. "Could you elaborate?"

"It was around one in the morning when I got out of bed to use the bathroom," Kaylynn said. "I guess you could say it was actually Tuesday when a flash of light caught my eye as I was washing my hands at the sink. Through the window I saw shadows, two people, the one in front holding a flashlight right outside Rosella's house."

"The front of the house?" Detective Toye asked.

"The west side, near the basement. But suddenly the light went out, and I couldn't see a thing."

"Are you sure of the time?"

"It was definitely somewhere between one and one thirty."

"Male or female?"

Kaylynn shook her head. "I don't know. Maybe both."

"Short or tall?"

"The one in front was taller. Like I said, I saw mostly shadows. The flashlight only came on for a few seconds. It all happened quickly."

"Anything else?"

Kaylynn shook her head. "I stood at the window for another minute. I even cracked the window open, but nothing happened. I decided I might have imagined seeing a light since I was still groggy with sleep. I went back to bed and fell asleep."

"We want to show you something," Detective Seicinski said as she used her chin to gesture at her partner.

Detective Toye reached into a tactical bag with a wide leather strap and pulled out a plastic bag with the word EVIDENCE written in bold, black letters across the top. He held the plastic bag up high enough so Kaylynn could see what was inside: a weird-looking doll made of thin branches and held together with twine. The doll had nuts for eyes, and a nail protruded from its irregularly shaped head. Kaylynn drew back, horrified. "Is that blood?"

"Nail polish," Detective Seicinski told her. "Do you recognize this object?"

"No."

"You've never seen this before?"

"No."

"Any idea how this might have ended up in the victim's home?"

"No idea." Did they think she'd made the doll? The detective was making her nervous.

"You do understand why this 'doll' might be significant in relation to the crime?" he asked.

"Um. I told you. I've never seen that thing before. Why are you asking me about it?"

"Please answer the question," Detective Toye prodded.

"Yes," Kaylynn said, answering the question. "I see why you would want to know who might have left that in Rosella's house. Whoever left it there probably wanted to scare her."

"Were you friends with Rosella Marlow?"

"Friends?" Moth wings fluttered inside her stomach. "I wouldn't say friends."

Toye glanced at his partner.

Shit. She was a horrible liar. But it was only a white lie, since Rosella simply tolerated her. They weren't friends. They never went out for coffee, or anything. Her palms were sweating. She would never pass a polygraph. It didn't matter that she'd done nothing wrong. She clamped her mouth shut.

Archer ran from the house. "Mom!" He ran to Kaylynn's side and held on to her leg, burying his face within the folds of her linen pants.

While Detective Toye put the doll back where he'd gotten it from, Detective Seicinski pulled out a card and handed it to her. "Thank you for your time. If you remember anything at all, please give us a call."

"I will," she said before ushering Archer back toward the house to gather the rest of their things, knowing she would never in a million years call either detective. She didn't like anyone meddling in her life, asking questions. She needed to protect her privacy, and her family, at all costs.

Chapter Fifteen

Shannon and Mac arrived at Chloe's house at six thirty. Chloe greeted them at the door. "Blake and Ridley are in the playroom with the little ones," she said, prompting Mac to head in the direction she pointed.

The foyer was spacious, and five or six women had gathered in the dining room already. Shannon took a moment to admire the floors, which were adorned with intricate, handmade ceramic tiles. From where she stood, she saw an enormous oak dining table surrounded by beautifully carved chairs with leather seats. And overhead was a magnificent wrought iron chandelier that cast a warm glow over the room. "Your house is stunning."

"Thank you."

Chloe pulled her into the dining room, introduced her to the women she had yet to meet, lots of names and faces she would do her best to remember. Chloe handed her a glass of red wine before running off to the foyer. A few more women arrived, including Kaylynn Alcozar, whom Shannon had met the other day. They made eye contact and waved at one another as Kaylynn passed by, taking her little boy to the playroom to join the others.

A few minutes later, Chloe clanked a piece of silverware against her crystal glass. "I'd like to get everyone's attention. There are a few ladies here tonight who can't stay long, so I'd like to make a couple of announcements. At this time, we have a dozen homes included in the tour. Balancing the number of houses ensures participants have enough time to appreciate each property. We might try to add a few more so we can showcase different architectural styles, interior designs, and so on. Last year, as many of you know, we attracted a few dozen participants, but this year, we've already sold over a hundred tickets."

"I'm going to have to decline," one of the women said.

Chloe looked straight at her. "What do you mean, *decline*, Peggy?"

"Demure. Reject. Send my regrets and pull my house from the tour," Peggy said, clearly exasperated. "I can't have hundreds of people walking through my home."

"But you have the oldest home in the area," Chloe said, clearly distraught. "It's one of the main attractions every year."

Peggy shook her head. "I never should have come tonight."

"Of course you should have come," Chloe said. "You are the pillar of the community. We look up to you as a role model and a leader."

"What if we get volunteers to stand, sit, whatever in every room of your house throughout the tour?" Becky asked.

"We can do that," Chloe said, her voice hopeful.

"Have you all lost your minds?" Peggy asked in a high-pitched voice. "A woman has been murdered. Does anyone care?" Her hands shook as she spoke. In her midseventies, Shannon guessed, she was a tiny woman, small-boned, with wispy silver hair and a weathered face.

"How is it possible that so many tickets have been sold already?" another woman asked. "I believe three dozen was the most participants we've ever had over the past decade."

"Sex and murder," Dianne said. "It's popular. Click on Netflix and you'll see what I'm talking about."

Dianne was Jason's wife. Another woman Shannon had met in her driveway the other day. She made a good point.

"Horrible," Peggy said. "If most of the people buying tickets are only there because Rosella Marlow was killed in the grisliest of fashions, I want no part of this." With a shaky hand, she set her wineglass on the table, hitched her purse higher on her shoulder, and headed for the door.

Chloe let her go without putting up a fight. "The good news is," Chloe said after Peggy left, "Shannon Gibbons has agreed to be a judge. And . . . the mayor's wife will also be a judge."

There was a mixture of groans along with claps of praise.

Chloe sighed. "About scheduling—"

"Nobody cares about the house tour," Dianne said. "Can we please talk about the elephant in the room?"

"I agree," a woman named Liliana said. "That's why I'm here."

Holly raised a hand as if she were in a classroom. "I heard Rosella was stabbed in the neck with a letter opener."

Becky stiffened.

"I can say whatever I want," Holly said in a whispered sneer, making Shannon think they were not happy with each other at the moment.

"You heard correctly," Chloe said. "Rosella was stabbed with her own letter opener. Whoever killed her must have snuck up from behind."

"If they snuck up from behind, that would tell me the killer already had the weapon in their possession?" Dianne wondered out loud.

Liliana said, "They could have grabbed the letter opener and struck fast before Rosella could react."

Shannon winced.

"I guess the detectives will have their work cut out for them," Dianne said. "Who do you think killed her?"

"That's the question we need answered," Chloe said. "How can we possibly move on with our lives, knowing there might be a killer in our midst?"

Holly paled. "You really think it might be someone in the neighborhood? Someone we know?"

"Of course it's someone in the neighborhood," Becky blurted, as if the two women hadn't already discussed this in the privacy of their own home. "She was a horrible person, and nobody liked her."

"I liked her."

All heads turned toward the squeaky voice across the room. Two boys were close to the table, gathering goodies. It was the smaller boy with three cookies clutched in his hand who had spoken. Shannon wasn't sure whose little boy it was until Kaylynn rushed over to him. "Of course you did," she said, taking his free hand and leading him back to the playroom.

"Rowan," Chloe said. "Is there something you need?"

Shannon knew Chloe had a twelve-year-old son. His light-brown hair was shaved around the ears. His bangs were thick and long, covering one of his eyes. "I liked Rosella, too."

"Rowan," Chloe admonished, "you only liked her because she handed out the big candy bars at Halloween."

"That's not the only reason," he told his mom, his cheeks turning red.

"What did you like about her?" Holly asked with genuine interest.

Rowan squared his small shoulders. "She was nice to me. And she would talk to me when I was sad." He teared up. "She made me cookies sometimes, and she gave me all of Daniel's video games after he died. She said I reminded her of him."

A strained silence settled around the room. Chloe went to him, but he turned and rushed from the room. After Rowan disappeared, she said, "I had no idea."

"I'm sorry," Becky said to the group, keeping her voice low enough so the children wouldn't hear, "but I'm sure Rosella was nice to Rowan for a reason, possibly to cause friction. You know, to drive a wedge between you and Rowan." Becky rubbed the back of her neck. "I'm sorry Rowan overheard us talking, but I know I'm not the only one in this room who didn't like Rosella Marlow. Please raise your hand if you did like her and I've got it all wrong."

Nobody made a move.

Becky said, "I don't think we need to hear the details of Rosella's murder. Word gets around fast. We've all heard about what happened. What we need to discuss is neighborhood safety."

"Monitoring the streets and reporting suspicious behavior is time consuming. Who's going to volunteer to be in charge of that?" Dianne asked. "Not me."

Liliana said, "I agree we need to do something. But we can't have my husband monitoring the streets, because he would be the first to run if he even glimpsed someone hiding in the shrubs."

Shannon thought of Trey, who was rarely home.

"How do we protect our kids?" Greta Knightley asked. "My daughter won't even go outside anymore. My husband is home with her right now, but she wouldn't come with me, and she cried when I left because she was afraid I might be killed. Her words, not mine."

Liliana nodded in agreement. "This sort of thing affects children physically and mentally."

"They need to suck it up," Dianne said, eliciting disgruntled murmurs.

"That's not how it works," Holly told her.

"I need to go," Greta said. "Maybe we can all think on it and discuss over Zoom." She headed for the door. Liliana and another woman Shannon hadn't met followed close behind.

"Why are we even discussing the murder?" Dianne asked Chloe after they left.

"I don't know," Chloe said. "I guess I thought it would be a good idea for us to all talk about what happened."

Dianne's eyebrows furrowed. "I know you. You were hoping to get us all together in hopes we could solve the murder somehow, weren't you?"

Kaylynn had returned to the room a while ago. She said, "I think we're all getting ahead of ourselves. The killer could be anyone, someone we've never heard of—a stranger from another city."

Holly jumped in. "I thought the same thing! It could have been a break-in that went horribly wrong."

Kaylynn nodded.

Becky spoke next. "I, for one, appreciate you bringing us all together tonight, Chloe, but I am perplexed by what you thought or still think this discussion will accomplish. As I already made clear, I did not like Rosella. But I didn't kill her, and neither did Holly." She raised her arms in exasperation. "God, I feel like I'm playing a game of Clue."

"Right?" Holly said. "I'm pretty sure it was Professor Plum, and he was in the conservatory."

Holly and Becky smiled at one another. Shannon smiled, too, glad there was no more tension between the two of them.

"What about Jason?" Chloe blurted.

"What about him?" Kaylynn asked.

Dianne's face reddened. "Yeah. What about him?" She stabbed a finger in the air in Chloe's direction. "Seriously? You think Jason might have killed Rosella? What the hell? How dare you."

Chloe set her wineglass on the table and walked over to Dianne. She rested her hands on Dianne's shoulders. "That's not what I meant."

"Don't touch me!" Dianne pushed Chloe away.

Chloe stumbled backward, right smack into Holly. Red wine sloshed out of Holly's glass and onto her blouse and the dining room rug.

Dianne was livid, her eyes dark, her face a maze of angry lines as she pointed a finger at Chloe. "How dare you accuse my husband of being a murderer when it's *your* husband who had the most to gain by her death."

Wide-eyed, Becky looked at Dianne, but Dianne was in another world and didn't seem to notice. *What did Becky know that the rest of them didn't?*

Chloe's face scrunched together. "What are you talking about?"

"Maybe you should ask Wesley why he's been making payments to Rosella every month," Dianne said. "If you can locate him. At least I know exactly where Jason is at this very moment."

Holly gave up on trying to get the wine out of her blouse and dropped the cloth napkin she'd been using on the table. "Stop," she said. "This is exactly what Rosella would have wanted, for all of us to start attacking one another. The truth is anyone in this room could be the killer. Rosella was downright evil." She shot a look toward the playroom, as if to make sure no kids were listening in.

There were murmurs of agreement before Holly added, "And there's something else. You should all know there are two detectives working the case, and they paid me a visit this morning. They asked a lot of questions and took notes. They even pulled out an evidence bag and showed me a doll with walnut shells for eyes and a nail stuck through its head. Whoever made it even took the time to apply red nail polish around the nail to make it look like blood. And guess what? I didn't make that doll, and I certainly didn't leave it inside Rosella's house. But someone in this room might have. If you did, be prepared to answer a few questions, because those detectives told me they were going to talk to everyone on the block."

"I saw it, too," Kaylynn said. "The detectives caught me outside in my driveway as I was packing up before work. I can't deny it—the doll gave me the creeps."

"If we start pointing fingers at one another," Becky said, "it will only cause animosity between us. I feel confident we're all safe."

"Says the woman with five dead bolts on her door," Chloe muttered.

"I agree with Becky." It was Kaylynn speaking again. "Let the detectives do their job."

"How can we assume we're all safe?" Chloe asked. "Just because Rosella was a nasty person and an obvious target?" She paused as if she wanted whatever she was about to say to sink in for a minute. "Nobody deserves to be murdered in cold blood. And what makes anyone in this room think the killer won't kill again?" She crossed her arms. "Because I really would like to know."

Nobody said a word.

Shannon spoke up for the first time. "I won't feel safe until someone is behind bars."

Chloe agreed before she turned to face Dianne. "I am sorry for accusing Jason. That was thoughtless and irresponsible of me to say. I don't think he's capable of killing anyone. I was trying to use him to stimulate more conversation, and it was stupid of me."

Dianne nodded, letting Chloe know she heard what she said, but she did not reply in kind with an apology of her own.

"I think we should take a vote," Becky said. "Who agrees that we should let the detectives solve Rosella's murder?"

Everyone raised a hand except for Shannon and Chloe.

"Okay," Chloe said, swiping two fingers across her mouth as if zipping her lips together.

Shannon took note of who was left: Dianne, Becky, Holly, Chloe, and Kaylynn. Women she hardly knew, but with whom she already felt a bizarre sort of connection, as if she were bonded to them by a disturbing event. Strangely, she did feel safe—at least, in this room. The thought of one of these ladies being a killer seemed implausible, and yet what would anyone do if they were pushed to the brink, left with no choice but to silence Rosella?

Shannon knew detectives were trained to approach investigations with open minds. To do their job correctly, they had to consider various possibilities and potential motivations behind a crime. They understood that people's actions were influenced by complex factors and that first appearances may not always reflect the truth of a situation. They had to gather information and evidence before drawing any conclusions. For that reason alone, Shannon knew she could not make assumptions based on outward appearance or initial impressions. Everyone in this room was suspect.

After Chloe apologized, they attempted small talk about kids, sports, anything other than Rosella Marlow. But the mood had been set, and it wasn't long before Dianne said goodbye and went to get Finn from the other room. Everyone else followed close behind, their kids in tow as they walked out the door.

Shannon started cleaning up by stacking dishes.

"That didn't go as I had hoped." Chloe sighed. "Accusing Dianne's husband probably wasn't the best way to get everyone to open up."

"No," Shannon agreed. "Probably not."

"I wanted to get people talking, and I got way more than I bargained for. Serves me right."

"Don't beat yourself up," Shannon said. "You invited everyone to your house tonight because you wanted to give all of us a chance to talk about what happened to Rosella. I think it was a smart decision to try and get it all out in the open."

"Thanks," Chloe said. "Becky did ask a good question, though."

"What question was that?"

"She asked what I'd hoped to accomplish by discussing Rosella's murder. It's one thing to talk to a detective and answer as truthfully as possible, but why would any of the women here tonight want to share details about their lives or their friends' lives?" She exhaled. "It was a stupid idea."

"I disagree. In fact, I think you and I should do our own investigation." Shannon had come to the meeting with the notion that the ladies on the block might want to work together to try and figure out who might have a motive to end Rosella's life. She had already decided she was going to do what she could to investigate Rosella's murder. Despite what she thought about not being able to judge a person by first impressions, for better or worse, she trusted Chloe. "Not liking Rosella is one thing," Shannon said, "but killing her? And who sent Rosella the note that said *I know what you did*?"

"What are you talking about?"

Shannon realized her mistake. "I didn't mention the note before?"

"No. You didn't."

"I'm sorry," Shannon said.

"Don't be. We hardly know each other. You probably don't know who to trust." Chloe sighed. "Tell me about this note."

"Rosella showed me the note and said it had been left in her mailbox a few weeks ago. It was written using a red marker. It could have been one of those paint pens, now that I think about it."

"That's so strange."

"Yes," Shannon agreed. "Rosella wanted me to help her figure out who wrote the note. She seemed sure the author of the note was the same person who was watching her."

Chloe was biting her lip.

"What are you thinking?" Shannon asked.

"To try and solve the murder as a collective group made sense to me. But if any of the women here tonight found out I was doing my own little investigation, some of them, probably most, would never talk to me again."

"You know these people better than me," Shannon said. "Do what you feel is best. As for me, I refuse to let it go. Rosella wanted my help. Attempting to figure out who left the note is the least I can do." She felt a sense of conviction, a deep-seated belief that she was doing the right thing, despite it not being a popular decision or even in her best interest.

"You're right." Chloe was fidgeting, as if an internal battle were happening. "I don't think I can move past this. Not without at least trying to do something about it," she said. "And truthfully, when you think about it, does anyone ever really know their neighbors or friends?"

"No," Shannon agreed, excited at the idea of working with Chloe. "Everyone has the right to keep certain aspects of their lives private, but together we might be able to determine who, if anyone, had a motive to kill Rosella."

Chloe nodded along. "Maybe you're right. If you and I are going to try and figure out who killed Rosella, or at least, determine who didn't kill Rosella, we're going to have to trust each other."

"No argument here."

Chloe offered a hand, and they sealed the deal with a handshake, which Shannon found endearing. "I do think it would be safe to say somebody living on this block knows something about what happened to Rosella."

"You're probably right," Chloe said. "And Dianne seems to know more than most . . . Accusing my husband of making payments to Rosella? What did she even mean?"

"I took it to mean one of two things: Either Rosella did work for him, maybe a writing project he was paying her for? What does he do?"

"He's an account executive for a tech company."

"Okay," Shannon said. "Rosella was a talented writer. Maybe she assisted him with crafting a clear and compelling proposal or report of some kind."

Chloe looked doubtful. "Or?"

"Or he was being blackmailed—making payments to her to keep her from revealing any damaging information," Shannon said.

"Wesley would have told me if she had ever done any work for him." Chloe stiffened as the alternative Shannon had mentioned appeared to strike her like a brick to the head.

Shannon picked up a pile of dishes to bring to the kitchen.

"Leave those," Chloe said. "I'll clean it up later."

Shannon quickly set the plates back on the table when she noticed Chloe tearing up. "It's okay. I was theorizing. Maybe Dianne is wrong about your husband making payments to Rosella. She seemed pretty upset with you."

Chloe used a napkin to wipe the corner of her eye. "It's not just that. It's everything. I didn't mean to upset Dianne. I wish I had kept my mouth shut. And what about Rowan? I had no idea he'd been talking to Rosella. I'm worried about Ridley . . . and I can't believe Rosella is dead."

Chloe began to cry in earnest. Shannon set a pile of plates back on the table and put her arms around her. "You're a wonderful mom. Blake is charming and sweet. And Ridley has been nothing but kind to Mac, welcoming her to the neighborhood and to her new school with open arms."

Chloe pulled away, sniffling as she talked. "Thank you. I didn't know Rowan had been talking to Rosella, but I do know Ridley has been struggling. She used to be so full of joy, but lately it's as if she has a black cloud hanging over her head. I don't know what to do about it. Is it normal teenage stuff—hormonal shifts, peer pressure, emotional growth? Or does her recent behavior indicate a mental health condition?"

Shannon had noticed the contrast between Ridley and Blake, but she hardly knew the girl, so she kept quiet.

"It's a tough balancing act," Chloe continued. "I don't know how to convince my daughter to see a therapist without giving her ultimatums."

"Maybe explain how worried you are, tell her you have to insist she talk to someone, at least a few times. After that, she can decide for herself if she would rather not continue. And if she doesn't want to talk to someone in person, there's always online counseling."

Chloe smiled. "The other day you thanked me for being a sounding board. Now it's my turn. Thank you, Shannon Gibbons, for listening and for being a good friend. I couldn't have asked for a better neighbor."

CHAPTER SIXTEEN

On the way home, Shannon was enjoying the cool breeze when Mac said, "Sounded as if there was some drama tonight."

"A little."

"Ridley and Blake were acting strange tonight, too," Mac said.

"How so?"

"Blake disappeared to get something to eat. When he returned, his face was pale. He and Ridley ended up huddled together in the corner of the room, whispering. Blake seemed worried about something. He was frowning the entire time he talked to Ridley, but she looked as casual as ever, leaning against the wall, hand in her pocket, as if she didn't care one bit about whatever he was telling her."

"Did you ask him what was wrong?" Shannon asked.

"He said he wasn't feeling well. But I don't know if I believe him." Mac gave a one-shouldered shrug. "Something else happened tonight that I thought was kind of weird."

Shannon stopped at the bottom of the steps leading to their front entry and turned to face her daughter. "What happened?"

"Archer, Mrs. Alcozar's little boy, tripped on a toy and fell. The floor was carpeted. He was crying and I knew he was being dramatic, but he said he had a boo-boo, and he was rubbing his left shin. As soon as I showed sympathy, he stopped crying. When I asked him if he was bleeding, he pulled up his pant leg. It wasn't bleeding, but I saw a pale-blue mark the size of a fifty-cent piece. It was an irregular shape, like the wings of a butterfly. Before I could ask him about it, his mom walked in. I wish you could have seen her face. She saw me looking at his leg, and she froze. It was weird, Mom. I didn't know what was going on. I thought maybe I had done something wrong."

"Did you say something to her?"

"No. I froze, too, because I thought she might faint. But she snapped out of whatever world she was in, walked over to me, and yanked his pant leg back in place. I told her he fell and I was making sure he wasn't bleeding. She didn't say a word. She wouldn't even look at me as she picked up Archer, gathered his things, and left without ever saying a word."

"She must have been stressed out after everything that went on tonight." Again, Shannon thought of what Rosella had said about secrets. She'd been so confident about the possibility of Kaylynn and Nicolas Alcozar hiding something. Why would something so insignificant cause Kaylynn so much grief? Maybe it would be wise to pay her a visit under the guise of simply wanting to get to know her new neighbor. "Come on," Shannon said. "Let's get inside."

After Archer had been put to bed and Holiday was in his room playing video games, Kaylynn finally had a chance to talk to her husband alone. She sat on the couch next to Nicolas and used the remote to mute the volume on the TV. In a low voice she said, "The detectives investigating the murder of Rosella Marlow talked to me today."

Nicolas's eyes widened. "What? Why?"

"I guess they're talking to everyone in the neighborhood."

"What did they want to know?"

She told him everything.

"And then they left?" he asked.

"Not before pulling out an evidence bag." She described the doll, then shuddered and said, "It unnerved me."

"Where did they find the thing?"

"Inside Rosella's house," Kaylynn said. "They kept pressing me for more. I was nervous, so I told them about the shadowy figures I saw late Monday night when I got up to use the bathroom."

"What? You never told me about any shadowy figures."

Because you weren't in bed when I returned, she thought but didn't say. After talking to the detectives, she'd remembered walking back to bed, intending to wake Nicolas and tell him what she'd seen, but he wasn't there.

Nicolas put a hand on her leg and gave her a gentle squeeze. "This whole thing has been tough on you, hasn't it? Are you okay?"

"I'm fine. But I do hope they don't come back."

"I don't see any reason why they would need to talk to you again. If they do return, don't talk to them without calling me."

"Why? Won't that make me look guilty, like I'm hiding something?"

"Just call me, okay?"

"Sure. I'll call you." She proceeded to tell him about Chloe holding a meeting at her house and the argument that broke out after Chloe accused Dianne's husband of murder.

Nicolas was stunned. "Why did you go?"

"Because I'm friends with most of these women. You and I rarely go out, and I feel trapped in this house sometimes."

"Things will get better," he said.

Nicolas had been saying that since the day they were married, promising her they would go out once a week and take a vacation every year. But nothing had changed. Even now, his focus was on the television screen. He was only half listening.

"Where was Archer during the hubbub?" he asked.

"In the playroom with all the other kids."

"Why didn't you leave him here with Holiday?"

Kaylynn raked her fingers through her hair. "We've been over this a thousand times. Archer spends three days a week with an elderly woman. He needs to spend time with other kids his age."

"But you know how I feel about Ethan. He's a bully."

Kaylynn rolled her eyes. "He's only five. Ethan is a sweetheart."

"Every time I see his little sister, she has at least one bite mark on her arm."

"Not every time."

"I'm telling you, something is seriously wrong with that kid."

"Ethan has never hurt Archer. In fact, Archer's friendship with Ethan and Finn helps him practice basic social skills."

Nicolas exhaled. "Okay. Okay. You're right. Sounds like Archer had a good time?"

She nodded, wishing she were normal and fertile and Archer had two or three siblings running around the house. All she had ever wanted was to be a mom. If she could stay home full time, she would, but they needed her small income to help keep a roof over their heads and food on the table. Nicolas made decent money as an attorney, but his income alone wasn't enough to be able to live in the Fabulous Forties. He had suggested they move to another area so she could stay home full time with Archer, but she wanted the best for Archer. She'd always thought if she did get pregnant, they would have no choice but to move, and she would be okay with that since Archer would have a built-in friend.

Nicolas must have sensed her sudden shift in mood because he slid closer to her and put his arm around her. "It's okay," he said. "Everything is going to be okay."

His voice was soothing. More than anything, Kaylynn wanted to believe him. But she wasn't so sure he was right. The constant feeling of sadness had been hanging on tight, grasping her ankles when she walked, tugging on her ear when she needed to focus at work, and tapping her shoulder to get her attention when she tried to sleep. For months now she'd felt irritable and frustrated over the smallest matters. She had even lost interest in drawing. She used to love to draw. It was a way to express herself and made her feel something. Lately, the only thing she felt was the walls closing in, squeezing out all the light. That same familiar despair was back with a vengeance, and it was coming for her.

CHAPTER SEVENTEEN

Early Thursday morning, Shannon pulled into the first empty parking space in front of the police station. Feeling anxious, she climbed out of the car, locked it, and headed for the entrance. Her heart was beating fast. The billowy clouds overhead blocked the sun, but the chill in the air didn't stop her palms from sweating.

Detective Seicinski had called after Mac had left for school and asked if she could come to the police station since they had a few more questions. Hadn't she told them everything she knew? Maybe they wanted to show her the voodoo doll Holly had mentioned, to see if they could get a reaction. Or somehow, they had found out about the envelope stuffed with random paperwork that Rosella had given her, which was why she'd brought the manila envelope with her. She would hand it off and let them deal with Rosella's scribbles. They didn't need to know she had scanned and printed Rosella's notes for her own use.

Less than a minute after walking through the door and giving her name to the clerk at the front desk, she was taken to the interview room and directed to take a seat at the rectangular wooden table in the center of the room. There were two empty chairs across from her. It wasn't long before Detective Seicinski, dressed in the same dark suit she'd worn to the murder scene, entered the room, followed by Detective Toye.

"Can I get you anything?" Detective Seicinski asked. "Coffee, tea, water?"

"No, thank you."

"You should know," Detective Seicinski said next, "that we will be digitally recording our interview with you today."

Shannon had seen the camera in the corner of the room near the ceiling. She nodded.

"You're free to leave at any time."

"Okay."

"Whether or not you decide to leave before the interview is over, we'll need you to be fingerprinted before you go."

Shannon winced.

"It's standard practice in a homicide case, allows us to eliminate the innocent. You are innocent, correct?"

"Of course. It's fine. I have nothing to hide."

Both detectives kept their eyes on her, as if trying to read every twitch, every breath she took. It was disconcerting, making her lose all train of thought.

Detective Toye took note of her hesitation. "But?"

"But," Shannon began again, "you should know that on Monday, when I met Rosella for the first time, I touched the letter opener."

"Touched or held?" Detective Toye asked.

"Um . . . *held* would be more accurate, I guess."

"You guess?" he asked. "Why didn't you mention this the other day?"

"I didn't think of it."

Detective Toye's eyes narrowed. His shoulders were squared and broad, and even sitting, he towered over her. Shannon was afraid to look away, afraid to blink.

"When you walked into Rosella Marlow's office on Tuesday morning and saw she'd been stabbed in the neck with a letter opener," he said, "it never dawned on you that it might be the same letter opener you held in your hand less than twenty-four hours before?"

She shook her head. "No. It never dawned on me."

"Why were you holding the letter opener?" The words flew from his mouth like bullets. "Did Rosella Marlow ask you to open her mail that day?"

Shannon swallowed. "No."

Detective Toye lifted a curious brow. "Maybe you simply decided to help her tidy up her desk?"

Shannon noted the glint in his eye and the sarcasm lining each word. It seemed Detective Toye was enjoying himself. He kept shooting off the next question before she could answer the first. She preferred talking directly with Detective Seicinski. When Detective Toye opened his mouth again, Shannon beat him to the punch with an answer: "Rosella's arm accidentally brushed the letter opener off her desk when she handed me a note. So I did what anyone would do. I walked over to where the letter opener had fallen, picked it up, and placed it back on her desk." Shannon tilted her head. "Do we—I mean you—have any idea when the murder took place? Some sort of time frame?"

Detective Seicinski didn't have to look at her notes. "We all know she died while you were there with her on Tuesday morning. According to the ME, the body was warm and no rigor was present."

"Does that mean I'm not a suspect?"

Detective Toye shook his head. "At this point in time, you're the number one suspect on our list."

"What? Why? I called 911."

"A common practice among first-time killers," Detective Toye said. "They kill out of anger or frustration, and when anger turns to shock, they call for help."

Shannon's eyes widened. "Are you going to arrest me?"

Detective Seicinski said, "It was also determined, based on the blood flow, clots, and congelation, that she was stabbed within a possible twelve-hour time frame prior to death."

Shannon visibly relaxed. "That proves my innocence, right?"

"Not necessarily," Detective Seicinski told her. "But it does expand the pool, so to speak." The detective opened her arms as she might do if she were going to hug someone. "It makes more room for additional suspects."

Shannon decided to keep her mouth shut.

"I'd like to back up a bit. You mentioned a note," Detective Seicinski said. "What did the note say?"

Shannon was digging herself a hole, and it was getting deeper. She sighed. "The note consisted of five words, written in big red, capitalized letters. It said, *I know what you did.*"

Detective Toye rubbed his face. Clearly, he had a few things to say.

"Do you know why Rosella showed you the note?" Detective Seicinski asked.

"Yes. She thought she was being followed and that whoever had left the note in her mailbox was probably the culprit. She wanted me to help her figure out who might have left the note."

"I'm confused," Detective Toye said. "Why was none of this mentioned when we questioned you on Tuesday?"

Shannon straightened her spine. "Because Detective Seicinski asked me to take her through the morning when I found Rosella slumped over her desk, and that's what I did."

"You're right," Detective Seicinski said before turning her attention to her partner. "Detective Toye. When I'm in need of your assistance, I will let you know."

"Yes, ma'am."

Detective Seicinski stiffened, apparently put off by her partner's use of an outdated honorific. Once again, she set her gaze on Shannon. "About the note. What did you think after you read the note Rosella handed you?"

"I felt bad for Rosella. The note bothered her. She felt threatened." Shannon reached into her bag, pulled out the manila envelope, and set it on the table in front of the detectives.

"What's this?" Detective Seicinski asked.

"Rosella gave it to me at the end of our first meeting. She said it would help me get to know the neighbors. Most of it looks nonsensical to me."

"And why didn't you give this to us earlier?"

"Because I had tossed it in the garbage and forgotten about it," she lied.

Shannon spent the next forty-five minutes relaying her first meeting with Rosella in detail, including everything Rosella had said about the neighbors and why she didn't like them.

Detective Seicinski's head tilted to one side while maintaining eye contact. Detective Toye folded his arms in front of his chest. They appeared to be not only bored but also skeptical. She didn't care. They were going in circles and getting nowhere.

Chapter Eighteen

As soon as the kids were off to school and the house was empty, Chloe made her way upstairs. As she walked down the long hallway, the wooden boards creaked beneath her feet. A shiver raced down her spine, causing her to pause midstride. The air felt heavy, charged with an inexplicable tension that prickled her skin and set her nerves on edge. She couldn't shake the unsettling feeling she got every time she thought of the doll with its twisted limbs.

Her mind raced, replaying memories of a time when her kids were small. Ridley had never been as artistically creative as her brothers; she'd never enjoyed drawing or coloring. But last night, Chloe had shot straight up in bed, her chest rising and falling, as it dawned on her what had been niggling at her about the stick doll. She would have searched the attic last night, but she hadn't wanted to wake anyone.

In the middle of the hallway, dangling from the ceiling, was a cord. She reached up and grasped it, giving it a hard tug, which released compact stairs leading to the attic. Since the holiday decorations were stored in the basement, she rarely made her way to the attic. Once she climbed up to the top and inside, she had to hunch over to see what was stored there. It saddened her to see all the plastic bins where she stored her children's keepsakes covered in dust.

Like many new moms, she had started off with good intentions. Blake and Ridley, being the oldest, had the most bins. They were well organized with folders, each grade labeled and color coded. But Rowan had only two bins, and one was only half-filled. Why? It wasn't as if Chloe had a full-time job or any interesting hobbies other than walking the dog or planning events with some of the women on her block. She did enjoy playing pickleball and decorating for the holidays. She used to spend time baking, but she couldn't remember the last time she'd made cookies. Something curdled inside her to imagine Rosella baking cookies for Rowan. Maybe the cookies had been store bought. Still, her chest tightened at the notion of Rowan spending time with Rosella, possibly telling her his thoughts and fears. She had no idea he'd ever spoken to the woman. She needed to have a chat with Rowan at the first opportunity.

But right now, she had other problems to deal with.

She easily located the bins marked with Ridley's name. Heart pounding, she opened the first one. It was stuffed to the brim with schoolwork, poems, and report cards. She took a giant breath as she pulled off the lid of the second bin. Inside were handmade cards and a bulky stuffed animal—a one-eyed raccoon with a ratty-looking tail. She breathed a sigh of relief, hoping her imagination had gotten the best of her as she pulled open the third and final bin. Inside, she found three thick photo albums filled with a mix of Polaroid and print pictures Ridley had taken with her friends over the years. She picked up the sequin-covered Minnie Mouse ears from their trip to Disneyland and smiled. Beneath the ears was a security blanket, soft and well worn. She pulled it out of the bin.

And there it was.

Her shoulders fell. At the bottom of the bin was the wooden stick figure made from branches. The one Ridley had made during a field trip with her class in the sixth grade. Her stomach cramped. When she had seen the evidence bag with the doll made of sticks, something about it had struck her as familiar.

Had Ridley made the stick doll left in Rosella's house?

If so, why? And how did the doll end up inside Rosella's home? Chloe wanted to destroy the doll staring up at her with its big walnut-shell eyes. But what if the investigators chose today to pay her a visit? She couldn't take the chance. And besides, she had a few more things to do before Wesley returned home from a business trip. After putting everything back the way she'd found it, she headed downstairs to her husband's office.

Sitting at Wesley's desk, another room in the house she rarely visited, she attempted logging on to his computer using his mother's maiden name as the password. That didn't work, so she tried their children's names along with the last four digits of his social security number. No such luck. Third time was a charm, she hoped. She tried the password Wesley had used when they were first married. No such luck.

Not surprising. Years ago, she had guessed the password to his cell phone and read multiple texts from a woman at his office. Wesley had been having an affair. When Chloe told him she was leaving him, he begged her forgiveness, assuring her he wasn't in love with the woman and promising to fire her the next day. Wesley kept his promise, and for a while, the time they spent together was magical. He planned weekly events and dinners out. Just the two of them. He even sent beautiful bouquets to the house each week.

Thinking on it now, Chloe couldn't remember the last time he'd sent flowers or taken her to dinner. Somewhere along the way, they'd both fallen into their old habits. He'd started working more and staying at the office late. Chloe went back to shopping with friends and planning events with the women in the neighborhood.

It wasn't until Dianne accused Wesley of having Rosella on his payroll that Chloe started to wonder about her husband. Talk of blackmail got her mind working overtime. What was Wesley up to?

She shut down the computer and merely sat there, thinking, fingers tapping. Her gaze fell on the acrylic calendar hanging on the wall across from her. It was a monthly calendar, sixteen-by-sixteen-inch dry erase. From where she sat, she noticed his chiropractor appointments fell on different days of the week. She knew he went to the chiropractor because of lower back pain, but now that she thought about it, when he was home, he played basketball at the gym and took morning runs on the weekend. It didn't add up. The Right Touch was the name of the company. She remembered because Jason Abbott had recommended the chiropractor to Wesley a few months ago.

She used her cell to look up the number and make the call. After introducing herself, since she didn't want to look like a nosy wife, she made up a story: she was surprising her husband with a dinner out on the town and needed to cancel his next appointment. The woman who answered put her on hold. When she returned, telling Chloe they had no record of Wesley Leavitt, Chloe apologized and pretended to have called the wrong chiropractor. Her heart sank. Although there hadn't been a spark in their marriage for a while, she had learned to trust him again. She felt like a fool.

After disconnecting the call, it didn't take long for Chloe to figure out what she needed to do.

CHAPTER NINETEEN

After leaving the police station, Shannon stopped at the store for groceries, hoping to calm her mind, but it hadn't worked. She pulled the car into the driveway, shut off the engine, and sat there, thinking about the expression on Detective Toye's face. He thought she was guilty of murder. The notion horrified her. Innocent people were thrown in jail every day.

She lifted the groceries from the trunk of her car and headed inside. After putting away food items that needed to be refrigerated, she went to her desk in the guest room. The first thing she grabbed was the article she had printed. The one Rosella had written about the Sierra Adoption Agency. Why hadn't the agency returned her call?

Twenty years ago, the news that her bio mom wanted nothing to do with her had been devastating. Shannon had felt as if she'd been abandoned not once, but twice. The deep-rooted rejection she had felt for most of her life was something she'd worked hard to hide from her husband and daughter. Her burden was not theirs. But she realized she would never be able to heal if she kept denying what she was feeling.

She talked to a therapist and found it helpful to learn that her bio mom couldn't reject her personally because she didn't know her. Shannon also came to recognize that although she had no control over what had happened to her as a baby, she could take control of her life from here on. And that's what she'd been working hard to do. Until now.

Seeing a connection, if you could call it that, between Rosella and the agency had been enough to set off old, familiar emotions, reminding her that the woman who gave birth to her couldn't even bother with a quick phone call. That's all she had wanted. To hear a voice. To ask a few questions. To let her know she had a granddaughter and that she was happy. But all the anger and resentment continued to bubble and simmer inside her, making her feel things she didn't want to feel.

Once again, she grabbed her cell and called the Sierra Adoption Agency. She left a voicemail, but this time, instead of merely giving them her name and asking them to return her call, she told them about the article Rosella Marlow had written and asked if anyone there knew who Rosella's contact might have been.

No sooner had she ended the call than her phone rang. It wasn't a number she recognized, but she answered, hopeful someone at the agency had received her message already.

"Hello. Is this Shannon Gibbons?"

"Yes. Who is this?"

"Mike Barilla. I understand you were one of my students before I retired from California State University, Sacramento."

"Yes. I took a couple of your classes."

"Wonderful. I was told you had a question for me."

"I do. It's about Rosella Marlow. She said the two of you were friends."

He chuckled. "I met her once. At a convention for journalists. They were giving out awards and she was one of the speakers. I would say we were more of acquaintances, but I'm flattered she remembered me at all."

Shannon quickly grasped, from what Mike Barilla had just told her, that Rosella had lied. "I hate to put you in an uncomfortable position, but do you remember me?"

There was a short pause before he said, "I'm sorry. But the answer is no."

"So it's safe for me to assume you never spoke to Rosella Marlow about me?"

A longer moment passed this time. "You sound perfectly lovely, Shannon Gibbons, but if it makes you feel any better, I can't remember most of my fifteen grandchildren's names, let alone my students from decades past. I hope you understand."

"Of course I do. I thought it was odd when *the* Rosella Marlow called me out of the blue and told me you had given me high praise, recommending me as a potential assistant. That's why I called you. I needed to know the truth."

"I must confess this news baffles me. I don't know what to say, other than to tell you this conversation between Rosella and me never happened." He sighed before saying, "I was saddened to hear the news of her unfortunate passing."

"Me too," Shannon said, feeling no need to bother him with details. "Thank you for returning my call. I appreciate it."

Once the call was disconnected, Shannon's shoulders slumped forward. Rosella had lied about Mike Barilla praising her work. What else had she lied about?

Shannon placed the article about the agency in its own file. As she sat thinking, Caroline Baxter's name came to mind. Ever since Janelle McKinnon said Rosella had paid Caroline to move, she couldn't stop thinking about her. If it were true, why would Rosella have done such a thing? She logged on to her computer. Fifteen minutes later, she couldn't find a number where she could reach her, but she had an address. Caroline Baxter lived twenty minutes away on La Honda Way in Carmichael.

The sound of the doorbell startled her. She wrote the address down on paper, tore it loose, and shoved it in her pocket. Praying it wasn't the detectives, she went to the door and peered through the peephole, relieved to see Chloe. She opened the door and Chloe rushed inside. Shannon followed her into the kitchen. "What's wrong?"

"Everything," Chloe said.

"Have a seat. It's my turn to make us tea."

Chloe pulled out a stool and took a seat while Shannon filled the kettle with water and set it on a burner. "Tell me," Shannon said. "What's going on?"

"It's about Wesley. After Dianne remarked about Wesley being on Rosella's payroll, I tried to log on to his computer. I never go into his office or snoop through his things, but I couldn't stop thinking about it. And to be perfectly honest, that's all bullshit. I did get into his phone a few years ago to read his texts. He was having an affair. I threatened to leave him, and he promised to change. I thought he had." Her head dropped. "I'm so fucking gullible."

"I'm sorry."

"Don't be. I never should have taken him back."

"It could happen to any of us," Shannon said. "We can't go following our spouses around every day. We have to trust the people we love."

"I know," Chloe said. "I know. But it guts me to think he might be up to his old tricks."

"You're not one hundred percent sure he's messing around?"

"I don't have any proof. Not yet. But I do know all the signs, and I haven't been paying attention. Wesley has been running again, something he did the last time this happened. He also started seeing a chiropractor once a week. I called the chiropractor's office this morning, and they had no record of Wesley Leavitt. His next appointment is Monday afternoon. I'm going to follow him."

"I'm sorry, Chloe. If you want someone to go with you, I'll tag along."

"Thanks, but I think I should go alone. Who knows what will happen if I catch him red-handed?"

Shannon met her gaze, concerned.

"I'm kidding," Chloe said. "I know we just met, but I swear, I'm not a violent person. I've spent well over thirty minutes before, trying to save a spider. I'm good."

Shannon paled.

"What's wrong? Is it something I said?"

Shannon shook her head. "The thing with Wesley got me thinking about what Rosella said about everyone in the neighborhood having a secret . . ."

"What about it?" Chloe asked.

"For starters," Shannon stated matter-of-factly, "if we're going to do this thing—"

"What thing?"

"Investigate Rosella's murder, remember?"

"Yes, okay. What does that have to do with Wesley possibly cheating?"

"Hear me out. If we're going to take this investigation seriously, we need to start thinking outside of the box. We need to think creatively and consider any and all possibilities."

"Okay," Chloe said, her features blank.

"That means *we*, but mostly *you*, since you know these people much better than me, can't let personal connections cloud our judgment."

Chloe appeared to relax. "I understand," she said. "Please go on. Tell me your thought process as far as Wesley is concerned."

"For a moment, let's go with the theory that Wesley is cheating."

Chloe nodded.

"And now imagine Rosella knew Wesley was cheating."

Another nod. "Go on," Chloe said.

"If we tie that information together with what Dianne said about Wesley making payments to Rosella . . ."

"Then blackmail would be a definite possibility."

Shannon nodded.

"Anything else?" Chloe asked.

"Yes. We need to talk about Caroline Baxter."

Chloe raised a brow. "You really think Rosella paid her to move?"

"I have no idea, but the only way to possibly find out is to ask Caroline Baxter herself."

"How are you going to find her?"

"I already did. She's living in Carmichael. I don't have a phone number yet, but I have an address." Shannon handed Chloe a mug of tea. "There's something else I wanted to share with you. Wait right here." A few minutes later, she returned with the pile of random notes she'd scanned and printed. She set a pad of paper and a pen on the counter, too.

"What's all this?"

"Before we decided to work together, I was holding back," Shannon said. "On Monday, when I met Rosella for the first time, she sent me home with an envelope stuffed with all of this. Rosella was obviously a notetaker, a maker of lists, the kind of person who jots things down on a whim . . . on napkins and receipts and whatever else they can get their hands on."

Chloe picked up a piece of paper and raised it higher, holding it at different angles as if that would help her decipher what it said.

"There's no shortage of slapdash scribbles," Shannon said as she went through the pile, muttering to herself. "Most of it makes little sense to me, but maybe I'm not looking at it through the right lens. I need to take my time. Organize the notes chronologically or by relevance."

"Oh my," Chloe said, reading some of the scribbles aloud. "Becky and Holly were both dating men when they met! Why would Rosella care?" Her eyebrows arched upward. "Did she tell you what she wanted you to do with all this?"

"She handed me the envelope and told me it would help me to get started. I was beyond excited to be leaving, so I didn't question her on its contents."

"She really did want you to know every little thing about all of us. I probably knew her better than anyone, and I just can't wrap my mind around all of this." She pointed at one of the pages, and Shannon leaned in to get a better look. "Look at this," Chloe said. "I am C's best friend, but she's not mine; C has never had to work hard for anything; C's daughter better stay away from Daniel."

Shannon didn't know what to say.

Chloe's face reddened. "This is confusing, and admittedly worrying at the same time. Ridley and Daniel were friends. I had no idea Rosella had a problem with my daughter hanging out with her son. But you know what?" Chloe slapped the palm of her hand on the counter. "I should have known. Just like I should have known every-fucking-thing else going on around me." She shook her head. "Have you shown anyone else any of this?"

"I handed it all over to Detective Seicinski this morning."

"But you took copies of everything first," Chloe said with a wink. "Brilliant."

"Before you showed up, my plan was to go through it all and see if there were any clues pointing to Rosella's killer."

"Let's do it," Chloe said as she grabbed half the pile and dug in.

Shannon took a seat on the stool next to Chloe, grabbed the rest of the papers, and started reading.

"Some of this is straightforward, but a lot of it isn't," Chloe said a few minutes later. "Maybe we should look for patterns, keywords, or references that could be relevant to the case." She chuckled. "Listen to me. Some might accuse me of having watched too many true crime shows."

Chloe was taking this all seriously, which made her a good partner. "That's a great idea," Shannon said. "When I skimmed over the notes the first time, I noticed Rosella had mentioned Jason Abbott multiple times. We could try to sort by people, too."

As they went along, they worked together, analyzing, talking, and trying to make sense out of every scribble. Hours later, Chloe sighed. "This isn't going to be easy."

"Look how far we've gotten," Shannon said. They had three stacks of papers. "This stack"—she rested her hand on the smallest pile—"represents information that needs further analysis." She moved her hand to the next. "This stack also needs to be revisited and scrutinized with fresh eyes at another time. And the last stack," she said, pushing it to the side, "is garbage."

"It's daunting," Chloe said. "We can't eliminate anyone as a suspect at this point. I find that mind-boggling."

"This is why so many cases go unsolved. Interpreting evidence isn't easy. But it's way too early to even think about giving up. We have to be methodical and open-minded if we hope to uncover the truth."

"I have to go, but this is a start," Chloe said, gesturing toward the stacks of paper. She reached into her bag and pulled out a new stack of papers. "Here are some flyers Dianne made for the BHOTB event to hang around the neighborhood—if you get bored," she said with a snort. She studied the interior of Shannon's house. "Maybe next time I come, we can get some of these boxes unpacked."

Shannon smiled.

"Should we get together again tomorrow?" Chloe asked.

"Sounds good." Shannon walked her to the door.

After Chloe left, Shannon went back to stare at the pile of papers needing further analysis. Maybe they would get lucky. She purposely didn't tell Chloe about the cold case crisis in the United States. The number of unsolved murder cases was high, reflecting an epidemic of failure to hold some of the vilest offenders accountable. Investigators needed to be patient, persistent, and leave no stone unturned if they wanted a fighting chance of solving a case. All she and Chloe could do was give it their best effort.

CHAPTER TWENTY

As Chloe walked home from Shannon's house, a heavy sense of unease settled in her chest, weighing her down with each step. Going through Rosella's notes had been rough—they represented a maelstrom of confusion and apprehension coming from a woman who seemed, judging by her endless scribbles, trapped in a maze of her own making. Shannon wasn't the only one who had once admired Rosella Marlow. The clarity and ease of her writing had always drawn Chloe in, but after looking through page after page of fragmented and disjointed thoughts, she couldn't help but think somewhere along the way, Rosella's words, like her thoughts, had escaped her, slipping through her fingers like grains of sand.

It made Chloe wonder whether Rosella had been one more person she had personally let down.

Chloe was the Forty-Fifth Street guardian, wasn't she? The person who took it upon herself to maintain a sense of order and vigilance, watching over the people who lived there—the people she cared about. Chloe had always enjoyed keeping track of the ebb and flow of daily life, noting when someone's routine deviated from the norm, which prompted her to check in. She was proud of her keen eye, taking notice of an overgrown lawn signaling a homeowner's absence, or the unfamiliar car parked in someone's driveway. By staying vigilant and watchful, she believed she was contributing to the greater good.

But Rosella's notes and scribbles told another story: *C is meddlesome and nosy. There she is again, walking, stopping, picking up garbage under the guise of keeping things neat and orderly while she peers into windows. Invasive, making residents feel as if they're under constant surveillance.*

Although Chloe tried not to care what Rosella believed, she did. She cared because there was some truth to what Rosella thought: Chloe was nothing but a bored housewife who was probably viewed by most as a nosy busybody.

She trudged onward, her feet feeling like cement blocks.

She needed to change.

The familiar street that before had provided her with comfort now seemed foreign. The once-friendly open windows and unlocked doors, now tightly shut, harbored shadows of uncertainty.

She stopped to look around, trying hard to conjure up better times. Smiling to herself, she thought of all the barbecues and Fourth of July parties they had enjoyed over the years: chairs lining the block, kids holding sparklers, laughing and drawing pictures in the sky. Sadly, the memories were tinged with nostalgia for a time that slipped further away with each passing moment.

The rapid growth of her children, once a source of great pride and joy, was another reminder of how fast time marched on. Whenever Wesley was away on business, she'd taken pride in being able to navigate the complexities of family life on her own. But lately, she realized, she felt alone. The sense of community that bound her and the neighbors together seemed to be dissipating, leaving a giant void in her heart. God, how she longed for the warmth of familiarity and the comforting embrace of the past. The large-paned windows where she would often see Rosella standing caught her eye. Chloe used to wave, which often prompted Rosella to look away. And now she was gone.

Chin up, Chloe thought. *Enough groveling in despair.* She'd done more than her fair share of feeling sorry for herself. It was time to brush herself off, get to the bottom of Rosella's murder, and hopefully find a way to move on. With a newfound resolve coursing through her veins, she decided it was never too late to start over. If she were going to attempt to change for the better, she needed to self-reflect. Maybe even get feedback. She cringed at the thought of asking her children; their list would be long. Catching a glimpse of Dianne's house as she made her way home, she had an idea about where to begin her journey to self-discovery and reconciliation.

CHAPTER TWENTY-ONE

An hour later, after a run to the bakery, Chloe knocked at Dianne Abbott's door. Dianne worked part-time at Sutter Hospital, and Chloe knew she had Thursdays off. In her moment of reflection earlier, she'd thought it might be nice to try to make things right between her and Dianne. Dianne, like her husband, Jason, wore an attitude of defiance on most days. But that little hiccup shouldn't come between their friendship.

The door came open. Dianne's gaze fell on the pastry box tied with a white satin ribbon. "It's about time," she said. "I wondered when you would come. Did you bring a vanilla latte with oat milk?"

Chloe smiled. "I did. It's in the car. I couldn't carry everything at once. Here. Take the pastries and I'll grab the coffee."

Chloe returned with two cups, shut the door, and went to the kitchen, where she found Dianne pulling plates from the cupboard. "Come on," Dianne said. "Let's go to the dining room."

Chloe felt the urge to blurt out another apology, but she held strong. She needed to learn to be patient, to see how things played out. She didn't have to wait long.

"I'm still extremely angry at you for tossing Jason's name out there," Dianne said. "Everyone knows he has a short fuse, but do you have any idea how tough it has been for Jason and me?"

Chloe said nothing. It was too soon to give her opinion, especially when Dianne was wound up tight.

"Ever since that bitch—sorry, I mean Rosella—sent a letter to Jason's boss accusing Jason of embezzling, his anger has increased ten-fold. And maybe that's why your words struck deep last night."

"Meaning?"

"Meaning, I've been wondering the same thing."

Chloe wasn't catching on. Dianne couldn't possibly be saying—

"Wondering if Jason killed her."

A bite of scone got stuck in Chloe's throat. She quickly took a gulp of coffee, her eyes tearing as the hot liquid burned her throat.

"Last week, after Rosella told Jason she had found his mail in her mailbox and tagged it all as 'return to sender,' he marched into the house, and under his breath so the kids wouldn't hear, he told me was going to kill Rosella."

"I'm sure it was only his anger talking," Chloe said, but was worried just the same.

Dianne blew hot air out through gritted teeth. "I know you're not here just to make amends."

"That's not true."

"I know you, Chloe Leavitt. We haven't always seen eye to eye, but I know you better than most. You're stubborn as all get-out, and you certainly don't have the patience to wait for the detectives to do their jobs. You're here to question me. I'm a small cog in the wheel of the investigation you're plotting in your head. I wouldn't be surprised if you got Shannon Gibbons to join you since she's new to the block."

Dianne took a couple of swigs of coffee before setting her cup on the table. "I'm going to make this easy on you and tell you everything I know." She jabbed a finger into the hardwood table. "I would never, ever have harmed that woman. She was insane—as loony as they come."

Dianne leaned closer. She met Chloe's gaze and held it captive. "I'm not as stupid as some people around here might think—"

"Nobody thinks you're st—"

Dianne sliced her hand through the air to shut Chloe up. "Let me talk. I know that hatred can be a destructive emotion. Hell, my husband is proof of that. Hatred can dehumanize a person. It eats away at a person's ability to feel empathy. And with all that said, I can tell you I hated Rosella with unbridled passion." Her eyes narrowed. "Don't you want to write that down? Did you bring a notepad with you?"

Chloe sighed but kept her thoughts to herself. It was good to see Dianne get it all out or, at least, rid herself of some frustration, even if it was at Chloe's expense.

"There you have it. Maybe Jason killed Rosella. Maybe he didn't. I don't care. In fact, if I'm honest, I'm glad she's dead." A tic set in Dianne's jaw. "You should know that I'll stand by Jason and do whatever I must to protect him. He's a good father to Finn. And I love him."

They spent the next few minutes in silence, eating their croissants and scones while sipping coffee.

"What else do you want to know?" Dianne finally asked. "Because this is it. After today, I won't be talking about Rosella, let alone thinking about her. I stopped talking to Rosella after she accused me of leaving a dead rat on her welcome mat. Why the fuck would I go out of my way to find a rat, let alone kill one and wait for the perfect time to leave it by her front door?" Dianne shook her head in disgust. "The old hag wouldn't stop harassing us. She didn't appreciate one of the tree branches in our backyard hanging over our shared fence, but when Jason cut the branch, hoping to shut the bitch up, she complained about the chain saw noise and told us we should have given her notice. She even called the police. And do you want to know something else?"

Chloe did, so she nodded.

"When Rosella's husband was in the hospital, on my floor, under my watch," Dianne said with an air of smugness, "and when she thought no one else was around, that horrid woman would lean low, close to his ear, and tell him he was an idiot. That he never should have been driving in snowy conditions. She told him he was old and decrepit. Rosella Marlow blamed Lance for killing her only son."

Chloe felt sick to her stomach. "That's horrible."

"It's beyond horrible. It's fucked up."

"How long was he in the hospital after the accident?" Chloe asked.

"Lance was in a coma for five days, and there wasn't a time I was there watching over him that I didn't hear her muttering under her breath, as angry as a cornered rattlesnake. She was always mean, but after her son died, she became insufferable." Dianne's hands clenched. "Do you think hatred is a motive?"

"For murder?"

Dianne rolled her eyes. "Yes. For murder."

Chloe sighed. "I don't know. If it is, that would mean the killer could be anyone on the block."

"Exactly."

"I've gone over and over the night Rosella was killed," Dianne said, her voice softer now. "Do you know why?"

"Why?"

"Because I've been practicing for when the detectives show up. All you have to do is a quick Google search to see what kind of questions they might ask. Like, *Where were you when the murder went down?*" Dianne spread her hands wide. "How the fuck can I answer that question when I have no idea when she was attacked? Monday night or Tuesday morning?"

"Good point," Chloe said.

"Good point or not, it's not going to be a good enough answer to send them away. I realized I better know where I was and what I was doing from, let's say, Monday eight p.m. until Tuesday eight a.m.?" Her eyes held on to Chloe's. "Can you answer me that?"

Chloe felt like a deer caught in headlights. "I don't know. I haven't thought about it."

"You might want to do some math before you go around checking on all of us, pretending to be the perfect little neighbor instead of the prying little busybody you've always been."

Chloe flinched. That one hurt.

"Um. Let's see." Dianne rubbed her chin. "Where was I during those particular hours? I didn't go to work until after I walked with all of you. I picked Finn up from day care at six p.m., and when I arrived home, Jason had already made dinner." She stopped talking. Just sat there quietly, giving Chloe a strange look.

"What?"

"Did I just tell a truth or a lie?"

Chloe wasn't sure she liked this game. "It was a lie."

Dianne laughed and gave the table a slap. "And why do you say that?"

"Because at least once a week when we walk, you talk about Jason never helping you make dinner."

She smacked her hands together. "Maybe you will be able to figure out who killed the old lady, after all."

"She wasn't old," Chloe said.

"Maybe not in the conventional sense that marks the number of years, but the resentment and bitterness inside her spoke volumes. It made the old hag look ancient." Dianne ate a piece of croissant and chased it down with coffee. "Anyway, moving on, I would tell the detectives about how Jason made spaghetti and french bread, because who can't make spaghetti and french bread? I might say he made a salad, too, trying to bore the shit out of them, then add stupid details like how he put too many onions in the salad. And I'll make a face because I don't like onions."

Even though the conversation had become worrisome, Chloe kept a straight face. Why in the world would Dianne go to all this trouble? Couldn't she simply tell the detectives the truth?

Chloe remained lighthearted as she asked, "You do have this down, don't you?"

Dianne clicked her tongue. "That I do."

"And I guess your answer would take care of Jason's whereabouts, too."

"Sort of." She shrugged. "He made dinner. We were home together. We didn't kill Rosella Marlow."

"Sort of?" Chloe asked.

"Well, it doesn't tell the whole story, does it?"

"Like what you did after dinner?"

"Bingo. Jason played with Finn while I tidied the kitchen," Dianne went on, as if reciting the Pledge of Allegiance. "We put Finn to bed. He's usually asleep by eight."

"And afterward?"

"And after that, we're fucked. Unless I lie again. You see, Jason had a sore throat, and we were out of throat lozenges and Nyquil, so he ran to the store."

"I don't see the problem," Chloe said.

"Neither did I until I went to check the medicine cabinet and the bathroom, the car, the kitchen, and every other cabinet in the house. Nothing. No Nyquil. No lozenges."

"I guess you'll leave the part about Jason going to the store out of the equation?"

"Yeah," Dianne said. "that's what I plan to do. The only problem is . . ." She pointed a finger at Chloe and waited for her to finish her thought.

"You're worried Jason *did* have something to do with Rosella's death."

"Correct."

Shivers coursed up Chloe's spine. She collected herself and said, "I really did come here to tell you how sorry I am for the things I said last night. I brought the pastries and coffee as a peace offering. Not because I wanted to interrogate you, even though I must say this impromptu visit satisfied something inside of me."

Dianne looked at her with renewed interest.

"You're right about me being the meddlesome, prying, nosy-as-all-get-up neighbor. I've been called 'security guard,' 'Forty-Fifth Street cop,' and 'guardian of this block.' Believe it or not, I'm going to change. At least, I'm going to try. You're also right about my preoccupation with wanting to know who killed Rosella. I'm going to do whatever it takes to figure it out. You can tell the neighbors what I said, or not, but I'm not going to let it go. We all deserve to go to bed at night feeling safe and protected."

Dianne crossed her arms. "What are you going to tell me next? That you're doing this for Rosella, because she cared about the community and that she was one of us?"

Chloe surprised herself when she said, "Yes. I'm doing this for Rosella, too. She was cruel. And maybe she won't be missed. But nobody, not even Rosella, deserves to be murdered."

Dianne walked her to the door. When they stepped outside, the sun's rays were shimmering off the pavement. Dianne said, "For the record, we're good. No need to bring me any more pastries."

Chloe was glad they had made up, but why did she feel even worse? She gave Dianne a hug, which felt like embracing a two-by-four. Chloe let go, but she couldn't leave yet. Not with one burning question begging to be asked. "Why did you tell me all of that about Jason, knowing Shannon and I are determined to find Rosella's killer?"

"Because I trust you. And although Jason might look guilty, I believe he's innocent. Besides, you're not the only one who wants the truth."

The roar of an engine caught their attention, and they both turned to watch Becky and Holly's college-age babysitter, Stephanie, pull to the curb in front of the Bateman house.

"I wonder what Stephanie is doing over there in the middle of the afternoon?" Dianne asked.

Stephanie was popular with all the kids due to the old Volkswagen van she drove. The kids thought the van was cool. It was orange and Stephanie called it Pumpkin, as if it were a beloved pet.

"She's probably watching the kids while Becky runs a few errands," Chloe said.

"Holly would be pissed if that were the case."

"Why would that upset Holly?"

"Are you kidding me? You must be losing your know-everything mojo. Holly and I are regulars at the cafeteria at Sutter," Dianne said confidently, as if she liked knowing more than Chloe, "and Holly is always talking about 'poor Becky' having to work at home with the kids, and how they rarely hire a babysitter anymore and never have time for each other. Holly has been working overtime because they need the money."

Stephanie disappeared inside the Bateman house.

Neither of them moved. Within seconds, Becky exited the house. She was wearing skinny jeans, white tee, and fitted blazer. Her hair was curled, makeup done. Chloe rarely saw Becky in anything other than sweatpants and moth-eaten tees. But she had looked nice the other day when Chloe had stopped by, too.

Dianne said, "What the hell am I doing?"

"What do you mean?"

"If anyone saw me standing here beside you, they might think we were collaborating. You know, coguardians of Forty-Fifth Street."

Chloe laughed.

"I'll see you later. I'm already regretting telling you my life story."

"Don't worry," Chloe said.

But she didn't mean it. Dianne should be worried. Very worried. Because at the moment, Jason Abbott was their number one suspect.

CHAPTER TWENTY-TWO

Once Dianne disappeared inside her house, Chloe headed down the walkway, surprised to see Wesley's car parked in their driveway. He must have returned from his trip early. About to check her phone for any missed texts or calls, she watched him exit the house, walk briskly toward his silver BMW, and slide behind the wheel.

Thinking fast, Chloe rushed toward the Abbotts' side yard and hid behind the tall shrubs. She pulled out her phone. He had messaged her a few minutes ago, letting her know he was going to the office. When they had talked last night, she'd told him she might be out running errands when he returned. He probably thought she was out and about. Hadn't he seen her car? Maybe he'd assumed someone else drove.

As soon as he made a right instead of a left, she knew something was up—that was not the way to his office. She ran to her car parked at the curb, jumped into the driver's seat, pushed the starter button, and hit the gas.

She made a right and sped until she caught up to the row of cars stuck at a red light. If she leaned to the left, she could see his BMW. She followed him from J Street to Fair Oaks Boulevard, then finally to

Howe Avenue. Exactly eleven minutes later, his BMW pulled into the parking lot of the Residence Inn by Marriott Sacramento.

Chloe pulled to the curb and shut off the engine. Wesley climbed out of his car and made his way into the hotel. She sat there, wondering what to do next. Did she really want to know who the woman was and what she looked like? No point in running after him and causing a scene. They were beyond that, weren't they?

Falling apart over a man she no longer loved made zero sense. She had fallen out of love with Wesley years ago. Every once in a while, they would drink too much wine and end up having sex. The shared intimacy always made her feel closer to her husband, made living under the same roof a little more bearable. At least for a while. He was obviously up to his old tricks, lying and sneaking off to be with another woman.

It was time to give him the boot. He stayed with her because of her bank account; Wesley liked living the good life too much to leave her for someone else. Chloe's parents were loaded, and they were generous, too. And opinionated and controlling. Chloe saw them once every few years, when they visited. With three children, a dog, and a cat that had since passed, staying at her house was too chaotic for them.

Despite her indifference toward Wesley, she felt numb. It saddened her to think of the passion they'd once had for each other. There were more good memories than bad ones. They had three great kids together. But if she stayed with him, it wouldn't be good for anyone. Least of all for her.

As she sat there, hands gripping the steering wheel, Chloe's mind swirled with a torrent of thoughts. She willed herself to sink into the stillness of the moment. And then she saw a familiar face. Becky Bateman was walking toward the entrance of the hotel. Every excuse for Becky's being there swam through Chloe's head. Maybe Becky was applying for a new job? Maybe the hotel was a client of hers? All her maybes were squashed when Wesley exited the double glass doors, all smiles as he wrapped his arms around Becky's waist and lifted her so high her feet left the ground.

———

Thirty minutes after returning home, Chloe heard a knock on the door. She peered through the peephole. She had thought the detectives might pay her a visit but didn't know when, and she had hoped not to see them quite so soon. Wishful thinking on her part. So far, her day had been more than enlightening. Her visit with Shannon, after reading dozens of pages filled with fanatical and irrational scribbles, had shined a bright light on Rosella's mental health. Talking to Dianne had also been eye opening.

But seeing Wesley with Becky Bateman was the icing on the cake.

A shitty, bitter icing that had left her with a sour stomach. Briefly, she considered not answering the door. But why? They would return eventually. She needed to answer their questions and put it behind her. As it was, she wasn't sleeping well, worrying about Ridley and the stupid stick doll, wondering whether her daughter had a deeper connection with Rosella because of her "relationship" with Daniel. The more she thought about it, she realized a lot of Ridley's problems began after Daniel's death. Her grades had dropped, she'd lost interest in extracurricular activities, and she'd been irritable and restless ever since.

Had Ridley and Daniel been more than friends?

No way. Ridley was sixteen when he passed. Chloe would have known if Ridley had felt something more than friendship for the boy. Wouldn't she have? At the moment, her husband's betrayal was the least of her worries.

Chloe smoothed out her apricot, V-neck Draper James blouse, made sure it was tucked neatly into her new Frank & Eileen denim pants, and opened the door to greet the detectives with the sort of smile that would hurt if held for too long.

"Hello," the female detective said. "Chloe Leavitt?"

"Yes."

They identified themselves, producing their badges. "We're here to talk about Rosella Marlow," Seicinski said.

"Yes," Chloe said. "Come in."

Carlin, Rowan's French bulldog, caught wind of visitors and came charging. He was a small dog, and cute as a button, but his bark was menacing. He jumped at the male detective, so high he was able to get saliva on the detective's tie. The giant of a man pushed Carlin away and drew his hand back. "He bit me!"

"Oh, no," Chloe said, waving it off. "I'm sure you're fine. He doesn't bite."

He showed the mark on the meaty part of his right thumb to Detective Seicinski. She didn't look overly concerned.

Chloe spared a glance over her shoulder as she walked toward the living room. "I'll put him in the backyard so he won't be able to frighten you."

He gave Chloe the side-eye and used a handkerchief from his pocket to wrap around his thumb.

"We would appreciate that," Detective Seicinski said.

When Chloe returned, she directed them into her living room. She gestured toward the sofa for them to take a seat, which they did. Chloe didn't offer them anything to drink; her mother would have been appalled. Chloe didn't care. She sat in the chair opposite them and asked, "What can I do for you?"

Detective Seicinski pulled a notebook and pen from the pocket of her blazer. "If you're ready, we'll get right to it."

"Please do."

"How would you describe your relationship with your neighbors?" Detective Seicinski asked.

"We're like one big happy family," Chloe answered. Mostly true, as far as she was concerned. Things had been rocky since Rosella's death, but Chloe's love and compassion for the neighborhood and its residents had not changed. Until the case was solved, everyone was innocent, including Jason Abbott.

"Did that happy family include Rosella Marlow?"

Chloe's nerves had calmed. She could do this. All she had to do was get through their line of questioning without rousing any suspicions about herself or her family. "Rosella might be described by some as the black sheep of our neighborhood family, but yes, she was part of the clan. She participated in most events held on our block, gave money to the charities Holly and Becky supported, and she was friendly to my youngest son."

"And yet we've been told you and Rosella, particularly, had no love lost between the two of you," Detective Toye chimed in.

"True. I was not fond of Rosella, but I never wished her harm."

"When was the last time you spoke to Rosella?" he asked.

"We might have said hello to each other at the fundraiser held at Holly and Becky's a month ago. It was for the American Cancer Society, I believe. We're holding another fundraiser on Saturday. If you would like to donate, please stop by."

"Thank you," Detective Seicinski said. "Could you tell us where you were, starting with Monday evening and ending Tuesday morning?"

"Sure. Between five and six thirty on Monday, I was at the store with my youngest son, Rowan. He's working on a science project. After the store, we picked up food from the Hidden Dumpling House in Midtown. The older kids were doing their own thing throughout the evening, homework, talking on the phone with friends, et cetera. Everyone was in their bedroom by ten. I read in bed for a few hours before falling asleep. My alarm clock went off at six thirty. I made coffee and said goodbye to Blake and Ridley before they left for school. Rowan and I were out the door by eight fifteen, and I was back home by eight-forty-five."

"What about your husband?"

The lying sack of shit, Chloe thought, *is fucking Becky Bateman in a hotel nine minutes away. Why don't you go ask him? They might still be there if you hurry.* "He's been away on business, but Wesley should be home this evening."

Detective Seicinski asked, "What does he do, and where does he work?"

"He's an account executive for SRX, a tech company in Sacramento."

While Detective Seicinski jotted the information in her notebook, Detective Toye asked, "What do you know about the details of the crime?"

"I know Shannon Gibbons found Rosella Tuesday morning slumped over her desk. Shannon told me Rosella had been stabbed through the neck with a letter opener."

"Did she tell you Rosella was dead?"

"Yes. She felt for a pulse and was certain Rosella had passed on."

Detective Seicinski spoke next. "Did you hear or see anything unusual the night before or the morning of the murder?"

"No. I didn't hear or see anything whatsoever."

"Have you talked to your neighbors about the murder?"

"Yes. Like I said, we're family. I called everyone together."

Detective Seicinski raised a brow. "Everyone?"

"Not the men," Chloe said, "since my husband was away on business and Shannon's husband works long hours at the hospital. I'm sure Jason Abbott would have come with his wife if he'd wanted to. Same with Nicolas Alcozar."

"What did you discuss?"

"I wanted to get everyone talking, maybe even find out if anyone suspected anyone else. Not my best idea. It didn't go well, and everyone left within the hour with the idea we would let authorities handle the situation."

"You and Shannon Gibbons planned this meeting because you were afraid the murderer might be someone you know?" Detective Toye asked.

Chloe gave his question some thought. "Maybe I wanted to hear it with my own ears—that nobody living on our block was capable of harming another human being."

"And were you reassured?"

Chloe sighed. "Not really. But the main thing is, I feel safe."

His squinty eyes opened wider. "You're telling me someone on your block could possibly be a killer, but you feel safe?"

"I *know* what Rosella was capable of, and therefore I feel reassured that if it was someone I know, someone on this block, then it was personal." Chloe made a face. "I'm not saying I condone someone killing another; I'm saying I don't think we have a serial killer running around the neighborhood." Her face felt heated. She took a breath, more upset with herself for letting this monster-size man get her riled.

"Can you think of anyone in the neighborhood who might be responsible?" Detective Seicinski asked. "Anyone who has been behaving unusually?"

"No."

"Can you provide any information about your neighbors' alibis or behavior?"

"No. How could I possibly know where every person in my neighborhood was at any given time?" Chloe took a deep breath. "Listen. I want to help. I want you to find whoever did this, but the fact is, Rosella was a public figure. She was not a nice person. In fact, she was spiteful and cruel, which tells me the two of you have your hands full because the killer could be anyone."

"We appreciate your cooperation," Detective Seicinski said as she leaned forward and handed Chloe a business card. "Please call us if you think of anything at all that might help us solve this case."

Detective Toye said, "We will need you to bring Blake and Ridley to the station to be fingerprinted. Anytime today would be best."

"Why?" Chloe wanted to know. "They're teenagers, for God's sake. They had nothing to do with this."

"It's standard procedure, ma'am," he said with a shrug. "You can voice any complaint you might have at the internal investigations unit of the PD."

"That's what I'll do."

"It's a matter of routine when there's reasonable and articulable suspicion of criminality."

"Until you show me reasonable and articulable whatever, it's not going to happen."

They all stood and Chloe followed them to the door, glad they were leaving but livid at the idea of taking her children to be fingerprinted. It wasn't happening.

"Oh, one more thing," Detective Toye said before they got too far. He pulled something from the leather case he carried, turned toward her, and stuck the evidence bag right in front of her face. It was the doll made of sticks.

Chloe had raised three children. Her kids were accident prone. Ridley had been only six when she fell out of the tree in their front yard and broke her leg and two fingers. At the age of seven, Blake rode his bicycle down the driveway and fell headfirst onto a decorative rock. He'd needed twenty-one stitches that day. Rowan was concussed after running smack into their glass sliding door. In all those instances, she'd remained calm and in control. Never fainted or felt the slightest bit woozy at the sight of blood.

And yet one glance at the stick doll inside the plastic bag, a doll she'd already seen through a vent, a doll with a nail protruding from its head and red polish dripping down the length of it, made her feel dizzy and lightheaded. A numbness rolled over her body, up over her face, and to the top of her skull before her legs gave out and everything went black.

———

Chloe woke up feeling disoriented. Her vision was blurry. It took her a moment to recognize the two detectives watching her closely. She was on the sofa where the detectives had been sitting earlier. Behind the detectives were her children. All three of them, plus Kristin Kilarski, the woman who dropped off Rowan every day after school.

Chloe tried to sit up but couldn't quite manage it. Blake came forward, squeezing between Detectives Seicinski and Toye so he could place a pillow behind her head. "Are you okay? Should I take you to the hospital?" he asked.

"No. I just need a few seconds." She saw Ridley behind the small crowd, looking at something in her grasp. It was the evidence bag. Her daughter was biting her bottom lip, something she'd always done when she was guilty of some small infraction.

Detective Seicinski followed Chloe's gaze, seemingly taking note of what Chloe was seeing, maybe even what she was thinking. The detective turned and walked that way, took the evidence bag from Ridley, but not before saying something to Chloe's daughter.

Panicked, Chloe knew she needed to get rid of everyone. As quickly as possible. She pushed herself upward until she was propped in a normal sitting position. She brushed the hair out of her face, then locked eyes with Blake. "Please see everyone out."

After the detectives were gone and before Ridley could hide in her room, she said, "Ridley, what did the detective say to you?"

Ridley folded her arms. "She asked me if I had seen the doll before."

"And what did you say?"

"I told her the truth. I said no." Ridley gazed at Chloe through narrowed eyes. "She had the same look on her face as you. She didn't believe me, either."

CHAPTER
TWENTY-THREE

It was Friday morning when Chloe stepped inside the house after taking Rowan to school. Wesley came downstairs carrying a hand towel. He was shirtless, his hair damp from a recent shower.

"Aren't you going to be late to work?" she asked him.

"I have some time. I heard the door and I wanted to see how you were feeling after everything you went through yesterday."

He had no idea.

He used the towel to dry his hair, his chest inflated like a male turkey with puffed-out feathers, strutting his stuff, establishing social dominance. Wesley might as well start gobbling. He hadn't returned home until after seven last night. Blake was the only one who had appeared happy to see him. Ridley had looked disinterested, and Rowan had been unusually quiet.

When she went to Rowan's bedroom later in the evening to say good night, she sat on the edge of the bed and asked him if there was anything he wanted to talk about. He shook his head. She apologized for not realizing he'd been hanging out with Rosella and asked him if he wanted to attend her funeral next week. He said he did. And that was all she got out of him. Trying to figure out what was going on inside

Rowan's head, or any of her kids', for that matter, was like trying to crack open a coconut on the beach without a rock or any tools at all.

"What's wrong?" Wesley asked as he followed her to the kitchen.

"I don't think you want to know."

"I do," he said. "I wouldn't have asked otherwise."

"Okay. Fine." She turned toward him, crossed her arms over her chest, and leaned against the marble counter. "Do you remember the doll Ridley made years ago out of tree branches and sticks?"

He laughed. "No, but it sounds like something Ridley would do. She loved climbing trees and finding the perfect branch to use as a sword. She always wanted to be the knight, never the princess."

The twinkle in his blue eyes as he talked about their daughter was one of many things she had once loved about Wesley. She shook off the thought. "Well, way back when, Ridley created a doll figure made from sticks. It had walnuts for eyes and a bit of moss for hair. She was never the creative one out of the three, which is why I saved it."

"Why do I get the feeling this conversation is going somewhere unpleasant?"

"Because that's what it has been around here lately. Unpleasant. Rosella's death has opened Pandora's box."

He sighed. "You're being dramatic."

"Am I? Since you asked what was wrong, I'm going to tell you. I'll start with Rowan. Did you know he was friends with Rosella? Apparently, she would make him cookies and talk to him when he was sad. She gave him all of Daniel's video games and told Rowan he reminded her of Daniel when he was Rowan's age."

"That doesn't sound so bad."

She ignored his comment. "Rowan wants to go to Rosella's funeral."

He raised a brow but said nothing.

"And then there's Ridley," Chloe went on. "Have you noticed a change in your daughter over the past year or so?"

"I put it down to teenage drama and hormones."

"I think there's more to it. In the past few days, I've learned Daniel meant much more to Ridley than I knew. It's starting to look as if they might have been more than friends."

"Ridley told you that?"

"No. I haven't talked to her yet."

"Okay. Who's next?"

"You are."

Both of his brows shot up.

"I invited the women in the neighborhood to our house the other night." His expression changed. He already knew this. Of course he did. Becky must have told him. "I was hoping to find out if anyone had suspicions about who might have killed Rosella—"

"Why would you do that?"

"Don't you want to know if someone on our block committed murder?"

"Not really. Not if it's someone we know."

"What if it is?" Chloe asked. "Doesn't it frighten you to think your kids might be hanging out with a murderer?"

He shook his head, all the while regarding her with a puzzled expression. "Not once did I think one of our friends, someone living next door, could have possibly killed that woman."

How could he make a judgment about anything going on in the neighborhood if he was seldom home? Lately it seemed as if he only cared about himself. Kids grew fast. Did he know Blake's favorite food was lasagna? Did he know Ridley's favorite color was red? Did he have any idea that Rowan had aced his math test?

"What about you?" she asked, feeling feisty, knowing he was a good dad to his kids but hating him just the same, ready to have it out with him and put it all on the table. "Did you kill her?"

He didn't chuckle or laugh. He guffawed. He sounded like a donkey.

"Is that a no?" she asked.

"No. I mean yes. It's a no . . . I didn't kill Rosella." He folded his arms over his chest. "Are you nuts?"

She considered his question, then shrugged. Maybe she had cracked. "After I accused Jason of having something to do with Rosella's death, Dianne became furious with me. She said I should be questioning *you*—the man who was making payments to Rosella."

He had nothing to say, but she didn't miss the flicker in his eyes and the way his body stiffened. He knew exactly what Dianne had been talking about.

"Were you paying Rosella to keep quiet about something?"

His eyes narrowed.

"You were. You are!" Chloe saw the answer to her question in every twitch of his jaw. "Rosella knew, didn't she? She knew you were having an affair with Becky, and she capitalized on it."

His face turned as white as her kitchen cabinets. "You're being irrational," he said.

"Don't bother denying it. I saw you and Becky at the Residence Inn yesterday afternoon. I couldn't believe how flexible she was when you lifted her into the air and she wrapped her legs around your hips. Impressive."

"It's not what you think."

That made Chloe smile.

"I told her I needed to end it. That I was in love with you." He reached for her, and she swatted him away.

"Stop it, Wesley. It's over. I don't love you, and you don't love me." She knew it would be beneficial if she took some time to cool down and gather her thoughts before engaging, but beneficial to whom? Not her. She didn't give a shit about his feelings—if he even had feelings.

Chloe's cell phone rang. She picked up the call, listened, and said, "It's perfect timing. No problem at all. I'll be right over." She grabbed her purse from the kitchen counter and headed for the door.

"Where are you going?" Wesley asked. "We need to talk."

She turned to face him. "We're done talking. I froze the credit cards and canceled your access to the main accounts. You still have your own checking account where you've had direct deposit from your work for years. It's a hefty amount. You'll be fine."

"You can't do this."

"I can and I did."

"You can't give up on the two of us without thinking things through. We can go to counseling together—"

"Years ago, after you cheated the first time, everyone told me I should leave you. Once a cheater, always a cheater. But I believed in you—in us. I thought we were different. I believed your lies, and look where it got me. Being the fool is a deeply unpleasant experience, Wesley."

There were a million things Chloe thought he should have said in that moment, including *I'm sorry*. But he said nothing.

"I have to go," she told him. "Becky and Holly need me to watch their kids. I guess the police want to talk to them." She lifted a brow. "Holly said they had to hire a lawyer," Chloe went on. "And that's a shame because they can't afford one, just like they can't afford to hire a babysitter whenever Becky feels the need to get laid."

CHAPTER TWENTY-FOUR

Chloe had been so eager to leave her house and be done with Wesley, she'd arrived at Becky and Holly's a little too quickly. Discombobulated, she walked right into the house without knocking first, surprised the house wasn't on lockdown.

Becky and Holly were in the kitchen, quarreling, and hardly spared her a glance. She walked straight past them to Charley and Ethan, who were watching television, and easily got them to follow her upstairs. In the loft, she grabbed the bin of Marvel characters, dropped a few Barbies on top, and went straight to Ethan's room, where she dumped the figurines onto the bed.

Charley clapped her hands with glee. "Can all the toys play on the bed?"

"Absolutely," Chloe said. "The more the merrier."

Both kids started running back and forth, grabbing toys from the loft, carrying them into the bedroom, and tossing them on the bed while Chloe listened to the conversation below.

If Dianne could see her now, she would be ashamed to see Chloe falling right back into her old habits. *These things take time,* Chloe told herself as she put an ear to the vent.

"Did you have to ask Chloe to watch the kids?"

"Yes!" Holly barked. "And thank God she could do it, because otherwise we'd have to reschedule and still pay the lawyer because he requires a twenty-four-hour cancellation notice."

"I was only asking a question," Becky said. "I don't know why you're so upset."

"Well, I don't know why you have a problem with Chloe watching the kids for free. You don't seem to understand what living within our means is all about. We don't belong in the Fabulous Forties. We can't afford it. But I went along with your idea because we agreed to stick to a budget, knowing it would be difficult for a few years. I used all of my grandmother's inheritance for the down payment for a giant house already in need of some serious upkeep. I work a minimum of sixty hours per week to make this work. And then you go and hire a criminal lawyer for three hundred and fifty dollars an hour."

"I'm not the one with my fingerprints all over the murder weapon," Becky said. "Which begs the question . . . Why are your fingerprints all over the murder weapon?"

"I never said they were."

"The second Detective Seicinski told you there were multiple sets of fingerprints found on the weapon, you turned white and agreed to get a lawyer."

Chloe couldn't see them. They were over by the refrigerator, out of sight. But she imagined Holly's shoulders slumping forward. She felt bad for her. Did Holly know about Becky and Wesley? Holly Bateman was the sweetest person she knew. She couldn't imagine Holly having anything to do with Rosella's death.

"We're leaving now!" Holly shouted from below, prompting Chloe to scramble to her feet and run to the loft.

"Okay. See you in an hour or two."

"We'll lock the door when we leave," Holly told her.

"Okay."

Chloe was back in Ethan's room when she heard Holly ask Becky, "Are those new?"

"What?"

"Your sunglasses. Are those Celine? When did you buy those?"

"Why does it matter?" Becky wanted to know.

Holly was standing by the table now, and Chloe saw her clicking away on her iPhone. "Those sunglasses cost five hundred dollars! What the hell?"

Chloe felt sick to her stomach. Wesley must have bought them for her.

"I'm sorry," Becky said. "I was tired and bored and needed something to cheer me up. I ordered them online. I'll send them back."

Tired and bored, my foot. Well, maybe tired, Chloe thought.

Holly said nothing in response.

Chloe heard footsteps, mostly stomping, then the sound of the door opening and closing before the lock rattled.

The house was peaceful. Even the kids were quiet as they sorted through their toys.

———

Shannon needed to get some air. She'd been spending way too much time reading over Rosella's notes and scribbles. So far, she hadn't been able to identify any connections between different pieces of information. But she had noticed a recurring name. *Bradley.* The name came up three times, and yet Shannon could find no relationship between Rosella and anyone named Bradley. The month of July was also mentioned six times, written in all caps and circled in the center of one of the pages. So far, those were the only two pieces of information that stood out. *Bradley and July.*

Shannon slid off the stool, plunked her hands on her hips, and did a side stretch. She and Chloe had a lot of work to do. She put on her sneakers and grabbed her crossover bag with her keys and cell phone. Mac would be home from school in a few hours, so she wrote her a note on the pad of paper in the kitchen, letting Mac know she would be back soon. After gathering some heavy-duty tape, a stapler, and the stack of flyers Chloe had left her, she headed out.

Nearly two hours later, it was hotter than hell and Shannon had already drained her water bottle. She had made it as far as Forty-Third Street. Sweat dribbled down her back. As she attempted to staple the last flyer to a thick oak, the bark crumbled.

"Stop what you're doing right now!"

A woman waved her arms overhead as she ran across a sizable expanse of lawn. She was coming straight for Shannon. It was the same woman from the meeting at Chloe's house the other night. Peggy was her name, and she was not happy. She got right up in Shannon's face, her eyes flashing, her breath reeking of garlic. "Who gave you permission to deface my oak tree with that flyer?"

"I was asked to hang the flyers. I'm sorry."

Peggy pointed a finger, the tip of her brittle nail nearly touching Shannon's nose. "You were at Chloe Leavitt's house. You two are friends. She told you to ruin my tree, didn't she?"

"No. Truly she didn't."

Peggy grabbed the flyer from her and read it. "They already sold two hundred tickets! How many people does she think the Knightleys and others want trampling through their homes?"

Shannon kept her mouth shut. Nothing she could say would make this woman feel better.

Peggy lost some of her bluster. "Well, I guess you're just a volunteer." She picked at a loose thread on her blouse. "You're new to the area?"

"I am. Not quite two weeks yet."

"My. Oh. My. You probably didn't get the chance to meet Rosella Marlow."

"I met her. She wanted me to assist her with a writing project."

Peggy's eyes twinkled. "Ahh! So maybe she told you about her son, Daniel."

"No. She didn't mention Daniel."

"Well, I'm sure Chloe has no idea, since she hasn't a clue what her kids are up to, but Daniel, bless his heart, was in love with Chloe's daughter, Ridley."

Shannon tried to hide her surprise. "How old was he when he passed?"

"Nineteen. Everyone who's been in the neighborhood long enough knows that Daniel and Ridley grew up playing together. But only a few of us were aware that their friendship had evolved into young love. The two lovebirds agreed to keep their friendship platonic until Ridley Leavitt turned eighteen."

"Who told you this?" Shannon asked.

"Not important. Do you want to hear the rest of the story, or not?"

Shannon wasn't sure. Because then she would have to tell Chloe, and Chloe was already feeling horribly disconnected from her children.

"Guess what Rosella did when she caught wind of their blossoming relationship?"

Oh no, Shannon thought. Curiosity got the best of her. "What did she do?"

"She invited Ridley to her home to let her know Daniel would be going away to college and it would be best for everyone if she stayed away from him. If she refused, Rosella would cut Daniel out of the will and kick him out of the house."

"Why would she do such a thing?"

"Nobody knows. I always felt sorry for the kid. Most people who knew the dynamics of the Marlow family felt the same way as me."

"I was under the impression that Rosella was a doting mom."

"You could say that. She showered the boy with attention and affection, fussing over his every need. From the moment he entered her life, he became her world."

"And yet she threatened to kick him out of the house?"

"I never believed she would follow through. An empty threat, if you ask me." Peggy swatted at a fly. "Anyway, Daniel was sent across the country to attend NYU, and to meet his mother's demands, he blocked

Ridley from his contacts. But kids are smarter than their parents. They both got burner phones." She laughed. "They talked every day."

"A happy ending," Shannon said. "I should go."

"You haven't even heard the worst part."

Shannon waited. How could she not?

"After Daniel died, Ridley changed. Once loud and animated at events held in the neighborhood, she became reserved, quiet. Her eyes no longer sparkled. And then Rosella was killed, and everyone I know"—her gaze followed the length of her street and back—"wonders if Ridley had something to do with Rosella's death."

Shannon's brow furrowed. "What proof does anyone have? You shouldn't be spreading rumors like that."

Peggy pointed at the telephone pole on the corner. "Please remove the flyers before you go, dear. Nice talking to you."

Shannon turned and walked away, leaving the flyers she'd already hung. Peggy could take them down herself if they bothered her. As she neared Kaylynn's house, their oldest son was being dropped off by a friend. He was a gangly kid, six feet tall with red, wiry hair. His friend drove off.

"Hi," Shannon said. "I'm Shannon Gibbons, your new neighbor."

He simply stood there, his eyes not quite meeting hers. He wore baggy denim pants and a heavy-metal tee beneath a checkered, button-down flannel shirt that hung open. There wasn't a drop of sweat on him.

"You must be Holiday."

He nodded.

"Nice to meet you." They shook hands. "Is your mom home?"

"No. She works on Fridays."

She sighed. "I was going to ask her about a woman named Peggy."

"Peggy Chandler," he said with distaste.

"Yes. I was posting flyers about the Best House on the Block award when she started talking about some of the kids in the neighborhood."

"Let me guess, she's still going on about Ridley Leavitt and Daniel Marlow being more than friends."

"That's exactly what she talked about. She seemed upset."

Without saying another word, Holiday started walking toward his house. Shannon followed him. "Did I say something wrong?"

They were standing at the front door. His gaze scanned the area as if to make sure nobody saw them. "Did you ask Chloe Leavitt about this?"

"No. Not yet."

"You might want to keep it to yourself," he told her. "If I were you, I wouldn't mention it to anyone."

"Why not?"

His face reddened as he reached deep into his pocket for his house key. "Because Ridley would freak out and probably go have a talk with Peggy Chandler and give her a piece of her mind." His eyes rounded. "If Ridley ever finds out I talked to you, I'll be dead to her."

He opened the door, and right as he stepped inside, she saw a hole in his shirt. The shirt was checkered. And the hole, a piece of gray fabric, big as a nickel, was missing.

She froze in place.

Holiday stepped inside and shut the door behind him, leaving Shannon to wonder what the hell she'd just seen. There was no doubt in her mind that the missing fabric from Holiday's flannel shirt was the same piece of material she'd found stuck in the woodwork at Rosella's house.

Why would Holiday have been inside Rosella's house? And why was he so afraid of Ridley?

Shannon recalled the look on Chloe's face after she'd read Rosella's notes about Rosella possibly having a problem with Daniel and Ridley's friendship. Much more than a friendship, according to Peggy Chandler. If Peggy and her friends thought Ridley had something to do with Rosella's death, why hadn't they called the police? Maybe they had.

CHAPTER
TWENTY-FIVE

Chloe and the kids were downstairs watching TV when she heard a key rattling in the door. She remained seated on the couch. The kids had fallen asleep, one on each side of her.

Becky entered, shut the door, and slid the dead bolt in place. When she saw Chloe on the couch, she said, "You're watching *Housewives Go to Miami*?"

"Close. *The Real Housewives of Miami*. It's pretty entertaining." Chloe didn't care what Becky thought about her choice of television viewing.

"No wonder they fell asleep," Becky said.

They had drifted off during a rerun of *Teenage Mutant Ninja Turtles*, but she felt no obligation to clarify. "Where's Holly?"

Becky put a finger over her lips, letting Chloe know she didn't want the kids to overhear. When Chloe joined her in the kitchen and grabbed a chair, Becky took a seat at the table across from her. Dark circles framed her eyes.

She said, "We were escorted into a room at the police station, along with our attorney, Jared Katz. The detectives didn't waste any time before they started asking questions. Was Holly ever involved in any criminal activities, did she have driving violations, yada, yada, yada. The questions went on for a while. And then they turned to me."

Chloe lifted an eyebrow.

"They wanted to know if there were things I kept from Holly."

Chloe didn't move a muscle.

"I scoffed, told them this wasn't about me. They disagreed, of course, and proceeded to ask me about my job and if I worked remotely. Then they asked me where I was yesterday between noon and five p.m."

Their eyes locked. Neither one of them blinked.

"You know, don't you?" Becky asked.

Chloe nodded.

Becky dropped her head, her chin hitting her chest. "It was awful . . . the expression on Holly's face as she told them they were mistaken." She lifted her head. "And then they brought out the pictures." Her brow creased. "I never meant for Holly to find out. Certainly not at a police station, in front of a lawyer and two detectives." Becky's gaze wandered before her attention shifted back to Chloe. "I was going to break it off, I swear."

"It doesn't matter."

"It does to me. I'm sorry, Chloe. I'm a horrible person."

Chloe didn't argue with her. "Wesley and I talked before I came here," she said. "You're not the first, and you probably won't be the last. I kicked him out of the house, and I won't be taking him back."

"Don't you want to know why or what happened?"

"No," Chloe said. "I don't care. He's all yours." And that was the God's honest truth. She felt relieved and free.

Becky didn't respond to Chloe telling her he was all hers, but she didn't look all that interested in keeping Wesley for herself.

"Poor Holly," Becky said, and Chloe did agree with that. "There's something else I need to tell you."

Chloe sighed. "I'm not interested in hearing about you and Wesley."

"It's not about that. It's about Holly."

Chloe waited for her to go on.

"After the detectives were done, another officer entered the room and whispered into the detective's ear. Detective Seicinski stood right up, staring at Holly the whole time. She unhooked her cuffs from her belt and said, 'I've just learned your fingerprints matched the ones found on the murder weapon. You're under arrest.'"

Chloe's mouth dropped open. "Holly is in jail?"

Becky nodded.

"Why were her fingerprints on the murder weapon?"

"I don't know," Becky said. "They didn't let me talk to her before they escorted her away."

"Holly told us she went inside Rosella's house but that she left after Rosella failed to answer when she called out. She lied to us."

Becky broke down into sobs, her arms folded on the table with her head on top. Chloe wanted to go to her, but she didn't know what to say, so she stood and walked out the door, shutting it quietly behind her.

CHAPTER TWENTY-SIX

Shannon was gathering her sunglasses and keys, readying to leave the house, when her phone buzzed. It was Chloe. She picked up the call and said hello.

"I saw that you called. I was hoping to stop by," Chloe said. "I'm leaving Holly and Becky's now. I need to talk to you."

"I was calling to see if you wanted to take a drive to Carmichael to talk to Caroline."

"Does she know you're coming?" Chloe asked.

"No. I don't even know if she'll be home."

"It's worth a shot. I'll be there in twenty seconds."

A few minutes later, Shannon was in the driver's seat, her eyes on the road, while Chloe told her about the conversation she'd had with Dianne the day before.

"She knows we're searching for answers concerning Rosella's murder?"

"Correct," Chloe said.

"And she bluntly told you Jason doesn't have an alibi for Monday night?"

"Correct." Chloe turned her body toward Shannon. "What if Rosella was killed between ten and twelve that night or early Tuesday morning? We can't eliminate him, but neither can we say he's our guy."

"That's true. I'm just surprised Dianne told you all of that."

"I was surprised, too. She said she believes Jason is innocent, but she's just as interested in knowing the truth as we are."

There was a long pause before Chloe broke the silence. "I followed Wesley yesterday."

"I thought that was happening on Monday?"

"After I left Dianne's house, I saw his car in the driveway. When he left, I followed him."

"And?" Shannon asked.

"And I was right about him having an affair."

A heavy weight settled in her stomach. Shannon didn't know what to say.

"It's Becky," Chloe said.

"What?"

"Wesley is having an affair with Becky Bateman."

"I thought you were just at their house."

"I was. It's a long story, but so much has happened since I saw you yesterday. After discovering Wesley was having an affair, I got home right before Detective Seicinski and Toye showed up at my door. They showed me the stick doll and I fainted."

"You didn't!"

"I did." Chloe's chin fell to her chest. "I think Ridley made the doll and maybe even left it inside Rosella's house."

A rush of helplessness washed through Shannon. "My God. I should pull over so we can talk about this."

"No. Please. Just keep driving."

Shannon couldn't believe what she was hearing. *Ridley* had made the stick doll? She needed a minute to think and sort it all out. Her mind was like a mini-tornado whirling about.

"There's more," Chloe said. "Holly's fingerprints were on the murder weapon. She was arrested."

Shannon kept her eyes pinned to the road. "She's in jail? This is absurd. Rosella was right about everyone having secrets, wasn't she?"

"Maybe so."

Shannon decided to wait on telling Chloe about what Peggy had said about Ridley and Daniel. How much more could one person take? And besides, they would be at Caroline Baxter's house soon.

———

Caroline's new residence was a one-story ranch-style home on a quiet cul-de-sac, with a substantial, grassy front yard. A burgundy Honda Accord sat in the driveway.

"That's her car," Chloe said.

As they walked up the stone pathway leading to the door, Shannon said, "I think you should do the talking since you know her."

"I'll give it my best shot, but on the off chance she was in cahoots with Rosella, she might not want to talk to me."

"Maybe you're right. Stand a bit to the side. If she opens the door, I'll try to put her at ease before you say hello." Shannon rang the doorbell. Uncertain whether Caroline would talk to a stranger, she was surprised when the door opened, revealing a middle-aged woman with wary eyes. "Can I help you?" the woman asked, her voice unsure.

Shannon began with a warm smile. "My name is Shannon Gibbons. I—"

Caroline's gaze fell on Chloe. Her eyes narrowed. "What are you doing here?"

"Hi, Caroline. Sorry for the unexpected visit, but we didn't have your phone number, and we only have a few questions."

"Questions?" Caroline asked. "About what?"

"About Rosella Marlow," Shannon said. "And the house you sold on Forty-Fifth Street in Sacramento."

A flicker of fear passed through the woman's eyes. "I'm sorry, I don't have time for this right now."

"Please," Chloe pleaded before she shut the door.

"Rosella Marlow is dead," Shannon said. "She can't hurt you any longer." It was a long shot, since Shannon had no idea whether Caroline's relationship with Rosella was good or bad, but she was going with her gut and the fear she'd glimpsed in Caroline's eyes. Shannon did not want to leave empty handed.

"I did hear about her death," Caroline admitted. "It was a shock."

"She was murdered," Chloe said. "If you have any information at all, please help us."

Shannon noticed Caroline's hesitation, her gaze darting nervously between Shannon and Chloe. It was clear she was torn between shutting the door and engaging in conversation. She knew something. "We're not here to cause you trouble," Shannon said.

Caroline's shoulders sagged with resignation. "Fine," she muttered, her voice tinged with defeat as she stepped back to allow them inside. "But we need to make it quick."

As they settled in the living room, no tea or coffee was offered. Caroline wasn't kidding about getting them in and out. Caroline sat on the couch. "What do you need to know?"

Shannon sat on the cushioned chair across from Caroline and gave Chloe a look that said, "Sit down." If they wanted the woman to talk, they needed to try to set the stage and make her comfortable. Chloe took the hint and sat in another chair closer to Caroline.

"I heard through the grapevine," Shannon began, "that Rosella paid you to move."

"It's true," Caroline said. "I won't tell you how or when or how much she paid me, but it was substantial enough that I was able to retire from my job at the bank."

Shannon didn't look at Chloe. They needed to keep things moving. "Did she say why she wanted you to move?"

"Yes. She wanted to make everyone suffer as she had suffered."

"She said that?" Chloe asked.

Caroline nodded.

"But how would getting you to move out of the neighborhood help her achieve her goal?" Shannon asked.

"She had someone in mind to buy the house," Caroline said. "*A mere pawn*, were her exact words. Someone to help her turn over every rock possible and leave nothing but destruction in her wake."

As the words sank in, a knot tightened in Shannon's stomach. She'd known in her gut that Rosella had wanted to use her, but having it confirmed was unsettling.

Chloe rubbed her face with her hands. "Seriously? That sounds like Dr. Evil talking."

"That's not all," Caroline said.

"What else did she say?" Shannon asked, tamping down the ugly truth.

"Rosella told me the work she was doing was important. I told her invading others' privacy and snooping on neighbors could have serious consequences, but she didn't care. In fact, she laughed when I said it. Rosella genuinely believed she was acting in the best interest of the neighborhood. When I scoffed, she leaned forward, her eyes piercing, and told me she was on the brink of figuring out who kidnapped a small child."

"What the hell?" Chloe said.

Shannon remained calm. "What small child?"

"I didn't ask. I knew then she had truly lost her mind. I threw up my arms and walked out of her house in a huff. After Lance and Daniel died in that tragic accident, I felt horrible for her. I tried to be there for her, but she was beyond help. Despite therapy and visits from everyone in the neighborhood, she lost all sense of reality. And I, for one, couldn't handle it any longer. I was happy to take the money and run."

———

Once they were back in the car, a heavy veil of silence settled around them. Shannon stopped at the light and looked Chloe's way. "Are you okay?"

Chloe's gaze remained on the road ahead of them. "No. I'm feeling a bit of Caroline Baxter's frustration at the moment. In fact, I'm not sure how much more I can take."

Shannon was worried. Chloe didn't move a muscle as she stared straight ahead.

"First Wesley," Chloe said after a while. "Our marriage was bound to fall apart sooner or later, but it's still hard. And Holly. She's locked in a cell. And you know what I'm thinking right now?"

Shannon said nothing.

"Maybe she did do it! Who the fuck knows anymore. I don't think we can cross anyone off the list. For all I know, *you* killed Rosella."

Shannon didn't take offense. Chloe was clearly exasperated. Out of the corner of her eye, she saw Chloe pull out her phone and tap away at the screen.

"Everyone has a secret," Chloe said, as if she were letting the notion sink in. "And Rosella was willing to pay Caroline to get out of Dodge so you could move into the neighborhood. To spy on us?"

The light turned green and Shannon put her foot on the gas pedal.

"What kind of weird bullshit is that?" Chloe asked. "And in the scheme of things, is that even a big deal? Becky is fucking my husband behind Holly's back. And what about that stupid stick doll and the ominous note?" She shook her head as she talked and tapped at the screen of her iPhone at the same time. "And now we get to throw kidnapping, of all things, into the mix.

"Oh, would you look at this. Not you," Chloe said. "You're driving. I googled 'kidnappings in California,' and it says here that 2,100 children are reported missing in the United States every day! Eight hundred of those cases are false alarms. After subtracting family member abductions, we're left with thirty-three children abducted by strangers." More tapping on her cell before she said, "Oh, wonderful. There's a map. A fucking map showing crimes in Sacramento. The city gets a D+ for kidnappings, which means the rate is higher than the average US county. This is ridiculous. They try to make people feel better by saying most of the kidnappings, not including family abductions, are either suspicious or unknown circumstances. It states that there are one or two stranger abductions in Sacramento County alone in any given year!"

"Sounds as if you're taking what Caroline Baxter said about the kidnapping thing seriously?"

"I'm thinking outside of the fucking box. We drove all this way to talk to Caroline Baxter, and she not only confirmed the rumors that Rosella paid her to leave the area but also tossed a kidnapping plot into the mix. That's why I'm going to spend the next five minutes analyzing the information in front of me and see if I can connect it to our investigation."

"How are you going to do that?" Shannon asked.

"I'm going to assume that what Rosella told Caroline was true, which would mean someone on our block kidnapped a small child. I'll start with me. I didn't kidnap any of my kids. I've got the stretch marks to prove it."

Shannon decided to go along with Chloe's thought process. Chloe obviously needed to focus on something other than Wesley and stick dolls. "What about Dianne and Jason?" she asked.

"When Dianne was pregnant with Finn, I went to Lamaze classes with her. We can cross her off the kidnapping list, too."

"How about Kaylynn?"

"Archer was a toddler when they moved into—"

"What is it?" Shannon asked when Chloe stopped talking midsentence.

"Charley and Ethan," Chloe said, breathless. "Holly never talks about their births, but according to Becky, they used a surrogate."

"The same one both times?"

"I have no idea. But why didn't one of them carry the babies?"

"There are many reasons a woman can't carry a baby to term."

"Okay. You're right. I get it. But the point is they *didn't* carry the babies. I never met the surrogate or surrogates, either." Chloe blew out a huff of air and straightened her spine. "Calm down," she said out loud. "Just thinking outside of the box."

"You're doing a good job," Shannon told her. "You're asking the right questions. We're almost home. When we get back, I'll do some searching and see what I can find."

CHAPTER TWENTY-SEVEN

After school, Blake and Ridley dropped Mac off at her house. Mac stood in the driveway, taking in the beauty around her. The entire block was canopied by trees. It was so pretty. And yet, Rosella Marlow's sudden death had changed things around here. Everyone was acting different, including her mom. She hardly ever saw Dad, which was sad because she missed him. Two new friends at school each had a parent who was a doctor. They told Mac she better get used to not seeing a lot of him. Another student said it would be fine and to make the most of the time she did have with him. That was good advice, Mac thought, especially since she would be going off to college in a couple of years. She headed for the house, hoping she could talk her mom into taking a bike ride with her, maybe explore the area a little, do something different, have some fun.

Inside the house, Mac called out for her mom. There was no answer. She grabbed her cell phone from her backpack and saw a text from Mom. She was running a few errands and would be back in an hour. Mac texted back to let her know she was going to take a quick bike ride to Compton's Market to get a sandwich. She was starved and had been craving their Philly Cheese Steak sandwich with marinated steak and onions on a superfresh roll.

She navigated her bike out onto the driveway, grabbed her helmet, and closed the garage door before making her way back inside the house. After putting on sneakers, she went back outside and was surprised to see a piece of paper taped to her bike's handlebar:

Meet me at Bertha Henschel Park on Forty-Fifth Street

—Blake

Mac looked around. Nobody was there. She used her phone to see where the park was located on Google Maps. It was close by. She could stop there on her way. But why, she wondered, hadn't Blake just knocked on her door or texted her? Maybe he wanted to tell her why he and his sister had been acting so secretive. Ridley did tell Mac today about her mom fainting after being interviewed by the two detectives making the rounds. That incident probably hadn't helped Blake's mood. But still, he'd been acting weird for a few days now. What was going on with him?

A few minutes later, Mac arrived at Blake's designated spot, a small neighborhood park, set in a residential area but superprivate because of all the trees. Mac walked her bike across a weedy lawn. There was a playground for kids under five. Southwest of that were a basketball court and lots of trees. Either Blake wasn't here yet or she couldn't see him within the shade of the trees.

Nobody was here.

She stopped to pull her phone from her pocket, ready to text Blake, when a man dressed in jeans and a hoodie appeared out of nowhere. He grabbed her from behind, his arms circling her waist. Mac's bike toppled over. Her phone slipped out of her hand and fell to the ground. Her adrenaline raced as she tried to get out of his grasp. She wriggled and screamed, slammed her foot down on top of his.

He yipped. "Tell your bitch mother and her friend to stay out of everyone's business, or someone's going to get hurt."

Bent over, Mac managed to loosen one of his arms and bring her head close enough to his forearm to bite him. She dug her teeth into his flesh.

"Shit!" He jerked his arm back and shoved her away from him. Mac fell sideways, tripping over her bike. The metal bars smacked against her side. Her elbow slammed into the hard dirt. Pain sliced through her hip. It took her a second to move.

Her attacker had disappeared. A man and woman ran across the field toward her. They were older but in decent shape, and they helped her untangle her limbs and get to her feet. She was bruised, but nothing was broken.

"Do you want us to call anyone? The police?" the woman asked.

Mac gingerly brushed the dirt from her clothes. "No. I'm okay. I only live a few minutes away."

The man picked up her phone and handed it to her.

"She lives close by," the woman told her husband. He grabbed her bike. "We're going to walk you home," the woman said. "I won't be able to go on with my day until I know you made it home safely."

Thankful to have them escort her home, Mac didn't protest. Her attacker had scared her more than she was letting on. Now that the shock was wearing off, her knees wobbled and her hands wouldn't stop shaking.

————

Shannon pulled into the driveway. They said goodbye. Chloe climbed out of the car and headed for home. Shannon was eager to log on to her computer and research kidnappings in the area. Her plan was to make notes about everything going on. There was a lot of information to take in, and it was becoming difficult to keep it all straight. But when she walked into the house, Mac ran into her arms. Her daughter was sobbing.

Shannon was furious to learn that she had been attacked in the park and that it seemed to have something to do with Shannon and Chloe's investigation. The first thing she did was call Detective Seicinski, who said she was in the area and would stop by. Before Shannon and Mac had a chance to go over all the details, the detective was sitting in their living room.

"If it's okay with you," Detective Seicinski said, "I would like to question your daughter."

"That's fine, but I'm not leaving the room," Shannon said.

Detective Seicinski nodded and turned her attention to Mac, who sat on the couch next to Shannon. "In your own words, go ahead and tell me what happened, starting at the point where you found a note on your bike."

"I thought the note was from my friend Blake."

"Blake is Chloe Leavitt's son," Shannon explained.

"He has a twin sister," Detective Seicinski said. "Correct?"

Shannon nodded. "Her name is Ridley."

Mac said, "I still have the note if you want to see it?"

"Yes," Detective Seicinski said. "I'll put on my gloves and bag it so I can take it to the lab to check for prints."

"I already touched it," Mac said. "More than once."

The detective nodded. "That's okay." After the note had been taken care of and Mac had finished telling the detective what happened, Detective Seicinski continued with her questioning. "How well do you know Blake Leavitt?"

"Um, not well, I guess."

"How long have you known him?"

"Only a week."

"Then it's safe to say you wouldn't recognize his handwriting?"

"No. I wouldn't. And I did think it was sorta weird he didn't just come over to the house if he wanted to talk to me."

"Did you have any idea about what he might have wanted to talk to you about?"

"I wasn't sure. But I was hoping to find out why he's been acting so strange lately."

Detective Seicinski wrote something down. "Strange in what way?"

Shannon could tell that her daughter felt awkward talking about Blake. He gave her a ride to and from school, and she probably didn't want to involve him.

"Not strange," Mac answered. "Just quiet."

"Okay. Let's move on for now. The man who attacked you. Did he speak to you?"

"Yes. He said, 'Tell your bitch mother and her friend to stay out of everyone's business, or someone's going to get hurt.'"

Shannon stiffened, shocked. The first time Mac had told her what happened, she'd said he didn't want her mom and her mom's friend in his business, but that was it.

"Do you know what he meant by that?"

Mac glanced at Shannon, who simply nodded. "I know my mom wants to find out who murdered Rosella."

"Okay," the detective said. "Did you recognize his voice?"

"No."

"Can you describe him for me?"

"I couldn't see his face, but I know he was white. Beneath his dark hoodie, he was wearing a black beanie. He also wore jeans and sneakers with holes in them. It looked as if he'd rubbed dirt on his face, and I thought maybe he was trying to disguise himself."

"And yet you're sure he was white skinned."

"Yes. Definitely. When I was fighting him off, I bit his arm. That's how I knew for sure."

"How tall would you say he was?"

"My dad's height."

"Trey is six feet," Shannon offered.

"Anything else you can think of?" Detective Seicinski asked Mac. She shook her head.

"Your mom has my number if you do remember anything that might be of help to us later on."

"Okay," Mac said.

Detective Seicinski stood. "One more thing. You said you fell. Any bruises?"

Mac stood and lifted her shirt high enough to see her belly button, turning both ways. There were purplish bruises on her right side.

"Do you mind if I take a picture?"

"I don't mind." Mac looked at Shannon, who gave the detective the go-ahead.

A few minutes later, as Shannon walked Detective Seicinski to the door, the detective's phone rang. She stepped to the side to answer it. "We can't charge her," she told the caller. "That's right. Let her go."

By the time the detective finished her call, Shannon was standing at the entry with the door open. The detective stepped outside. "You should know your fingerprints were indeed found on the murder weapon."

Although it wasn't a surprise, since she'd already told the detective that she'd touched the letter opener, that didn't stop Shannon's insides from twisting.

"Holly Bateman's fingerprints were also found on the murder weapon."

Shannon said nothing.

The way the detective was staring at Shannon made her think she was searching for something. Maybe she expected a reaction, but Shannon already knew about Holly.

"She was arrested this morning, but we've decided to let her go for now."

"What happens next?"

"This is a case surrounded by unusual circumstances. We're considering polygraph tests, but we still have a lot of work to do. If I were you," Detective Seicinski said, her expression grave, "I would tie up any loose ends you might have around here. Just in case."

"Are you saying I might be arrested?"

Detective Seicinski's shrug said it all.

"But you know why I was at Rosella's house. I didn't do it."

"Holly said the same thing . . . that she didn't do it." The detective stared at her. "Let it go. Let the professionals do their jobs. Okay?"

No way in hell, Shannon thought. Her daughter had been attacked, and her own freedom was now on the line. The clock was ticking.

"Let me know if your daughter remembers anything more about the man in the park." Detective Seicinski turned and walked away.

CHAPTER
TWENTY-EIGHT

Chloe answered the door thinking it was Wesley, back to beg her forgiveness. Instead, she found herself staring at Detective Seicinski. She was not happy to see her. "I answered all of your questions yesterday."

"And again," Detective Seicinski said, "I thank you for your cooperation."

A dark sedan pulled up to the curb in front of Chloe's house. Detective Toye emerged from the vehicle. As he approached, he said to his partner, "Came as soon as I could."

Detective Seicinski nodded at him before turning back to face Chloe.

"What do you want?" Chloe asked.

"MacKenzie Gibbons was attacked at a nearby park."

"What?" Chloe felt the blood drain from her face. "Is she okay?"

"She's bruised and shaken up, but she'll be fine. We would like to talk to your son Blake."

"Why?"

"The note left on MacKenzie's bike was signed by Blake."

"What does a note have to do with Mac being attacked?"

Detective Seicinski didn't move. "It's best if we all talk inside."

Chloe sighed. "Fine. Let's get this over with. Come in."

"While we're at it, we'd like to talk to your daughter, too."

Chloe narrowed her eyes, but she didn't stop them from entering. No reason to draw this whole thing out. She shut the door and gestured toward the living room. "Make yourself at home. You know where to sit. I'll get the kids." Chloe made her way upstairs. She found Blake in his room, told him what had happened to Mac and how the detectives were here to talk to him because of a note. "You didn't leave a note for Mac asking her to meet you at the park, did you?"

"No," he said. "Why would I do that when she lives two houses away from us?"

"That's what I thought. They're going to be asking you the same question."

"I don't mind," Blake said. "I have nothing to hide. But I am worried about you. Are you okay, Mom?"

"I've been better. But don't worry. I won't faint, I promise."

"How long have they been here?"

"A few minutes," Chloe told him. "I have to find your sister. They want to talk to Ridley, too."

"Why would they want to talk to Ridley?"

Blake's concern for his sister worried her. "I don't know, but everything's going to be okay. We need to stay calm, answer their questions to the best of our ability, and hope this is the last time we see them."

"I'll get Ridley and meet you down there," Blake said, avoiding eye contact.

Chloe pointed to Carlin. "Make sure the dog stays in your room. He doesn't like the male detective."

Chloe headed downstairs, thankful Rowan was at a friend's house. She offered the detectives something to drink. They declined. A minute later, Blake walked into the room with Ridley right behind him. They were seventeen, Chloe thought, but they were still her babies. She wanted to protect them, and yet she felt powerless.

The detectives were sitting in the same spots on the couch as where they'd sat yesterday. Once again, Detective Seicinski took the lead. "Blake," she said. "We'll start with you, if you don't mind?"

"That's fine."

"Your new neighbor, MacKenzie Gibbons—"

"We call her Mac."

"Okay, after returning home from school, Mac decided to take a bike ride. After running back inside the house to get her sneakers, she went back to her bike and found a note taped to the handlebar." Detective Seicinski handed him an evidence bag. "Go ahead and read the note."

As he did so, Ridley leaned close and read along with him.

"Is that your handwriting?" the detective asked.

"No," Blake said. "If I had wanted to talk to Mac, I would have walked two houses down and knocked on her door."

"That's what she told us."

Chloe noticed his shoulders relax.

Detective Seicinski asked, "Could you please pull up your shirt-sleeves and extend both arms?"

Blake did as the detective requested.

"What are you looking for?" Chloe asked, her heart racing.

"While at the park," Detective Seicinski continued, "Mac was attacked by a man about your son's height. She was able to fight him off, but not before he gave her a warning."

"What was the warning?" Chloe asked.

The detective pulled out her notebook and read verbatim, "Tell your bitch mother and her friend to stay out of everyone's business, or someone's going to get hurt."

Goose bumps sprang up on Chloe's arms.

The detective directed her attention on Blake. "Mac mentioned you've been quiet lately. Is anything wrong?"

"I don't know what she's talking about," Blake said. "I'm fine."

Chloe stiffened. "You said specifically the attacker was my son's height, and now you're talking about him being quiet for some reason. Are you suggesting Blake attacked Mac?"

"No. I'm not suggesting that at all. Merely asking questions, trying to get to the bottom of this."

Chloe wanted to kick them out but figured it would only make things worse.

"What about the doll made from sticks?" Detective Toye asked, taking Chloe by surprise.

"What about it?" Blake asked, still composed.

"Did you or your sister have anything to do with the doll left at Rosella's house?"

"No."

"Are you sure? We have a witness who saw two people with a flashlight outside Rosella's house on Monday night. Forensics has been back to the house to collect footprints from the area pointed out by the witness."

"I'm sure."

"Are we finished here?" Chloe asked.

Detective Seicinski shook her head. "Almost." She fiddled with her phone and placed it on the coffee table. "Ridley, would you mind taking a look at the letters on my phone?"

Chloe walked over to her daughter, once again hovering as she read the letters, her stomach curdling. It took everything Chloe had inside her to stay composed.

Mrs. Marlow,

I know you think I'm a child, but I'll be sixteen soon, only a few years younger than Daniel. We love each other and I don't think it's fair of you to keep us apart. With or without your approval, we will be together someday. Love always finds a way. We both know that Daniel would do anything for you, so please, I'm asking . . . begging you to let us spend some time together.

—Ridley

The second letter was short, but not so sweet, written months before Daniel's tragic death fifteen months ago.

Mrs. Marlow,
You are mean and cruel. Your son hates you. I hate you. And more than anything, I wish you were dead. —Ridley

"Did you write these letters?" Detective Seicinski asked Ridley.

"Yes," Ridley answered before Chloe could stop her.

"You and Daniel were in love?"

"Yes. I still love him. Rosella had no right to keep us apart. I'm glad she's dead."

Her daughter's words sucked the air out of the room. It took everything she had not to crumple to the floor with guilt and concern for her daughter's well-being. Her suspicions about Ridley had been confirmed. Ridley had been suffering on her own, without Chloe's support. How had she missed the signs? And why hadn't Ridley felt comfortable sharing her feelings?

"Stop," Chloe said, her heart racing. "We're done here. Get out of my house. Now." The note left on Mac's bike wasn't the only reason the detectives had come. In her opinion, they also came here to get a rise out of her daughter. They were increasingly intrusive, and as far as she was concerned, this was an abuse of authority.

After the detectives left, Chloe stopped Ridley from heading upstairs and steered her back into the living room, where Blake still sat, his gaze on nothing, as if in a trance. Ridley took a seat in the same chair next to her brother. Chloe sat on the couch, leaned forward, and said, "You're both going to tell me what's going on." Every muscle in her body hummed. Enough was enough. She needed to know everything.

"Nothing is going on," Ridley said, her tone defiant. "Daniel and I loved each other and now he's dead. All because of Rosella."

"Rosella was murdered," Chloe reminded her.

"She got what she had coming to her," Ridley said, her tone flat. "She never should have kept us apart."

Ridley didn't look at Chloe. She sat there emotionless—no tears, no more words.

Chloe was her mom, and despite Ridley's apparent lack of compassion or empathy for Rosella, she understood Ridley's reaction had more to do with grief and teenage love. Closure, Chloe thought, was an important part of grieving, and her daughter hadn't gotten that. She loved her daughter, and it broke her heart to see her in pain.

"Daniel and Ridley had burner phones," Blake told Chloe, his face reddening as he appeared to come back to life. "Rosella sent Daniel away to college back east to keep them from being together, but they still found a way to talk to each other every day."

"Big deal," Ridley said, clearly annoyed at her brother for speaking up. "Rosella called me to her house to talk with me and told me I was never to see Daniel or talk to him again. She called me a whore and a slut. Even Daniel hated her, but he wanted to finish school and get a job before cutting all ties with her."

Elbows propped on his knees, Blake rubbed his hands over his face, as if he hoped to scrub away his frustrations. "You just needed to be patient," he muttered.

"What do you mean?" Chloe asked him.

"Ridley needed to calm down and wait for Daniel to finish school. That's all she had to do. Instead, she spent every moment of her life worrying about their relationship and being kept apart. She changed, and I didn't like it. After Daniel died, Ridley blamed Rosella for Daniel's death." He shook his head. "It's stupid to blame someone for an accident nobody can control. But Ridley couldn't let it go. Not before his death, and certainly not after."

"Blake's never been in love!" Ridley cried. "He has a new girlfriend every month."

Blake went on as if his sister hadn't said a word. "Ridley made that stupid stick doll you saw the other day, the one with the nail through the head and the red polish made to look like blood. She asked me to go with her to put it inside Rosella's house. I didn't want to do it, but I knew if I didn't go with her, she would do it alone."

Ridley had lied to her when she'd asked her about the doll. Somewhere along the way, Chloe had lost her daughter's trust. She shut her eyes for a long moment before opening them. "Where did you leave the doll?"

"Next to the knife block in the kitchen," Ridley said without remorse.

"But neither of you saw Rosella that night?" Chloe asked.

"No," Blake said. "After Ridley put the doll in the kitchen, we left through the basement window, the same way we entered."

"And you didn't see anything unusual when you were inside her house? An open window or a door ajar?"

"Everything looked the same to me," Ridley said.

Blake nodded his agreement. "The lights were all off. Rosella had to be asleep."

Or dead, Chloe thought.

CHAPTER TWENTY-NINE

Kaylynn Alcozar sipped her coffee as she stared out the window overlooking Forty-Fifth Street. It was Saturday and everything appeared eerily tranquil and serene. Their block was usually bustling with activity on the weekends—people walking their dogs, entire families riding bicycles in a neat little row, waving at passersby as they rolled along.

The fundraiser was set for today. There would be lots of spaghetti and garlic bread. Kaylynn had signed up to bring pies, which she had baked last night. Others had been assigned salad and cookies. There would be plenty of food for anyone living within or even outside the Fabulous Forties. The price for a plastic stick-on bracelet to get in line for food was twenty dollars, free for children under five. All proceeds would go to Children's Receiving Home of Sacramento (CRH), a charity dedicated to helping children by providing hope and healing for kids who needed it most. This was the first time since Kaylynn and Nicolas had moved here that Becky and Holly Bateman weren't already outside setting up. Eventually, the entire block would be sectioned off with orange cones and ribbon. Two ten-by-twelve-foot canopies would provide cover for the tables laden with food.

But it was already nine o'clock. And nothing was happening out there.

It had been a stressful week. Kaylynn wondered whether the fundraiser had been canceled. She hoped so. The one thing she was grateful for today was that Detectives Seicinski and Toye hadn't reached out again. She'd heard from Dianne, who heard from Jason, who heard from Wesley, that Holly Bateman had been arrested yesterday morning and then released by late afternoon. Apparently, nearly everyone in the neighborhood had been in and out of Rosella's house in the days leading up to the murder. The killer could be anyone.

Kaylynn kept thinking about Monday night, though. How she'd awoken after midnight to go to the bathroom and seen two figures outside Rosella's house. At first, because of the sizes of the silhouettes, she'd thought it might be the twins, Blake and Ridley. Over the past year, she'd sensed Ridley's animosity toward Rosella. And Rosella never talked about Ridley, which was odd. Rosella talked about everyone, including the small children. So when Kaylynn had talked to the detectives about seeing someone outside, she hadn't wanted to point fingers. But lately, she couldn't stop thinking about returning to bed and finding it empty. She hadn't asked Nicolas about it because a part of her didn't want to know.

But not knowing was eating her up, interfering with her ability to concentrate on daily tasks. She knew what needed to be done. She needed to protect her family. She left her coffee cup on the table and went in search of her phone and the business card Detective Seicinski had given her.

———

Shannon had spent the entire morning baking homemade chocolate chip cookies while thinking about what her daughter's attacker had said.

Trey was adamant about her stepping back and letting it go: no more asking questions or looking for clues. He was worried sick, and understandably so. But how could she move on as if nothing had happened to Mac? How would she ever allow Mac to go on a walk or ride her bike without monitoring her closely?

If she and Chloe *did* let it go, was that a guarantee this person would simply leave them all alone? No way! She refused to live in fear. The attack had made her more determined than ever to take proactive steps toward solving the mystery of Rosella's death.

"I'm feeling much better," Mac told her. "I'm walking without a limp."

"Let me see."

Mac pulled up her shirt. The bruise on Mac's hip had yellowed around the edges. It was hard to tell anything had happened to her. But that didn't mean Shannon thought her daughter should go to today's neighborhood event.

"I don't think she should go," Trey said.

Mac looked from her dad to Shannon. "I promised Holly I would be in charge of watching after the kids. I want to do it!"

Shannon knew Mac also wanted to talk to Blake to make sure he wasn't mad at her for saying he'd been acting different. That was, if the detectives had repeated what she'd said.

"It's up to you," Shannon told her husband.

"Please," Mac begged. "I'll stay with the smaller kids the entire time. I promise."

"Fine," he said. "But don't go anywhere, not even back to the house, without telling one of us, okay?"

Mac agreed and Shannon handed them each a foil pan filled to the brim with cookies and covered with Saran Wrap.

She and Trey exchanged looks. After a string of stressful days, they were both craving a reprieve from the chaos. It felt like ages since she'd woken up with Trey at her side. They had made love and enjoyed coffee in bed. She knew he wasn't excited about spending his one day off with the neighbors, not with everything going on, but when he smiled at her, his eyes were bright, and she could tell he was happy to do his part.

Shannon grabbed the last two pans of cookies and followed them out the door. If her daughter hadn't been threatened and Rosella's murderer weren't running free, she might have taken a moment to enjoy the blue skies and sunshine. But as it was, she walked on, feeling confident that at least things couldn't get any worse.

Shannon stood with Kaylynn and Dianne as the party wound down. Chloe had run off to pour champagne into some clear plastic cups to celebrate a record-earning fundraiser. The event had gone smoothly, better than any of them dared hope, with way more attendees than expected. There were games for the kids: cornhole and face makeup. Plenty of food and drinks. Once the festivities dwindled down to predominantly the people on their block, they would start to clean up.

"I can't believe you're still not talking to me," Shannon overheard Becky say from close by.

"I can't believe you've been fucking Wesley Leavitt," Holly shot back, her voice a low growl, but not so low that Shannon and the others couldn't overhear.

Kaylynn and Dianne nudged one another.

"If you don't want to help clean up," Holly said, "feel free to run off. Maybe you should give Wesley a call and see what he's up to."

"I told you, it's over."

"Probably a good thing since he won't be able to afford expensive restaurants or nice hotels. No more high-end, ridiculously expensive sunglasses."

"What are you talking about?" Becky asked.

"I heard from Dianne that Chloe closed off Wesley's access to her bank accounts."

They all looked at Dianne, who made a face. "It's true. I can't deny it."

"Yep," Holly said. "That's what happens when you mess around. You destroy lives. Good job."

"Our cute little block is falling apart," Kaylynn said in a quiet voice.

Chloe returned and passed a plastic cup to each of them. Her forehead wrinkled when she turned to face Shannon. "What's wrong?"

"Don't do it," Shannon said, mostly to herself, as she watched Trey walk right up to Jason Abbott. She'd had no idea Trey still intended to talk to the man until she saw him approach Jason and heard raised voices. She watched closely as things quickly spiraled out of control.

"Don't do what?" Chloe asked, prompting all of them to follow Shannon's gaze.

Jason's face had turned bright red. "How many different ways can I tell you, buddy. Rosella and I had a history that went way back. All I wanted to do was talk to your wife and tell her my side of the story."

"My wife had a traumatic morning and didn't want to talk to you. When someone tells you no, it means no," Trey said.

With two kids in tow, Mac appeared at Shannon's side. "Mom. You have to stop them. What is Dad doing? This is embarrassing."

Jason grabbed hold of the top of Trey's button-down shirt. "Big Doctor Man thinks he's going to teach me a lesson, is that it?"

Trey's gaze fell to the fistfuls of his shirt in Jason's grasp. "Get your hands off me."

"What are you going to do about it?"

The minute Shannon saw the look on her husband's face, his stiff jaw and piercing eyes, she knew there was going to be trouble. "Please," she said, handing Chloe the plastic cup and running toward them. "Stop this nonsense."

But it was too late.

Trey's fist made contact with Jason's jaw, sending him to the ground. Jason scrambled to his feet, ready to duke it out.

Shannon had seen Trey angry before, but she'd never seen him actually use his fist to strike a man. She didn't like it one bit. She was furious with him.

Dianne joined the feisty group just as someone called out in a loud, slurry voice, "One big happy family!" It was Wesley. He stumbled drunkenly through a small crowd that had gathered, people Shannon didn't recognize who no doubt lived on another block.

As Wesley approached, he tripped on his own feet, giving his body enough momentum to careen forward, right into Dianne's chest. Her arms were like windmills as she tried to catch her balance. Becky, appearing out of the blue, shot forward in time to catch Dianne and stop her from toppling over.

Wesley's gaze fell on Becky. He frowned. "Why haven't you answered my calls?"

Becky ignored him. She made sure Dianne was good on her feet before she walked away.

"Come back," he cried before meeting Chloe's gaze. He swayed slightly but managed to keep his balance. "My love," he said. "My darling wife. The only woman for me."

Blake appeared. "Stop it, Dad. Enough."

Shannon froze when she overheard Kaylynn and Nicolas Alcozar talking less than a few feet away.

"It's time to go home," Nicolas told his wife.

"No," she said. "We're going to stay and help clean up."

"Well, I'm going home."

"Surprise, surprise." She sounded resentful. "It's a great life, isn't it? Always hiding, afraid of our own shadows. All because of you."

Shannon wondered whether anyone else had heard what they were saying, but all eyes appeared to be on Wesley and whatever he was saying to his eldest son. Shannon found it interesting Rosella had said the same thing to Shannon . . . *The Alcozars are afraid of their own shadows, and they're hiding something.*

"Tell Holiday I went home," Nicolas told Kaylynn. "It's getting hot."

"I told you not to wear a long-sleeved shirt," she said. "And Holiday never came to the party. He's in his room. Your son is always in his room. Do you know why?" Before Nicolas could answer, Kaylynn said, "Because you've made it impossible for him to go anywhere without being scared to death he might say the wrong thing."

When Shannon began to think this day could not possibly get any worse, it did. Detective Seicinski and Detective Toye had arrived. Maybe they had come to donate money to their cause? She was kidding herself, of course, and at the same time, praying they weren't here to arrest her.

Shannon couldn't find Chloe in the crowd. She saw Kaylynn pull on her husband's shirt and say, "Those are the detectives I told you about."

"I'll go check on Holiday," he said. "I'll see you at home."

Nicolas was gone in a flash. But Shannon no longer had any interest in the Alcozars. Her focus was on Detective Seicinski, whose gaze was laser-focused as she scanned the crowd for her prey. She stiffened before taking long single-minded strides. Shannon followed the detective's gaze, surprised to see her walking toward Ridley Leavitt. Why? And where was Mac?

Panic began to set in until she saw Mac with three-year-old Charley propped on her good hip. She was talking to Rowan, no doubt trying to keep the boy's attention away from his father. Once Shannon knew Mac was fine, she made a beeline toward Ridley, hoping to draw her away before Detective Seicinski got to her. Blake must have had the same idea because he was at his sister's side in a flash.

"Stand aside, please," Detective Seicinski told Blake. "We're here to arrest Ridley Leavitt for the murder of Rosella Marlow."

"Fuck off!" Ridley said. "That's stupid."

"You have nothing on her," Blake told the detectives. "It's all circumstantial. An ugly stick doll I made myself."

"You made the doll?"

"Yes!" he cried.

He looked wide-eyed and scared. *He is lying*, Shannon thought.

"We have a witness who saw you and your sister at Rosella's house around one thirty in the morning on the day of the murder. Ridley's fingerprints are on the doll and all over the house."

"So are mine," Blake said.

Shannon gave up looking for Chloe. "This is silly," she told the detective. "You're talking to a couple of teenagers. Everyone's fingerprints were on the murder weapon, including mine."

"Move out of the way, Mrs. Gibbons, or you'll be handcuffed and brought to the station, too."

Blake no longer held any emotion on his face when he said, "I returned home with Ridley the night you're talking about. When she fell asleep, I went back to Rosella's house and killed her."

Ridley stepped forward and grabbed her brother's arm. "Stop it, Blake." Tears started to fall. "He didn't do it. Neither of us killed Rosella. You and Lurch"—she gave Detective Toye the evil eye—"don't know what you're doing. Blake is innocent. He wouldn't hurt a fly."

"No," Blake said, using one hand to push his sister out of the way. "I killed Rosella Marlow. I had no choice. Ridley wasn't even there."

Another sob escaped Ridley. "Stop it, Blake." Her gaze fell on Detective Seicinski, her eyes pleading. "He's lying and you know it!"

Detective Toye began to read Blake his rights while Detective Seicinski handcuffed him.

Shannon ran to get Chloe, who was helping Holly with cleanup inside the house. The door to Holly's house was open. She ran inside. "Chloe! You have to come. Quickly!"

Chloe was wiping her hands on a towel when she appeared. "What's going on? What has Wesley done now?"

"No. It's Blake. The detectives showed up. They came to arrest Ridley, but Blake confessed to the murder of Rosella Marlow, and they're putting him in handcuffs."

Chloe's face turned as white as chalk. The towel dropped to the floor as she walked past Shannon. As soon as she hit solid ground outside, she started running.

By the time Shannon got back outside, Rowan and Ridley were clinging to Chloe as the crowd watched Blake being escorted away in handcuffs. Some people were crying, while others clung to their children and whispered to the person standing next to them. Chloe's eyes were vacant and hollow. Her face was pale. She was hanging on by a thread.

CHAPTER THIRTY

Shannon, Trey, and Mac headed back home after the spaghetti fund-raiser. Nobody said a word. Everyone except the Alcozars and the Leavitts had stayed to help clean and put everything away. Jason and Trey had worked as a team, taking the canopies down and putting away folding tables. Somebody had called a taxi to take Wesley to the hotel where he was staying. They never did get the chance to celebrate Holly raising a record amount of money for a good cause.

Once they were inside the house, Mac told them she was going upstairs to take a long, hot shower.

"Wine?" Trey asked Shannon. She nodded. He filled two glasses, and they carried their wine out to the back patio and took a seat overlooking a well-manicured lawn bordered by colorful flowers. It was only the second time she and Trey had sat in their backyard together. Shannon's body ached. She felt as if she'd spent the day weeding.

Trey released a heavy sigh before saying, "I think it's in our best interest to put the house up for sale and find somewhere else to live."

Shannon shook her head.

"Don't you?" Trey frowned. "Our daughter has been hanging out with a murderer."

"Blake did not kill Rosella."

"How do you know that?"

"I guess I don't, but I feel it in my bones. I don't think Ridley had anything to do with it, either."

"Intuition can only take you so far."

"I understand, but he's a sweet, charming kid."

"Didn't someone say that about Jeffrey Dahmer, too?"

"Nobody ever called Dahmer sweet. Blake comes across as genuine. He reminds me a lot of our daughter."

Trey shook his head. "Don't do this, Shannon. I like the kid, too, but—"

"You've never met him. And besides, my fingerprints were also on the murder weapon. So were Holly's, which is why they arrested her for a hot minute."

"Okay. You're right," Trey said. "We'll wait and see what happens. But you have to admit nobody on this block likes anyone else."

Over the years, Shannon had tended to listen to Trey but keep quiet about stuff she thought might get her husband riled. That was on her, though, not him. It all needed to change. Since moving here and meeting Rosella and the other women on the block, including Peggy Chandler, who seemed at ease with speaking her mind, Shannon wasn't in the mood to keep her thoughts to herself. It was way past time she started sharing her observations and opinions.

"I think you're wrong about our neighbors. They have formed strong bonds and friendships over the years. I do believe the block as a whole is struggling right now, what with everything going on." Shannon sipped her wine. "The residents seem to be acting more like squabbling siblings than neighbors, because they truly care about one another."

He pointed in the direction of the front of their house, where the fundraiser had taken place. "That's what you call caring? Everyone attacking each other, everyone happy about the death of Rosella Marlow?"

"What I saw out there was everyone coming together to support Holly and her fundraiser." Shannon set her glass on the table. "And in case you didn't know, our neighbors weren't the only people who didn't like Rosella. Google her name and you'll find a large number of people who despised her."

Trey said nothing, but she could tell he didn't agree with a word she was saying.

"Did I ever tell you what Rosella said about all men, including you, being cheaters?"

"She didn't know me. I never met Rosella."

Shannon shrugged. "Rosella didn't care. You were a good-looking doctor, so it was bound to happen."

"Why are you telling me this?"

"Because I think I've been holding in too much, and I need to get it all out." Telling him that, letting him know she'd been suppressing her feelings, made her feel empowered. Her husband was someone she loved and trusted. She should have opened up to him a long time ago.

"Okay," he said, meeting her gaze. "I've never cheated on you. Never would cheat on you because I love you."

"I love you too."

"Anything else?" Trey asked. "You can tell me, Shannon. I'm here for you. I always have been."

"Did you know that when I was twenty, I reached out to the Sierra Adoption Agency to see if my bio mom would be interested in meeting with me?"

"No. You never told me."

"You're right. I never did, and I should have. Opening up about my past has always made me uncomfortable and even ashamed."

"I had no idea you've been struggling. Keeping it all bottled up inside can't be good for you. What happened to you as a child was beyond your control. You didn't choose to be given up for adoption, and it's not your fault."

"Thank you. I never wanted to burden you with my problems."

"I want you to always feel comfortable enough to share anything at all with me."

She nodded, her heart filling with gratitude.

"Did your bio mom ever respond?" Trey asked.

"Two weeks after I had gotten in touch, I received a letter from the agency letting me know she wasn't interested in meeting me."

"I'm sorry."

She smiled, but it was strained. "I'll be okay. I feel better now that I've told you."

"I'm glad."

"I've never felt a connection to anyone other than you and Mac. But something strange happened when we moved here to the Fab Forties." Shannon placed a hand over her heart. "Something clicked, and I felt an instant connection with this place and these women."

"Don't you think maybe you're being naive?" Trey asked.

"Why do you say that?"

He sipped his wine, his gaze set on hers. "These people are not your friends. You can't trust them because you don't even know them."

"Says the man who asked me to marry him within twenty-four hours of meeting me." Effective communication took work, and in this moment, humor came easily. If she was going to open up to him, she knew she might not always get the reaction she desired.

"That was different."

Shannon smiled. "Maybe. But these people have made me feel welcomed and accepted. I already feel a strong sense of community." She reached over and touched his arm. "We have been married for twenty-two years, and yet sometimes I think you are the one who doesn't know me."

"Believe me," Trey said. "I know you."

"If you did, if you listened to the things I have shared with you in the past, then you might understand why I could feel a connection to these women, even in such a short time."

"I get it. You didn't have biological parents or siblings. But you had the Fergusons, and they loved you."

"Mr. Ferguson wanted to get rid of me the minute his wife died. He became someone else altogether. I had to lock my door at night to keep him out of my room." She tried not to think about Mr. Ferguson, but when she did, she felt a tightening in the muscles of her shoulders and neck.

"You said he never touched you."

"I told you he never raped me." She allowed the fear and shame to rise up from her chest and travel through her body before dissipating.

"You're right," Trey said. "I should have asked more questions. I do feel uncomfortable talking about your past at times because I can't do anything to fix it."

"I appreciate you telling me," Shannon said, a weight lifting from her shoulders. "Mr. Ferguson wasn't a good man. I never felt safe, but we don't need to discuss it again."

"No. I want you to be able to talk to me."

A tremendous wave of hope swept over her. "I want that, too," she said. "I know you've always worked hard to make a good life for our family. You continue to work long hours. But we have both made sacrifices. You know that, right?"

"Do you know how many women would give a limb to be you?" Trey asked. "To get to stay at home with their child? To live in a luxurious house in a fabulous area? I moved here because you asked me to. All I've ever wanted was for you to be happy."

His words hit a nerve. They had been doing so well, too. She had a feeling his frustrations stemmed from being unable to make her past traumas disappear like a snowflake that evaporated the second it made contact with the ground. Either way, she couldn't let it go without a response. If they were going to communicate at a deeper level, they needed to say how they felt.

"Do you know how many men would give a limb to be you?" she asked. "To have a wife who appreciates her husband and who was willing to give up a career to raise their daughter? A wife who works to make everything nice for when he comes home after a hard day's work?"

"Come on," Trey said. "You know I didn't mean it that way."

"Well, I did. You're a revisionist," Shannon said, feeling good about getting everything out in the open. "When I first met Rosella, I asked you if you would be open to looking at properties in the area. You said no. It wasn't until you got the job offer at Sutter Hospital that you agreed to move."

"And your point being?"

"You didn't move here solely for my benefit."

"Listen," he said. "I don't want to fight with you."

"I don't want to fight, either. I just want you to understand me. To know what it feels like to be missing that parental connection, to know you are loved unconditionally, no matter what."

He opened his mouth to protest, but she stopped him. "Hear me out. Please."

He clamped his mouth shut, impatience scrawled all over his face.

"You have two parents who have loved and supported you since the day you were born," Shannon reminded him. "The only thing they didn't like about you . . . was *me*. They thought you deserved better because they knew I was broken."

He said nothing. Probably because he knew it was true.

"Do you have any idea what it's like to grow up alone . . . completely alone? Some foster homes—at least I've heard—are wonderful, filled with kind and loving people who want to help children like me. But whether you want to believe it or not, there is a dark side to foster care. The foster homes I ended up in were operated by greedy people who were looking for a way to cash in each month. Some of them wanted a cook, a laundress, someone who could help keep the house tidy or keep an eye on their younger kids. Before I was adopted by the Fergusons, I spent the first thirteen years of my life being abused and neglected. I never felt safe. I certainly never felt loved. Not until I met you."

He set his glass on the table, got to his feet, and held his hands out for her to take, which she did. He pulled her into his arms. "I'm sorry."

She couldn't stop a lone tear from falling. "It's not all your fault—the miscommunication. There were many times when I could have opened up to you but didn't. I should have tried harder to communicate what I was feeling."

"I wish I could wave a magic wand and make everything better for you," Trey said, "but I can't. You need to agree to tell me when you're feeling abandoned or unseen. I also want to acknowledge your trauma."

The tears were falling now. Talking about her past and knowing she had his support was overwhelmingly cathartic.

"I wish my parents hadn't been so hard on you and that they saw what I saw and still see. I don't want anyone but you. And you're right. I'm the lucky one out of the two of us." He held her close enough for her to feel the beat of his heart. "I'm also glad you feel a weird connection to this place and these women."

"It's not weird," she said with a lighthearted laugh.

He chuckled. "Okay. You're right. And no more talk about moving. Not unless Jason Abbott touches me again."

She held him close, glad she'd found the courage to finally open up. "I've missed you."

"I've missed you, too."

CHAPTER THIRTY-ONE

The next day, minutes after arriving home from the police station, Chloe's cell phone rang. It was Shannon. She tapped the screen to answer the call. "Hi," she said, trying hard to hold herself together. It was impossible to comprehend how her child could have ended up in this situation. The guilt she felt for not being able to prevent this from happening ate at her insides. She'd never felt so helpless in her life, unable to figure out what to do next. It hadn't helped when Wesley showed up at the police station, hungover and begging her forgiveness, causing her even more stress.

"I'm not even going to ask how you're doing." Shannon told her. "But I do need to talk to you. Trey and Mac are out playing pickleball. Can you come over?"

"What's this about?"

"It's about getting Blake out of jail. To do that, we need to figure out who the killer is."

Chloe's shoulders fell. Figuring out who killed Rosella was like paddling a canoe across Lake Natoma in hopes of finding a lost diamond ring. "How do you propose we do that?"

"We revisit the notes to search for overlooked details or new insights."

Instead of cleaning, Chloe wanted to go back to bed, stare at the ceiling, and disengage. "I don't know, Shannon. This feels worse than searching for a needle in ten haystacks."

Shannon didn't seem to be listening to a word Chloe said, because she kept right on talking.

"Rosella must have given me those notes for a reason. If her instincts were anywhere near as good as she thought they were, she probably felt there was a chance I might find a clue or a piece of information she'd forgotten about."

"She could have gone through the pile of crap herself. Why did she need you to go through her notes?"

"Being too close to a project can limit a person's perspective. Maybe that's why she gave it all to me."

Chloe exhaled. "I don't have much of a choice, it appears, but to do my darndest to try and figure this mystery out, do I?"

There was no response.

"I'll be there soon."

Chloe felt sick to her stomach. Seeing Blake in an orange jumpsuit, handcuffed, and looking so damned resigned to sticking to his story, had been too much. She'd pleaded with Detective Seicinski, tried to make her see that Blake was innocent, but she wasn't budging. The detectives wanted to close this case and move on.

Fuck Seicinski and Toye. Chloe might be Blake's only chance of getting out of jail. It didn't matter that she hadn't slept more than five hours in two nights. She couldn't remember the last time she'd eaten, either. Sleep and food were overrated; she didn't have time for them. With renewed energy, Chloe grabbed her purse and headed out.

The door to Shannon's home opened before Chloe had a chance to knock. They said nothing. No point. This was business. Shannon made her way to the two stacks of papers sitting on the kitchen counter. A pad of paper with Shannon's notes, organized and neat, rested on the counter, too.

Chloe tapped on the name and date written at the top of the pad. "Bradley. Who's that?"

Shannon was across the way, pouring coffee into mugs. "I don't know. I've read through those notes dozens of times, and I noticed the name Bradley was mentioned more than once." She absentmindedly played with a strand of hair. "Too bad Rosella didn't give us more insight into what her scribblings meant."

"And what about the month of July?"

"Rosella scribbled the word *July* a total of six times. She even made a box around the month. So I wrote it down." Shannon set a cup of hot coffee in front of Chloe and took a seat on the stool next to her.

"What about the kidnapping?"

"I couldn't find a kidnapping involving a child in the area."

"It could have happened anywhere," Chloe said. "But what I'm trying to say is maybe *Bradley* was kidnapped in *July*." She started tapping on her phone.

Shannon did the same.

"I had no idea a Bradley was a fighting vehicle," Chloe said.

"I see a Stephen Bradley," Shannon said. "Oh, never mind. He was the kidnapper. Apparently, he kidnapped an eight-year-old boy. It happened a long time ago."

"There's a long list of Bradley kidnappings, but I don't see any children under the age of ten. And most of them happened a decade ago or longer."

"Maybe we should spend more time on this later, since there are so many Bradleys." Shannon took a swallow of coffee. "I think it would be a good idea to cross people off our list. People we know who we believe had nothing to do with what happened to Rosella."

Chloe noticed the list Shannon had made of all the names on the block. Everyone living close to Rosella, including teenagers. "Okay. Where do we start? Who do we cross off first?"

Shannon didn't pick up the pen, so Chloe did. She drew a line through Peggy's name. "She's too old."

"Okay," Shannon agreed. "Leave her crossed off. She seemed legitimately upset about Rosella's death. We can cross off our names because we both have alibis."

"You could have killed Rosella the first day you met her," Chloe said. She puffed her cheeks and blew the air out. "This isn't going to get us anywhere."

"Stay focused. I could not have killed Rosella on Monday morning because the ME report stated she was stabbed within twelve hours of my being there on Tuesday, but she didn't die until I arrived."

"So you could be the murderer," Chloe said.

"Technically, yes. Leave my name on the list."

Chloe crossed her name off. "I have an alibi. Wesley was out of town and my kids would have heard me leave the house." Her body sagged. "Okay, I'll leave my name on the list, too." She wrote her name at the top again.

"Can I cross out Mac, Blake, Ridley, or Holiday's name?"

"No. I met Holiday a few days ago," Shannon said. "He was wearing a shirt with a hole in it."

"So?"

"I didn't think much of it at the time, but while I was in Rosella's house waiting for Detective Seicinski to talk to me, I spotted a piece of torn fabric. It had gotten caught in the woodwork in the archway between the living room and the bottom of the stairs."

"And?"

"And I'm positive it matched the fabric of the shirt Holiday was wearing when I talked to him."

Chloe blew air through her teeth. "Okay. I need to try and be unbiased."

Shannon nodded.

"The piece of cloth, assuming it's the same bit of cloth from Holiday's shirt, means Holiday was inside Rosella's house," Chloe said. "Rosella had a cleaner at the house once a week. The cleaning lady is thorough. She used to clean my house. And so this tells us Holiday was not only inside Rosella's house but also there recently."

"I agree."

Chloe reread the list. "Mac didn't know Rosella, but that doesn't mean shit." She tossed the pen to the side. "We can't cross anyone off the damn list."

"I agree," Shannon said. "It's too soon."

"Yeah," Chloe said. "You know what's really far-fetched?"

"What?"

"I don't think a day has gone by that we haven't done something together since we met. I already feel as if I've known you my whole life." Chloe not only had confidence in Shannon but also felt a fondness and warmth toward her. "With everything going on lately, I'm grateful to have you around."

"I feel the same way," Shannon said. "You make me feel understood and appreciated. It's comforting to feel valued by another human being."

"Agreed."

"Aww." Chloe put an arm around Shannon's shoulder and gave her a squeeze. "Too bad I can't cross your name off our murder list."

"That does suck."

Chloe watched Shannon pick up her phone and begin to scroll. "What are you doing?"

"I'm looking at pictures I took at the spaghetti fundraiser yesterday."

Chloe scooted closer so she could look at the pictures with her. "Holly did such a good job yesterday. Too bad she didn't get to enjoy it."

"Mm-hm," Shannon said. "What about Jason Abbott?"

"What about him?"

"He used to be my number one suspect, but now he blends in with everyone else."

Chloe leaned closer to take a look at the picture of Dianne, Jason, and Finn standing outside their house before yesterday's event.

"What about Dianne?" Shannon asked.

"Wait a minute." Chloe pointed at the picture, more particularly at the roofline near the garage. "See those wires?"

Shannon nodded.

"Where's the camera? They used to have a security camera out front." Chloe jumped to her feet.

Shannon's eyes widened. "What are you doing?"

"What do you think? We need to talk to her. The Abbotts had cameras everywhere, and their house is right smack next to Rosella's. We need to see if Dianne has video of the night Rosella was killed."

Minutes later, Shannon and Chloe were standing in front of Dianne's door, knocking. Dianne opened the door and frowned. "What do you guys want? I have to get ready for work soon."

Chloe tried to peek over Dianne's head. "Where's Jason?"

"At the park with Finn. If I remember correctly, I'm the only one in the neighborhood who has to work on Sundays."

"I'm sorry," Chloe said. "We have a couple of questions, and then we'll leave."

Dianne let them in. She crossed her arms over her chest. "You've got five minutes, Sherlock."

Chloe said, "Security cameras. Where are they?"

"I don't know what you're talking about."

"Yes, you do." Chloe knocked Shannon's arm. "Show her the picture. Please."

Shannon pulled out her cell, tapped her finger on the screen, and handed her phone to Dianne, who said, "What am I looking at?"

Chloe pointed to the garage. "See those wires? You and Jason installed cameras over a month ago, so where are they?"

Dianne stiffened. "Jason removed them. I don't know when."

Dianne couldn't even maintain eye contact. She obviously thought her husband had killed Rosella. Maybe he had. Upon seeing desperation in the woman's eyes, Chloe decided she needed to stay composed. "Have you even looked at the app?"

Dianne shook her head.

"Please, Dianne? I'm begging you. Blake is in jail. I need to see the videos."

"Come on," Dianne said. "Follow me."

Chloe and Shannon exchanged a quick glance before they followed Dianne into the kitchen. Chloe noticed the peeling vintage wallpaper and the wood cabinets that needed a good cleaning. Even when distressed, these things drove her nuts. *What was wrong with her?*

Dianne held her phone. She input a passcode, tapped the app, and handed the phone over to Chloe. "You have the same cameras at your place. You'll probably be able to find what you need faster than I will."

Chloe was surprised she was letting her look at all. Was it because of Blake? It could be any number of reasons. Chloe didn't ask. She needed to hurry before Jason returned or Dianne changed her mind. She scrolled through the tiny thumb-size photos, which was getting her nowhere fast. She selected videos on camera number two, since it overlooked Dianne's side yard, which should pick up what was going on outside Rosella's basement.

"Rosella was killed Monday night or Tuesday," Shannon said. "The videos are dated. Start with the video on Sunday night."

Shannon stood on one side of her, and Dianne stood on the other.

"There won't be any video recordings unless someone was in the yard or an animal activated the camera," Chloe said.

Dianne reached over Chloe's arm and clicked on the video taken on Friday night. "Oops. Wrong one," she said.

For ten seconds they saw nothing but basement windows and shrubs illuminated by moonlight. Seconds later, someone appeared holding a flashlight. The person wore a camouflage hoodie and held a tool in their hand.

"Is that a crowbar?" Shannon asked.

"Fuck," Dianne said.

A house light came on. The person in the hoodie stopped whatever they'd been doing and ran off.

"Rosella told me someone tried to break into the basement window," Shannon said. "The police were called, but nothing came of it."

"I bought Jason that hoodie for when he goes hunting with his buddies."

Chloe's head tilted. "You're acting very calm about the whole thing. We just saw your husband trying to break into Rosella's house. We can't—"

"It wasn't Jason."

Shannon said, "But you just told us you bought him the hoodie."

"I did. But Jason wasn't wearing it that night. I was. That's me in the video."

Chloe scrunched her nose. "What the hell?"

"I wasn't going to kill her," Dianne said, her shoulders sagging. "I only wanted to scare her."

"What in the world!" Chloe said. "What were you going to do once you got inside?"

Dianne was trembling. "I don't know. I hadn't gotten that far. When the light came on, I ran. If it makes you two feeling any better, I regretted doing it."

"Well, thank God for that," Chloe said before tapping on the next video. The video was dated Monday night. It was triggered when Jason entered the side yard carrying bags of trash and tossed the bags into the garbage bin.

Next, Chloe clicked on one of three videos taken Tuesday morning. It was dark out, but the stars made it possible for them to see shadows until a flash of light suddenly illuminated the grass and shone on Rosella's basement window. This time two figures appeared, Blake and Ridley. Chloe knew their silhouettes just as Dianne had known the hoodie belonged to Jason. When the video ended, Chloe tapped her finger on the next one. Blake opened the window before he and Ridley slipped through it and into the garage. The video ended.

Chloe thought she might be sick. She clicked on the last video and saw both Blake and Ridley crawl back through the window and run off.

"Look at the time," Shannon said, pointing. "They were only inside the house for four minutes. No way was that enough time—"

Before she could finish her sentence, another figure came into view.

"Who is that?" Dianne asked, pressing into Chloe's arm.

A darkly clad figure had appeared seconds after Blake and Ridley headed toward home. Too soon to have been Blake, Chloe thought, since he'd told the detectives he had gone back home with Ridley and returned after she fell asleep.

"Is it Holiday?" Shannon asked.

"I don't know," Dianne said as the person climbed through the same window Blake and Ridley had used.

"Can you go back and pause it?" Shannon asked.

Chloe did as she asked.

"It looks like he's wearing a baseball cap underneath the hoodie."

There was an emblem on the cap. The person disappeared inside Rosella's garage. The video shut down after ten minutes and there were no further videos.

"Nobody ever came out," Dianne said.

Shannon frowned. "Was he still there when I arrived before eight the next morning?"

"No telling," Chloe said.

"It tells me it wasn't Jason," Dianne said excitedly. "He was in bed next to me all night. I'm a light sleeper. I would have known if he'd been gone for that long."

"I'm going to copy and send this video to my phone, okay?" Chloe asked.

"Sure," Dianne said.

Chloe's shoulders sagged as if a heavy weight had been lifted from them. Tears welled in her eyes as she exhaled a breath she hadn't realized she'd been holding. She prayed the video would be enough to prove Blake's innocence.

CHAPTER
THIRTY-TWO

They were back at Shannon's house and she was reeling with the heaviness of it all. All signs, in Shannon's opinion, pointed to Holiday. The piece of fabric caught in the woodwork at Chloe's house. The same piece of fabric missing from Holiday's shirt. And what about the person who showed up at Rosella's house right after Blake and Ridley disappeared? If Holiday was responsible for Rosella's death, what could possibly have been his motive?

She'd met him only once. She knew you couldn't judge a book by its cover, but seriously, besides his height and build, he was a kid. She thought Dianne and Chloe had been leaning toward Holiday being the culprit, but neither of them had said a word.

"What did you think about the baseball hat with the emblem on it?" Shannon asked.

"I thought it could be anyone's."

"Have you tried zooming in on the picture?"

Chloe nodded. "It's even blurrier when I enlarge the photo."

Shannon saw the pain etched in Chloe's face, and she felt a profound ache of empathy. Her son was in jail. Shannon couldn't imagine being in her shoes.

"The video proves Blake didn't kill Rosella, doesn't it?" Chloe asked.

"We're getting closer," Shannon said.

"The pressure is on to find the killer, but we have to get it right." Chloe pulled out her phone and tapped on the screen. "Why do I feel as if Rosella has won? Even in death? She was so sure I wanted to steal Lance away from her." Chloe shook her head in disbelief. "She hated me."

"She hated everyone," Shannon reminded her.

"The hate she carried for me was different, though. I saw it in her eyes. She wanted me to suffer from the beginning."

Shannon's mind filled with snapshots of her meeting with Rosella, how calm she'd appeared one moment, then how desperate and paranoid in the next. Shannon knew from her work helping to solve online crimes that it helped to always go back to the victim. Personal conflicts were always a red flag. Unfortunately, Rosella had more red flags than most. "Do you think Rosella truly wanted the entire neighborhood to feel her pain?"

"Definitely," Chloe said without hesitation. "I don't think I would have said that a few years ago. She was always mean, but Daniel's death had a detrimental impact on her, steering her down a very dark path."

They were sitting at the kitchen island. What Chloe said did seem to be the consensus. While Shannon sifted through the stack of notes, Chloe kept rewinding and watching the video of her kids crawling from Rosella's basement window and running off seconds before a third figure showed up.

Another image of Shannon's day with Rosella surfaced in her head—this one of Rosella gesturing for Shannon to turn away while she fiddled with her husband's antique desk. "Rosella had been hiding the envelope of scribbles she gave me. What else had she been hiding?"

Chloe didn't respond.

"Isn't a paranoid and suspicious person usually the one hiding secrets?"

"Not necessarily," Chloe said. "But what do I know?"

"When Rosella said everyone in the neighborhood was hiding something, I wonder if she was projecting."

"What do you mean?"

"Maybe Rosella was attributing her own thoughts and feelings to others? Maybe she was hiding the biggest secret of all."

"Like what?"

"I don't know."

Chloe went back to watching her video.

"I think we need to find a way to get inside Rosella's house," Shannon said matter-of-factly.

Chloe grimaced. "Are you serious? Why would we do such a thing?"

"Hear me out. When I first met Rosella, she made me look away while she fiddled with her late husband's antique desk. It had a bunch of compartments, and she needed a key to get into it." Shannon paused. "Why would she have me turn away? Unless," she said, raising her brows for emphasis, "she was hiding something."

Chloe asked, "Why are you so sure Blake isn't responsible for Rosella's death?"

The question came out of nowhere, taking Shannon by surprise. "For starters, you also know Blake is innocent."

"But I'm his mother. I know him inside and out. I know his heart."

"The video you keep watching is our first real clue," Shannon said, pointing at Chloe's phone. "There's no way Blake had enough time to return home and run back to Rosella's before the third person appears." She paused. "It wasn't Blake. Mac would have known if he was the one who attacked her."

"Detective Seicinski has been through Rosella's house twice now," Chloe reminded her.

"I don't care. We need to get inside and open Rosella's desk."

Chloe frowned. "It's a long shot, and you do realize you're talking about breaking and entering?"

"I'm talking about possibly getting Blake out of jail. We have a video, and we both know it's a great start, but we need more. If we do get inside Rosella's house, and we find nothing inside her desk, we call Detective Seicinski and tell her everything we know."

Chloe was quiet.

Shannon pushed a strand of hair out of her face. "You started this conversation by saying it was over—that Rosella had won, which means we lost. Are you ready to give up?"

"No. Let's do this."

"You used to be friends with Rosella," Shannon said. "Any idea how we might get into her house?"

"The Marlows used to keep a spare key under a loose brick on the patio in her backyard."

"How long ago?"

"Ten years. Maybe longer."

Shannon tried to rub the kink out of her neck, but it was no use.

"It was Lance who told me about the key," Chloe explained. "They were away on a family trip, and Lance called to ask if I would unplug their kitchen appliances and the air-conditioning. Rosella was a stickler for that sort of thing, and he didn't want her to know he'd forgotten to do it. When I told him I didn't have a key, he told me about the one hidden under a loose brick in the backyard. There's a good chance he never told Rosella, since she would not have been happy about having a spare key lying around. But if she did know about the key, it's probably gone."

"It's worth a shot," Shannon said. "I'll bring a picklock, just in case."

"I'm not even going to ask," Chloe said. "Let's do it tonight. I'll tell Ridley to watch Rowan."

"Where are you planning to say you're going?" Shannon asked.

"To the police station to talk to Detective Seicinski and to see Blake."

"Call me when you're ready to go. I'll tell Trey and Mac you need me."

"Okay," Chloe said. "Wear black. Meet me on the corner of Forty-Fifth and M. I'll be sitting in my car. We'll drive to the next block over, then sneak back to our block and make our way through the side yard, past the garbage bins."

"I'll be waiting for your call."

CHAPTER THIRTY-THREE

Sunday night, as she watched television with Trey and Mac, Shannon tried to play it cool when her cell rang. "It's Chloe," she said as she stepped out of the living area. A minute later, she returned to let them know Chloe was upset and needed her. If they didn't both feel so bad for Chloe with Wesley's cheating and Blake being in jail, they might have protested. But not tonight.

"How long will you be?" Trey asked.

"An hour," Shannon said. "Maybe longer."

Mac said, "We won't watch *Barbie* until you get back."

"No. Don't wait up, okay?"

"Okay," Mac said.

"Let Chloe know we're thinking of her," Trey said.

"I will." Shannon grabbed her backpack on the way out the door. The last time she'd peered out the window, it was still dusk. Now it was dark. The only sound was her footfalls on the sidewalk. As she approached Chloe's house, she picked up her pace, almost at a jog, until she saw Chloe's car parked at the corner of Forty-Fifth and M.

She opened the car door and hopped into the passenger seat. Expecting to see a tired, broken woman behind the wheel, she saw instead the same woman who had chased off Devin Hawke when the

Channel 10 News van showed up. Chloe looked sharp in her black leggings, black turtleneck, and black combat boots. Her hair was pulled back into a tight bun at the nape of her neck. "Did you bring your picklock?" she asked.

"I did," Shannon said as she gathered her hair and tied it in a ponytail. She reached into her backpack and pulled out her phone and put it on silent. The picklock came out next. When they got out, she would carry it in her back pocket. Everything else would stay in the car.

Chloe turned on the engine and pulled onto the road. "I'm going to park near the Hansons' around the corner. The family is in Hawaii." No sooner had she turned onto the next street over than she pulled to the curb and turned off the engine. "When we get out, follow me. Stay close. Don't look around. Make like we do this every night. Nothing to see here."

Shannon was taken aback by how effortlessly Chloe slipped into the role of amateur detective, as though it were second nature to her. Clad in all black, Chloe exuded a sense of confidence, focused on the task ahead of them. Shannon felt proud of her for agreeing to the plan. And yet, it niggled at her because she knew they were taking a big risk. If they got caught, they could be arrested. What then?

Within minutes they were standing outside Rosella's side gate. Chloe reached over the gate and undid the latch. So far, so good. Their footsteps echoed against the silence as they crept past a neat row of garbage cans. Shannon was just beginning to relax when her foot hit an empty bottle and sent it rolling across cement. She tried to reach for the bottle, but it rolled closer to the fence, out of view. Five steps later, the neighbors' light came on.

Chloe yanked on Shannon's arm, pulling her to the ground next to her.

"The Abbotts," Chloe whispered into her ear.

They heard footsteps. Someone drew closer, the beam of a flashlight shining through the slats in the fence separating his property from Rosella's.

"Do you see anything?" a woman asked.

It was Dianne. There was worry in her voice.

"Must have been a stray cat," he said.

Once they heard the squeak of a sliding door, they remained still. Shannon started counting to herself. She got to thirty when Chloe gave her a tug. Time to get going.

Her heart was racing. The thought of breaking and entering was much different from actually doing it. She breathed through her nose and out through her mouth as they moved onward until they arrived at the brick patio. Shannon had hoped for a much smaller patio. This one was at least twenty by fifteen feet.

"Where was the key last time?" Shannon asked, her voice a whisper.

"I don't recall. We're going to have to get on our hands and knees," Chloe said. "Take it slow. Use your hands to feel every brick. I'm going to start over there. You start here."

Shannon did as Chloe said. *Haste makes waste*, the one thing she'd learned from Mr. Ferguson, she thought, as she used the tips of her fingers to try and wriggle each brick. She took her time, time they didn't have. Trey would begin to worry if she was gone for too long. She was on number twenty-seven when a brick came loose.

She felt butterflies in her stomach as she wriggled the brick free and set it to the side. She felt around inside the gap. Her palms were sweaty. Her fingers brushed over metal. Her heart pounded against her ribs. The key. After all this time, it was still in its hiding place. Shannon crawled over to Chloe and held the key up, in front of her face. "I found it!" Shannon felt a profound sense of triumph.

Chloe let out a squeal and then slapped her hand over her mouth. They threw their arms around each other and got to their feet. Once again, Shannon followed Chloe back the way they had come. They slipped through the gate, squeezed their way between the hedges and the front of the house. "Stay here," Chloe said. "When you see the door open, get inside as quickly as possible."

Shannon nodded and waited. They were so close, and yet so far. If the detectives hadn't been able to find any clues inside Rosella's desk, what made her think she could find something? The door came open. Bending over, she rushed inside. She could hardly believe they had made it this far without being seen.

"No lights," Shannon said.

Chloe nodded. "Hang tight to the railing as we head upstairs."

When they made it to the top of the landing, Shannon began to feel queasy. Images flickered through her mind like an old black-and-white film. Seeing Rosella slumped over her desk, all that blood, her finger twitching, and the gurgling sounds she'd made as she tried to tell Shannon something. Something important.

"Are you coming?" Chloe asked.

Shannon shook it off. She needed to keep going. As soon as she stepped into the office, she pointed at the brass statue on the desk. "There it is. The skeleton key."

Chloe slid the key off the statue, located the hole to the lock, and slipped the skeleton key into position. There was a small click. The center drawer opened.

The inside of the drawer was pitch black. Shannon turned on her phone and used the flashlight app to locate the lever. Without waiting for Chloe to tell her what to do, she tugged on it. A tiny drawer at the far right of the desk sprang open. Shannon peered into the small space but didn't see anything.

"Here!" Chloe whispered. Between a stash of unused envelopes was a small cord with a bronzed bead at the end. She pulled on it. A long whirring sound ensued, but no drawers or compartments sprang open. Shannon used the flashlight to look over the desk, but she couldn't find anything. And yet the whirring sound was the same noise she'd heard the day she'd turned away while Rosella fiddled with the desk.

"It has to be here somewhere." Shannon turned off the flashlight and slipped her phone into her back pocket. Blindly, as she had done with the bricks outside, she swept her fingertips over every nook and crevice until her fingers brushed over a small round piece of brass. She pressed down on it. Nothing happened.

Refusing to give up, she used both hands to feel around. Bingo!

There were two round discs, both cold to the touch. When she pressed down on both metal discs at the same time, another drawer, this one the length of the desk but only a quarter inch in height, came partially open.

"You did it!" Chloe whispered into her ear.

Shannon tugged gently on the face of the drawer until it slid all the way open. Inside was a single piece of paper, an article cut from a newspaper. Once again, Shannon used the flashlight from her iPhone to have a look. They leaned close, their heads touching as they read the newspaper clipping.

"What is this?" Chloe asked before she had finished reading. "Blake," she said, clearly disappointed. "What does this have to do with Blake?"

Shannon raised a hand to silence her. Rosella must have saved the article for a reason. She was meticulous. Shannon started from the beginning and read the article again, this time aloud, word for word. "Bradley Wilson," she said. "He was eighteen months old when he went missing on July 21, 2020. The mayor of Elk Grove continues to shed light on his disappearance. The boy was taken four years ago, vanishing from Oak Street in broad daylight on a weekday."

"Bradley," Chloe said. "July!"

Chills swept over Shannon as she continued to read. "His mom, single, died a year earlier of an overdose. Bradley was living with his grandmother, who had since passed on. The boy had an unusual birthmark shaped like butterfly wings on his leg. Oh my God!"

"What is it?" Chloe asked.

"Bradley *Wilson*. This whole time I thought Rosella's last words were *Willis* and *son*. She also said, *He's here.*" Goose bumps raced up her legs and arms. Shannon grasped Chloe's forearm. "The night you invited everyone over to discuss what happened to Rosella, Mac was watching over the smaller kids when Archer tripped and fell. When she lifted his pant leg to see if he was bleeding, she saw a pale-blue mark that looked like the wings of a butterfly."

"You think Archer might be Bradley Wilson?"

"I'm saying *he is* Bradley Wilson. How many little boys have a birthmark resembling a butterfly? Rosella was adamant when she said the Alcozars were hiding something. She was onto them."

A noise sounded somewhere on the first floor—a rustling, creaky sound.

Chloe grabbed her arm so tight it hurt. "Someone's trying to get inside. Did you lock the door?"

"I did," Shannon said. "Maybe that was a branch scraping across a window."

Chloe looked out the window across from her and shook her head. "There's no breeze."

"We need to hide." Shannon started for the closet, but Chloe grabbed her hand and pulled her along with her. They exited the office, hurried across the landing, and made their way into what appeared to be Rosella's primary bedroom. The curtains were pulled open, and moonlight poured in through the windows. Rosella's bedroom was massive. There was a fireplace set in stone, a hand-knotted, abstract wool rug, and a leather couch with a row of decorative pillows. Chloe dragged her across the room and into a walk-in closet the size of Shannon's own bedroom.

Shannon was about to question Chloe's idea to hide in such a wide-open space when Chloe reached behind a designer bag on the shelf above the shoes and pushed a button. There was a whirring sound as a solid wall of mahogany to their left began to slide open, revealing a ten-by-ten-foot room with a bar and a small couch. Chloe pulled her inside and quickly flicked the switch on the wall. They didn't say a word as the door began to close. Shannon's pulse jumped when she heard a loud crash from downstairs.

The article, Shannon thought. Had she left it on Rosella's desk or dropped it along the way? *Shit.* She slid her phone from her back pocket. There was no cell service. The reinforced walls were too thick. There was no intercom system or ham radio like she'd seen in a movie once. The house was built sometime in the early 1900s. They didn't have cell phones then, and nobody had bothered to update the safe room.

Chloe was scrambling around in the corner of the room, behind a small table.

"What are you doing?" Shannon asked.

"I found a safe, but I don't know the combination. Maybe there's a weapon inside. Maybe a gun."

"How did you know about this room?"

She continued fiddling with the safe as she talked. Shannon took a seat on the couch in order to hear her better.

"When Rosella and I were friends, I came to the house to pick her up for lunch. She said she had to grab something and disappeared upstairs. Fifteen minutes passed with no sign of her, so I headed up the stairs in search of her and heard frantic knocking. She had locked herself inside this room and had forgotten the code to get out." Chloe pointed toward the door. "She had the switch installed a few weeks later."

"I wish I had known Rosella back then."

"Yeah." After a few minutes, Chloe gave up trying to open the safe. She plunked down on the floor. "We have nothing to use to protect ourselves with."

Shannon held up her picklock, which resembled a small screwdriver. It could do some damage, she thought, if she held strong and stayed focused. "Whoever is out there could be harmless," she said. "Rosella's murder has been all over the media. Everyone knows the house is empty. Maybe they'll take a few things and run off."

"I hope you're right."

Shannon tried to pick the lock on the safe. It was no use. She sat down next to Chloe and gave her leg a reassuring pat. "We need to sit tight."

"I can't stop thinking about Blake." Chloe exhaled. "We wouldn't be here now if he hadn't confessed to something he didn't do. What was he thinking?"

"He was protecting Ridley."

Chloe sighed. "Ridley would never have killed Rosella. She's going through something, but she's my daughter and I know her better than anyone. She's hard on the outside and gooey soft inside."

They fell silent and listened.

"I don't hear anything," Chloe said.

Shannon nodded. "This will probably sound stupid, but if someone had asked me in the past few days who I would want to be stuck in a safe room with, it would have been you."

"Why me, for heaven's sake?"

Shannon shrugged. "When I first met you and the others, I felt an instant sense of belonging. A warm and welcoming feeling. With you especially."

Chloe smiled. "You're sweet. I felt the same way about you when we met. We have compatible personalities."

"I told Trey I felt a connection to you and the other women on the block. He believes it has something to do with my traumatic childhood." She shook her head. "I'm not so sure."

"What happened?" Chloe asked.

"Like millions of other babies, I was given up for adoption."

Chloe stiffened.

"It's okay," Shannon said, thinking Chloe was feeling bad for her. "Nobody wanted me, and I don't blame them. I was rebellious. I convinced every foster mom I was with that my bio mom was out there looking for me. I just wanted someone to help me find her."

Chloe paled. "You were never adopted?"

"At the age of thirteen, the Fergusons adopted me. I regret never calling Mrs. Ferguson 'Mom.' She didn't deserve that. I was sixteen when she died of cancer. Looking back, I should have moved out, but I was a minor and had nowhere else to go."

"What about Mr. Ferguson?"

"Mr. Ferguson fell apart. He began to drink. It got ugly, and he would come into my room late at night. I had to start locking my bedroom door. He died on the second anniversary of his wife's passing. Soon after, I reached out to Sierra Adoption Agency. I was twenty, too old to be pining for my mother." Shannon released a laugh tinged with bitterness. "I thought I could handle the truth. But the agency sent me a letter letting me know my bio mom was not interested in meeting me. The whole thing sort of messed with my head. I had Mac and Trey. I had my own family. I thought I had everything I needed, but then why didn't I ever feel whole?"

Shannon covered her hands with her face, unable to stop her emotions from getting the best of her. She'd never learned to find a way to simply be herself. And she thought she knew why: so many adoptees struggled with attachment issues—they became clingy, or they were distrustful and avoided people altogether. Because of this, Shannon walked on eggshells in her attempt to not be either of those things. She was aware of her sensitivity to rejection and abandonment, which was why she hadn't opened up to Trey until earlier. Her lifelong journey to search for her biological roots had caused her nothing but anxiety and apprehension.

Shannon lifted her head and wiped her eyes. "Lots of people were given up as babies and went on to lead amazing lives," she said to Chloe. "What is wrong with me?" She sighed. "I'm sorry. All of that was to say I'm glad we met, and I'm happy you're here with me now." She tried her best to regain some sense of composure. "I hope I haven't freaked you out."

Chloe hadn't said a word, which made Shannon start to feel even more uncomfortable. "Don't worry," Shannon told her. "I'm not the clingy type. I won't follow you around like a puppy dog after we get out of here."

"Do you know your birth date?"

"Yes. I was born on May 26, 1983."

Chloe swallowed.

A long stretch of silence followed. Had she upset Chloe?

"The agency contacted me when I was going through tough times," Chloe said as she stared at her hands in her lap. "Wesley was having an affair at the time. I was devastated."

Confusion settled around Shannon's shoulders like a scratchy blanket. "What agency?"

Chloe didn't answer, but she kept on talking. Shannon's brows furrowed. Chloe was obviously distraught, but why?

"I was fifteen years old," Chloe said, "when I gave birth to a beautiful little girl. The date was May 26, 1983."

Shannon's sharp intake of breath didn't stop Chloe from continuing with her story.

"One peek at her and I knew I couldn't give her away. I wanted to keep her." Chloe looked at Shannon, her gaze searching. For what? What was she saying?

"She was my own flesh and blood. She was mine. Nobody could take her from me. But my parents had paid a lot of money to make sure I didn't bring my baby home." Chloe was looking at her hands again. "I had a fit. I told every nurse who entered my room that I was keeping my baby. Nothing they could say would change my mind. Finally, a kind-looking nurse with gray hair and green eyes told me it was crucial they check the baby's heart rate and take measurements. She promised me she would bring her back. But she never did. And I never saw my daughter again."

The hairs on the back of Shannon's neck rose. She had been watching Chloe the entire time she was telling her story. For the first time since meeting her, Shannon saw the resemblance—the wider forehead and narrow chin. She thought of Blake, Ridley, and Rowan, all with the same heavy lower lip and turned-up nose as herself. Half siblings? Why hadn't she noticed the likeness before? This couldn't be happening. She wanted to pinch herself to make sure she wasn't dreaming. Her muscles tensed. "You're my mother, aren't you?"

"I believe so. Yes."

"It can't be true," Shannon said, the fog clearing from her head.

"But it is."

"This had to be Rosella's doing," Shannon said, her adrenaline surging. "This was her way of making you suffer, too."

"I'm not following."

"Rosella must have known you had given me up as a child." Shannon set her narrowed gaze on Chloe. "She knew, didn't she? She even did a write-up on the Sierra Adoption Agency."

"We did talk about it," Chloe said. "It was Rosella who brought it up. I was shocked that she knew."

Shannon's muscles tensed. "I think I know why Rosella went to all the trouble of finding me."

"I thought you said your professor had highly recommended you?"

"I talked to him. Rosella lied. The professor had never had a conversation with her about me." Shannon couldn't take her eyes off Chloe Leavitt. "You were right about one thing."

"What's that?" Chloe asked.

"Rosella Marlow didn't dislike you—she *despised* you. She must have known you didn't want to meet me. And after losing Daniel, she decided it might be interesting to find a way to bring me here and introduce us." Shannon did her thinking out loud as she tried to piece the puzzle together. "Rosella must have had access to the agency's files when she wrote the story. She must have seen the letter they sent to me letting me know you didn't want to meet me."

"It wasn't because I didn't want—"

Shannon talked over her, determined to finish her thought. "Rosella called me within months of losing her only son and asked me to work with her. After Caroline Baxter moved, Rosella contacted me again to let me know there was a house up for sale. A house on her block. A house two doors away from my long-lost mother," she said bitterly. Shannon couldn't take her eyes off Chloe as the cold, hard truth of the matter settled inside her. Heat rose to her face. "You told the agency you didn't want to meet me?"

Chloe said in a voice she could barely hear, "It was bad timing—"

Shannon's heart started beating fast. "You could have contacted the agency at any time, though. You could have changed your mind."

Chloe reached for her hand, but Shannon pulled away, unable to contain the urge to react impulsively, her anger building and getting the best of her. "You should know we're moving," Shannon lied. "We've already picked a house in Midtown, a stunning Victorian."

"You can't move now," Chloe said. "We've only just found each other."

Shannon balked. "*Found each other?* You have no idea what it's like to spend your life questioning your self-worth and your value as you wonder why someone would give you up and not even consider taking a call. What did you think I was going to do? Barge into your house and fuck up your perfect life? All I wanted was ten fucking minutes to say hello and hear your voice. That's all I wanted."

"I'm sorry. I never wanted to give you up. I wrote you letters. And I thought of you every day."

"Bullshit." Shannon pushed herself to her feet and slapped the dust off her pants. "I'm leaving." She jabbed a finger in Chloe's direction. "Don't worry about me, okay? I've made it this far without you. I'll be fine." She walked toward the switch she'd seen Chloe push earlier right as the door to the safe room came to life, whirring open on its own.

Shannon's eyes grew round. What was happening? She grabbed hold of the picklock and held it out in front of her.

Chloe jumped to her feet.

Standing on the other side was Nicolas Alcozar. The man had transformed from a preppy attorney with slicked-back hair and fashionable eyeglasses into a man with a crazed look in his eyes. His hair was disheveled, his clothes rumpled. In one hand was the newspaper clipping they had found in Rosella's desk. In the other was a gun.

Before he had a chance to point his weapon in their direction, Shannon lunged for him, gouging him in his side with the picklock. "Run!" she told Chloe.

Nicolas grabbed a fistful of Shannon's shirt as she tried to get past him. She kicked him hard in the chest, got as far as Rosella's bedroom door before she glanced back and saw that he had Chloe in a bear hug. Chloe bit his arm. He cried out, but she was unable to escape.

Shannon didn't think; she simply reacted, running toward them and trying to jab him again with the picklock. He jumped, stumbled, and ended up bringing Chloe to the ground with him. Her head made a sickening thump when it hit the floor.

Nicolas got to his feet, the gun still in his grasp. His gaze was locked on Shannon's as she sidestepped toward the fireplace, where she saw the wrought iron utensils out of the corner of her eye. She grabbed the poker and swung at the same time he fired a shot.

The poker hit the floor, clunking loudly as it rolled. Shannon had no idea who or what Nicolas had fired at until she felt a trickle of warmth running down her right arm.

Droplets of blood hit the floor.

She'd been shot.

Shock overrode any pain as her vision blurred. She thought she was hallucinating when a woman stepped into the bedroom. She was holding a gun, and it was aimed at Nicolas. "Drop the gun, Nicolas."

He pivoted fast. "Kaylynn. What are you doing? Put that down."

"It's over, Nicolas. I told you to take him back home. I begged you. But you wouldn't listen."

"Archer is our son. I'll never let them take him from us. Go home," he told her. "Now!"

Leaning against the wall near the window, holding the hole in her arm to try and stop the bleeding, Shannon noticed Chloe crawling toward the wrought iron poker.

Every muscle in Shannon's body quivered. Across from her, Chloe grabbed hold of the utensil, scrambled to her feet, drew back her arm, and swung straight and true, hitting Nicolas in the back. The gun flew from his grasp, clunked against the floor, and disappeared under the bed. Instead of going in search of the gun, Nicolas took two long strides before he reached his wife and swiped the gun out of her hands.

He turned toward Chloe, the barrel of the gun aimed at her head. One shot rang out.

"No!" Shannon called, her heart sinking.

The thought of losing Chloe, the mother she'd been searching for her entire life, made her legs turn to mush as she melted to the floor. It was her fault Chloe was here, her stupid plan to break into Rosella's house. With her back against the wall, Shannon's gaze fell on Nicolas. He teetered on wobbly legs as if trying to catch his balance. What was going on? He pivoted slightly before falling forward, his body as stiff as a newly cut tree. The sound of his head striking the corner of the stone mantel was nauseating. His legs buckled and he toppled to the ground.

Shannon didn't understand what had happened until she saw Jason standing inside the bedroom, legs set, gun drawn. He'd shot Nicolas.

"I never loaded my gun," Kaylynn said before she rushed to her husband's side and dropped to the floor so she could cradle his head in her lap. "Don't leave me, Nicolas. I'm sorry. I just wanted it to stop."

"I called the police," Jason said. "Right after hearing the first shot fired. Who got hit?"

Chloe was fine, Shannon realized when the woman came to her aid. Chloe pulled her bloodied sleeve up in order to see the wound. "Shannon's been hit." Chloe pointed to the bed. "I need the bedsheet."

Jason made quick work of pulling off the sheet. He used his teeth to rip the cloth into wide strips, the two of them working together to stanch the blood. By the time the police arrived, Jason was watching over Kaylynn and Nicolas, checking for a pulse. He made eye contact with Shannon and shook his head.

CHAPTER THIRTY-FOUR

It was the third day since she'd been released from the hospital. Shannon had been lucky—the bullet had gone through her upper arm cleanly, missing bone and nerves. Trey had been notified and had met her at the hospital, insisting she stay overnight. Medical staff took X-rays, cleaned the wounds, and hooked her up to an IV to administer antibiotics and medications. She was released the next morning.

Things could have turned out much differently. Her arm was in a sling. She felt stiff and sore, and there wasn't much she could do but sit and think. Mostly about Chloe being her mom. Despite the horrible loss she'd felt when Nicolas had aimed his gun at Chloe, Shannon was still pissed off. She couldn't help it; she'd been rejected twice by the woman.

To make matters worse, Chloe Leavitt had been spending a lot of time with Mac, making sure she got to and from school and did her homework. Chloe came over every chance she got, bringing hot meals for the entire family, making sure everyone was eating and getting plenty of rest. Acting as if she were a mother-of-the-year contender!

There was a knock on the door. Shannon didn't budge. She knew it wasn't Trey because she had just talked to him on the phone. And Mac would be in school for another hour.

The door came open and she heard Chloe's voice. "Hello. Is anyone home?"

Shannon tossed the book she'd been reading and heaved herself off the couch. Red-hot pain shot up her arm, making her wince. She headed for the door, livid. Sure enough, Chloe was walking right into her home. "What are you doing here? Did Mac leave the door unlocked?"

"Trey gave me a key," Chloe said, "in case there was an emergency and someone needed to get inside."

Shannon grunted. When Trey had found out that Chloe was her biological mother, he'd been delighted. *You found her!* But then Shannon explained how angry that made her. Chloe had given her up not once, but twice. Shannon wanted nothing to do with her. Trey felt she just needed time, but Shannon wouldn't listen.

"There is no emergency. Please leave." Shannon tried to use her arm to gesture toward the door. A searing pain coursed through her.

With concern lining her face, Chloe came rushing toward her, cradling a shoebox. "What is it? Do you need to go to the ER?"

Shannon wasn't falling for the frantic act. "Why are you doing this?"

"Doing what?" Chloe asked.

"Pretending to care about me and trying so hard to be my mother, when we both know you suck as a parent. You're my bio mom, the person I thought would change my world and make me whole again. It's inconceivable."

"Why?"

"Because you being my mom is a joke," Shannon said, going for the dagger and driving deep. "We both know you can hardly take care of the three kids you have at home. What makes you think you have room for me, too?" Shannon's phone buzzed. She walked back to the living room, where her phone was, and saw that Trey was calling again. She picked up the call.

"I thought you might want to know your mother is on her way over."

"She's not my mother. And she's already here. Did you really give her a key?"

Trey said, "I was worried about you being home alone."

"Have you talked to the contractor about making those changes to our new house in Midtown?" Shannon asked, sticking to the lie she'd already told Chloe about her plans to move—something she and Trey had not discussed.

"What are you talking about?" he asked.

"Wonderful," Shannon said, as if he'd responded to her question. "A new house. A new—"

"I get what you're doing," Trey said. "You might want to know that Chloe asked me about our plans to move. I set her straight. She knows we didn't buy a house in Midtown."

"Thanks a lot," Shannon said. "I have to go. I love you. Goodbye."

"I'll see you tonight. Give her a chance," he said before hanging up.

Shannon put her phone on the coffee table. Chloe was staring at her. "I wanted to buy a house in Midtown," Shannon said, unable to let the fabrication go. "It was a purple Victorian on Nineteenth Street, but someone else got it. Fuckers."

"I know you're angry at me," Chloe said. "I get it. I do."

Shannon looked away, her gaze settling on the wall.

"My reluctance to meet you was a mistake. It was never a reflection of my feelings toward you, but rather my own fears and uncertainties. I was wrong to have closed myself off to the possibility of meeting you. I deeply regret it. Please," Chloe said, taking one step closer. "I apologize for any hurt or disappointment my actions caused." She swallowed. "I do hope you can find a way to forgive me and we can start over."

Although the speech sounded rehearsed, some of the tension in Shannon's shoulders left her. "Please go," she said, turning toward the window overlooking Forty-Fifth Street, not wanting Chloe to see her eyes welling and her heart melting. Shannon had wanted to hurt Chloe just as Rosella had wanted to hurt everyone in the neighborhood. For the first time since she'd come to live here, she knew how Rosella might have felt. Frustrated. Angry. Alone.

Footsteps sounded as Chloe made her way to the kitchen before heading for the door. Shannon didn't look up until she heard the door click shut. She sank back onto the couch, wiped her eyes, and didn't bother to get up when she saw the shoebox sitting on the kitchen island.

———

Shannon took a pain pill after Chloe left and went to bed. Two hours later, she heard someone enter the house. It had to be Mac, since it was that time of day. She climbed out of bed.

"Have you read these?" Mac asked as Shannon made her way downstairs.

"No. What is it?"

"Letters. Lots of them."

Shannon stopped at the landing, where she noticed Mac pull a letter from the shoebox Chloe had left. Chloe had been bringing food over for days now, and Shannon had assumed the box was filled with more baked goods.

"I think these are from Nana," Mac said as she slid a letter from its envelope.

Shannon frowned. "Who's Nana?"

Mac stared at Shannon, unblinking, until suddenly her shoulders sagged and her expression softened. "You really are upset with Chloe, aren't you?"

"I am."

"Dad and I thought you would be so excited to have found your biological mom." Mac sighed. "I don't think I ever stopped to imagine how difficult it must have been for you growing up without a stable family." Mac's head tilted slightly. "I admire you so much for everything you've overcome and for the amazing person you are. I know it's not easy for you to talk about your past, but I want you to know that I love you, and I'm so grateful to have you as my mom."

Shannon's eyes welled as Mac came to her and hugged her good side.

When Mac pulled away, she said, "I won't talk about Chloe anymore. I don't need to go over there after school, either."

Shannon wiped her eyes. "It's okay. I'll be fine. We'll get through this."

Mac looked down at the letter in her hand. "What are these letters?" she asked.

"I don't know."

Mac started reading aloud:

> My Dearest Daughter,
> I have written to you so many times over the years, wishing I could explain myself. I was fifteen when I gave birth to you. I didn't want to give you away. My parents forced me to leave school for a year and gave me no choice but to hand you over to the Sierra Adoption Agency. When you were sixteen, I was thirty-one and getting married, and I called the agency in hopes of learning more about your life. They assured me that you had a childhood filled with joy and security and were living your best life.
>
> Four years later, the agency reached out to tell me you wanted to meet. I panicked. I had just miscarried after learning of my husband's infidelity. And yet as I write this, it sounds hollow . . . like an excuse. The truth is, I was afraid to meet you. Afraid of the unknown. Afraid of the questions you might ask and the disappointment I might see in your eyes. I was afraid of dredging up so many painful memories of the

past. Afraid to tell my husband since he didn't know about you. I was afraid of being judged. Afraid of how you would fit into a life I was struggling to build.

It wasn't until my older children reached the age of fifteen that I thought more of how the adoption might have impacted your life. It seemed suddenly like yesterday that I was fifteen myself, navigating the difficult journey that took me from child to adult. I remembered how confusing the teenage years could be. How they can make you question yourself, make you wonder what your future holds. I began to worry you might have grown up feeling lost and that maybe you wondered at times why the woman who gave birth to you not only gave you away but also refused to meet you.

When I do finally muster the courage to make the call that I should have made twenty years ago, my hope is I'm not too late and that you'll give me the chance to be in your life in whatever form is comfortable for you.

Your Mother

Shannon was speechless, overwhelmed with emotion. She felt deprived of air.

Mac riffled through the box. "It looks like she wrote you a bunch of letters." She slipped the letter into the envelope and put it back inside the box. She brought the shoebox to Shannon. "I think you should read these." After a short pause, Mac said, "Do you remember the quote you read to me when I was super mad at Dad for not letting me go camping with my friend?"

"You were only eight."

"Well, you told me the same quote more than once: 'The weak can never forgive. Forgiveness is the attribute of the strong.' It's a quote by Mahatma Gandhi."

Rolling her eyes, Shannon took the box and headed back upstairs, where she went to her bedroom and shut the door. Sitting on a cushioned chaise near the window where the sunlight poured into the room, she found a letter written on her first birthday and began to read.

CHAPTER THIRTY-FIVE

Three weeks after Shannon found Rosella slumped over her desk in her office, a funeral was held for Rosella Marlow at the East Lawn Memorial Park. No words were said before her casket was lowered into the ground. Rosella had bought the plot thirty years ago, at the same time she bought her husband's. From the looks of it, the staff at East Lawn Memorial Park had gone to a lot of trouble to excavate and exhume Lance Marlow's body. The ground right next to Rosella's plot was no longer level, and wooden planks covered the deep hole where her husband's casket had been put to rest fifteen months ago.

A dozen people Shannon didn't recognize had come to watch Rosella's casket being lowered into the ground. Also in attendance were Chloe and Rowan, because Chloe had made a promise to her son. Trey and Mac stood next to Shannon. Jason and Dianne had also come. It might have seemed strange to some if they knew the man who despised Rosella and who nine days ago shot a man in Rosella's bedroom stood among them. But Jason Abbott had purposely aimed for Nicolas's leg, never intending to kill him. He'd only wanted to stop Nicolas from harming anyone else.

Nobody had known Kaylynn's gun wasn't even loaded. And how could Jason have known Nicolas would pivot and fall at the precise angle necessary for his head to hit the sharp corner of the stone mantel? Nicolas had ruptured an artery and suffered what the doctors called an epidural hematoma; he had bled quickly, which exerted pressure on the brain and proved fatal.

When Shannon had found out there was a bite mark on Nicolas's arm, she'd felt a mix of emotions. Detective Seicinski had written in her report that Nicolas Alcozar, afraid of being found out, had attacked Mac in the park, hoping he would frighten her enough to stop Shannon and Chloe from continuing with their probe. How sad to think the man had felt the need to attack a child in order to protect his own.

Shannon was thankful Mac was okay but insisted her daughter speak to an online therapist once a week. Experiencing a traumatic event could lead to a range of emotional responses, making it difficult for her daughter to feel safe and comfortable in public spaces.

As far as Shannon was concerned, there were two loose ends in the investigation. One being a piece of information never brought to Detective Seicinski's attention—the torn bit of cloth Shannon had discovered on the broken fragment of wood within the entrance to the living room. Nothing warranted bringing it to anyone's attention, Shannon decided. Chloe hadn't mentioned it, so she let it be. The other loose end was the note Rosella had found in her mailbox. Shannon couldn't think of any reason why Nicolas would have left such a note for Rosella, and for now, she decided it was best if she let it go. But she did have a question for Holly.

The casket stopped moving downward. It was over.

Chloe grabbed a fistful of dirt and tossed it onto Rosella's casket. The rest of the people in attendance did the same as a show of solidarity. There would be another funeral in the coming days for Nicolas Alcozar. Shannon and Chloe had been spending a lot of time with Kaylynn. In fact, Holly, Becky, and Dianne had joined them in helping Kaylynn get through this trying time. They were working on raising money to help her with legal fees and living expenses since there was no way she could afford to support the boys on her meager income. Kaylynn appreciated the help until she could figure out what to do next.

Holiday's mother had contacted him the other day to see whether he wanted to move in with her and her new boyfriend, but he'd told her he'd rather live with Kaylynn and Archer if Kaylynn would have him. Kaylynn was happy he wanted to stay. Although nobody knew the legalities of what would happen with Archer, for now, she kept both her boys close.

When they were done, their little group from Forty-Fifth Street, made up of seven people, headed back to the Leavitt house, where everyone else was waiting. When they arrived at Chloe's home, Becky and Holly were there with their two children. The two women had been working hard to stay together, Becky bending over backward to please Holly, which seemed to be working.

Becky played with the kids while Holly set up the trays of food Chloe had ordered from Mother, a restaurant on K Street. Today, in Rosella's honor, they would be feasting on lasagna, collard greens, mushroom Bolognese, and oyster and mushroom po'boy sandwiches. When Becky left the kitchen, Shannon went to speak with Holly. "Holly," she said. "Thanks for doing all of this."

"Glad I could help." Holly looked her over. "How's your arm?"

"A little stiff, but I'm doing well." Shannon shifted from one foot to the other. "I have a question for you. It's been keeping me up at night."

Holly stopped working and met her gaze. "What is it?"

"Your fingerprints were found on the murder weapon, and I was curious as to why."

Holly made sure nobody else was around before she said, "I was hoping nobody would ask."

"I'm sorry."

Holly sighed. "I was there at Rosella's house before you came. That's when I must have lost the mask I had hooked to my wrist. I went upstairs to find Rosella and talk to her. She was sprawled on top of her desk—blood everywhere. When I heard her say, *Help*, I knew she was still alive." Holly inhaled a shaky breath.

Shannon remained still, her heart beating fast.

"I told Rosella I would call for help if she answered my question: Was she the one who sent the complaints about me to CDPH?" Holly wiped her hands on the small towel she was holding and said, "Rosella told me very bluntly, as if it were of no consequence, that it was her." Holly closed her eyes tight. "I wrapped my fingers around the letter opener with the intention of driving it deeper. I hated that woman. The hatred I felt clouded my judgment and made me irrational. And I knew it, which is why I didn't do it. I released my hold on the letter opener and ran. I ran as fast as I could. I'm not proud of it. The thought that maybe I could have saved her will never leave me. I regret what I did, but I can't change the past." She glanced over her shoulder again. "I haven't told Becky or anyone else. And I don't plan to."

"Understood," Shannon said. She wanted to tell Holly how much she appreciated her honesty, but Holly turned back to what she'd been doing before Shannon had interrupted.

Shannon walked away, leaving her alone. Every nerve ending felt numb as she made her way back to the main room. She was grateful to Holly for answering her question, but she found it unsettling to acknowledge that Rosella's maliciousness had such a profound effect on so many. The damage she'd caused the community was hard to swallow.

When she entered the living room and saw Wesley talking to Ridley, she felt awkward. Chloe had mentioned Wesley had called to ask if he could come today; she'd told him it was fine as long as he didn't drink or make a scene—those were the rules. Shannon didn't know the man, but she had seen firsthand the hurt he'd caused not only his family but also Holly, and she didn't know what to think of him. Maybe he wondered about her, too, after hearing Chloe was Shannon's biological mother.

Shannon and Chloe had talked for hours since Shannon had read all the letters. Each one had been meaningful, happy, and sad. Despite the initial hurt she'd felt upon realizing Chloe hadn't wanted to meet her, she was beginning to understand what her mother had gone through. Shannon wasn't the only one who had struggled. In spite of everything Rosella had done, Chloe and Shannon were thankful to the journalist for bringing them together. Nobody would ever know what Rosella's endgame had been. Had her plan involved setting Shannon against Chloe before dropping the bomb?

Shannon picked up a flute of champagne from a tray. Blake was coming downstairs. He stopped before he got to the landing, frowning as he asked in a voice loud enough for the roomful of guests to hear, "Is this a celebration of Rosella's life?"

Everyone grew quiet.

It was Rowan who spoke first, his voice cracking. "Yes," he said. "She was nice to me, and I liked her."

Cute little Archer stepped forward and stood close to Rowan. "I liked her, too."

Everyone looked at Kaylynn, who merely shrugged as if to say, "Each to their own."

A few halfhearted cheers sounded, and everyone raised their glasses and then took a sip of champagne or punch.

Shannon couldn't keep her eyes off Blake. Although many days had passed since his arrest, it was good to see him home where he belonged. And it was difficult not to stare. He was her half sibling. Same with Ridley and Rowan. It would take some time for all of them to get used to it. Except for Mac, who was thrilled to now officially be part of a large family, something she'd always longed for.

The sound of the doorbell had Chloe rushing to the door, already back to being the perfect hostess. It surprised everyone but Shannon to realize Chloe had invited Detective Seicinski and Detective Toye. After asking Rowan to please take Ethan and Archer to the playroom and turn on cartoons, Chloe handed each detective a glass of champagne. "Is there anything either of you would like to say?" she asked. "Anything at all?"

"Don't worry," Detective Toye said to all in an unusual moment of friendliness. "Nobody is under arrest."

Laughter erupted, along with a few forced chuckles.

"We stopped by to let you know," Detective Seicinski said, "we were given the go-ahead to exhume Lance Marlow's body, and the results have come back."

Dianne moved closer, eager to hear what the detectives had to say. She had decided to talk to the detectives a while back, telling them everything she had witnessed of Rosella's treatment of Lance Marlow while he was in the hospital. During another sweep of Rosella's house, the detectives had found more than a dozen nonfiction books all having to do with wives killing their husbands. Inside the books were highlighted sections and notes in Rosella's handwriting. Tucked inside *Before He Wakes* by Jerry Bledsoe was a printed list of books from Goodreads, titled "True Crime—Wife Killing Husband."

"An autopsy was done," Detective Seicinski said. "Lance Marlow died of asphyxiation and not of complications from the accident."

"Does that mean what I think it means?" Jason asked.

Dianne nodded. "Rosella killed him."

"We're celebrating the life of a murderer?" Blake asked, obviously still angry with Rosella for causing him and everyone else so much grief. "This party is lame."

Chloe went to her son and whispered in his ear. When she noticed the detectives already heading out, she went after them, took hold of Detective Toye's thick arm, and led him back to the table laden with food. "At least take a sandwich for the road."

While they each selected a sandwich and a cookie to go, Shannon approached the table and asked, "What happens now?" What could they do, she wondered, to a dead murderer?

Detective Seicinski shrugged. "There won't be a trial. No criminal charges, either. Our commanding officer could decide to make an announcement, but it's unlikely."

"And from a civil perspective," Detective Toye said, "there's nobody left to sue Rosella Marlow's estate for damages."

Shannon checked to make sure Kaylynn wasn't within earshot. "What about Kaylynn Alcozar? What's going to happen to her and Archer?"

"Kaylynn is sticking to her original story. She didn't know her husband kidnapped Bradley Wilson," Detective Toye said.

Detective Seicinski must have noticed Chloe's and Shannon's confusion, because she added, "According to Kaylynn, Nicolas told her he had a one-night stand with a woman at the office where he used to work. Eighteen months later, the woman was diagnosed with stage 4 cancer, and she asked Nicolas to take care of the baby."

"Makes sense," Chloe said, but Shannon could tell she was going along with the story because she didn't want Kaylynn to get in trouble.

Detective Seicinski shrugged. "Kaylynn Alcozar is a smart woman who has hired one of the best criminal attorneys in the state. She is the only mother the boy has ever known, at least that he remembers. He has no family, no aunts or uncles. Nobody knows who the father is or was. If Archer is taken from Kaylynn, he'll be put in foster care."

"That would be a shame," Chloe said.

Detective Seicinski heaved a weary sigh, making Shannon wonder if the woman might finally get a chance to sleep. "In the end," the detective said, "it will depend on the judge's ruling. Kaylynn is not viewed as a flight risk, so for now, the boy stays with her."

Shannon's gaze was now focused on Mac and her husband, who was whispering in their daughter's ear, making her laugh about something. A few feet away, she spotted Kaylynn running after Archer, who'd grabbed two cupcakes from the tray instead of one. Finally, her eyes settled on Chloe, who was now walking the detectives to the door. Instantaneously, Shannon felt something she hadn't expected to feel: a profound sense of accomplishment, a quiet pride in having worked with her mom to unravel clues and secrets to form a coherent picture that had once seemed impossibly out of reach.

The mystery had been solved.

Nicolas Alcozar, a young man who had never been spanked as a child, who did well in school and didn't know the humiliation of being called to the principal's office, a man who had never before had trouble with the law, had come home early one Thursday afternoon only to discover, without anyone being the wiser, that his wife and son had been visiting Rosella Marlow. He'd known then, had felt a deep conviction and understanding based on past experiences with Rosella, that she was onto him. She'd known Archer had once gone by the name Bradley Wilson.

But had she known, he pondered in his writing to Kaylynn, that the boy had shown signs of abuse? He hadn't kidnapped Bradley Wilson, he wrote. He had saved him—given the boy a chance at living his best life. And yet he also knew it hadn't been his choice to make. So he'd done the only thing he could think of to protect his family: he had killed Rosella. Once he discovered Chloe Leavitt and Shannon Gibbons hoped to uncover the mystery of Forty-Fifth Street, he'd felt trapped, panicked, and determined to leave no loose ends. He was deeply entrenched by then.

Shannon knew all this because she had seen the letter Nicolas had left for Kaylynn, detailing what had happened in the event things didn't go well, which they did not. His written message began with Nicolas declaring his love for his wife and ended with his apologies for causing her and the boys so much pain and disappointment. After Kaylynn showed Shannon and Chloe the letter, they followed her outside and watched her put a match to it, saw it turn to ashes within the firepit Nicolas had built out of stone.

In this fleeting moment of clarity and resolution Shannon was experiencing, she allowed herself to bask in the satisfaction of a job well done. The mystery may have been solved, but the memories of the journey, the lessons learned, and the friendships forged along the way would stay with her forever. And it wouldn't be long, she thought, before her life would go back to the mundane routines of everyday life.

Or would it?

Despite Rosella's flaws, Shannon was grateful for the woman's impact on her life, whether her intent had been a positive one or not. Reflecting on Rosella's life and the choices she'd made, the good and the bad, allowed Shannon to think about the nature of forgiveness, the complexities of human behavior, and the chance she had now to live her life to its fullest.

From across the room, Trey winked at her. She smiled back at him and found herself wondering what new mysteries awaited. Filled with determination and a newfound sense of freedom, she stood poised, ready to conquer the world, knowing the best was yet to come.

CHAPTER
THIRTY-SIX

It was late February, not yet spring, and Shannon was walking to Dianne's when she stopped to take a good long look around the neighborhood. She'd never been happier. Even Trey had come around and thought of their neighbors as family. From where she stood, she could see Chloe's house. She would never refer to Chloe as "Mom" or "Mother," but inwardly, in her heart, that's how she thought of her. Not only as her best friend but also as her mom, the woman who had birthed her.

She and Chloe saw each other every day. They walked Carlin, the cute little Frenchie who was fond of nipping strangers. Shannon and Chloe went to hot yoga together and baked and spent time with the kids. Mostly, they talked about everything, details about their lives, the positives and the negatives, catching up on all the lost years.

Standing outside Dianne's house, she was about to go inside and help with the posters Holly needed for the yearly nonperishable food drive. Her gaze fell on Rosella's beautiful home. Everything Rosella had owned had been removed from the house months ago. Her house was tall and regal, exuding an air of vigilant guardianship over all the other homes. Even so, she had not won the competition. The Best House on the Block award had gone to Mr. and Mrs. Knightley. The winner had been announced a few days after Rosella's funeral. Chloe said she didn't care about winning or losing. She even admitted to submitting her home for consideration simply to goad Rosella. Every time Shannon walked past Rosella's house and noticed the enormous windows on the top floor, she saw in her mind's eye Rosella standing there, peering through binoculars.

The arched door of the blue cottage with the diamond-shaped glass in the windows came open. Dianne waved. "Come on in," she said. "Get out of the cold."

Shannon made her way inside. The kids were in school. Jason was at work. It was quiet. Peaceful. They hugged. Dianne guided her to the kitchen and poured her a cup of coffee. After a bit of small talk, they refilled their cups and went to the dining room table, where Dianne had laid out paper and pens. It wasn't until Shannon took a seat and set her coffee on the coaster that she noticed the poster Dianne had already made. Huge, capitalized letters. Red letters. Next to the poster was a pack of seven acrylic paint pens, minus the red marker resting near the poster. The marker used was the same color and texture as the one utilized to write *I know what you did*—the note Rosella had received in her mailbox.

Dianne must have noticed the surprise on Shannon's face because she kept looking from Shannon to the poster to the red marker. "You saw the note?" she finally asked, appearing deflated.

"Yes. Rosella showed it to me. Did you write it?"

"I did." She straightened her spine, as if to show defiance. As if she had no regrets. "I did it because I knew Rosella had been watching everyone in the neighborhood. Jason and I saw her on multiple occasions with those binoculars held up to her eyes while she stared out her office window. I was tired of her spying and judging every one of us. I strongly suspected her of killing Lance. I decided to show her what it felt like to be watched, and to let her know someone out there knew she had secrets, too."

Something else dawned on Shannon. "I have a question."

Dianne waited.

"You confessed to being the person who tried to break into Rosella's basement, so were you also the one watching her from afar?"

"No. That was Becky. She was pissed off about the complaints Holly was getting at the hospital. She and I talked about it. I told Becky I was going to leave a note for Rosella in hopes of giving her a taste of her own medicine. Becky wanted to help, so she started dressing in all black and watching Rosella whenever she would see her standing at the window. Neither of us are proud of what we did. Rosella went out of her way to make our lives miserable, and we wanted to return the favor." Dianne shook her head. "I'd never encountered anyone like Rosella Marlow before."

Shannon was stunned. Nearly everyone in the neighborhood, it seemed, had had a hand in trying to make Rosella uncomfortable. Rosella hadn't been paranoid after all. "Chloe told me it was you who reported Rosella to the director at Sutter Hospital."

"Yes. Twice. During Lance's stay and after he passed away. Lance was in a coma when they brought him to the hospital. By the third day, they took him off life support." She reached across the table and grabbed hold of Shannon's arm. "Because he was getting better every day. I wasn't the only one who saw his eyes twitch. I knew it was only a matter of time before he woke up. We all knew. Lance Marlow's attending physician was thrilled to give Rosella the good news. And after the doctor left the room, guess what she did? She leaned low and whispered into her husband's ear, told him he killed their son and didn't deserve to live. The next day, when I returned from lunch, I saw Rosella exit the hospital and head for the parking lot. When I walked out of the elevator and heard the alarms going off, I knew. Before I even walked into Lance Marlow's room, I knew he was dead."

"Why didn't the hospital inform the police?"

"I'm not sure," Dianne said, "but I do know that Rosella contributed significant funds to the hospital. If I want to keep my job, it's best I leave it at that."

Shannon didn't know what to say, except, "I'm sorry, Dianne, for everything you and Jason have been put through. I'm sorry for everybody on the block, including Lance Marlow. And I'm sorry for Rosella, too. After her son died it seems she snapped and lost all sense of reality."

Dianne nodded, her eyes downcast. "Rosella did pay the ultimate price for her actions."

Silence hung between them before Dianne asked, "Did you hear the news yesterday?"

"What news?"

"The judge ruled in favor of Archer staying with Kaylynn. She can start the adoption process."

"That's wonderful." It was a miracle. Truly a miracle, because Shannon and Chloe knew something no one else did. When they were inside Rosella's bedroom, before Nicolas fell and hit his head on the mantel, Kaylynn had said, *"It's over, Nicolas. I told you to take him back home. I begged you. But you wouldn't listen."*

Kaylynn had known exactly what her husband had done.

But no one needed to know. There was no family to return Archer to. Kaylynn loved her son more than anything. She was a good mother, and Chloe and Shannon never talked about what they had overheard. They didn't need to, because like many mothers and daughters, whether biological or adopted, they were linked by the strongest bond of all.

EPILOGUE

The sunlight forced its way through wispy clouds, casting a warm, golden glow across the beach. A gentle breeze whispered through the air, carrying the scent of water and damp earth along with the faint tang of sunscreen. It was mid-April, the air chilly whenever the clouds hovered for too long. But Chloe had wanted to get away for a few days, spend time with her kids before the school year ended.

Blake and Rowan threw a Frisbee, playing with boundless energy. They laughed and shouted joyfully as they tossed it back and forth. They looked happy and carefree.

Ridley stood at the water's edge, the cool water reaching her toes. A boy with his little sister in tow stopped to chat. Then he handed Ridley something. It was a rock. With the flick of his wrist, a stone in his hand skipped across the surface of the water, sending outward ripples. Ridley watched him throw another rock before she gave it a try. Her stone skipped and hopped. His little sister jumped up and down excitedly. For the first time in more than a year, Ridley's laughter rang out, her animated gestures and bright smile a stark contrast to the melancholy that had shrouded her since Daniel's passing.

Chloe watched her daughter chat with the boy. He was an inch taller than Blake, and he had a boyish face. Chloe guessed his age to be the same as Ridley's. They were only a short distance away, and Chloe took joy in the way the sunlight peeked through the clouds and caught her daughter's profile. She felt a renewed sense of hope stirring within her. Despite all the obstacles they had faced, witnessing her daughter's joy filled her with a sense of gratitude and optimism.

The serene surroundings of Lake Tahoe were a fitting backdrop for reflections on life, with all its trials and tribulations, twists and turns, the challenges of divorce, the profound bond she shared with Shannon and Mac, and knowing that beyond every bend were new hurdles and opportunities. It was moments like this that Chloe had been missing. She had always been running from one thing to the next, her life a blur until now; the laughter of loved ones and the beauty of nature reminded her that life was a delicate balance.

Only one thing was missing.

"Look, Mom," Rowan shouted from across the way. He pointed at the row of pines and redwoods hiding the small parking lot behind her. Chloe shifted in her beach chair, surprised to see Shannon and Mac.

They had made it after all.

With a glance heavenward, Chloe sent thanks to Rosella for taking matters into her own hands and illuminating a path she had never thought she'd tread, leading her to exactly where she needed to be. She stood, brushed the sand off her, and opened her arms wide.

ACKNOWLEDGMENTS

I am forever grateful to Cathy Katz, sister extraordinaire, without whom I am certain I would not be an author of eighteen thrillers and multiple other novels. You are heaven sent, the person who has always made me feel loved and seen. Thank you. Thank you. Thank you.

I am also immensely grateful to my agent, Amy Tannenbaum, for her unwavering support and encouragement over the years. Thank you, Amy, for your expertise and tireless advocacy on my behalf!

Much appreciation goes to Liz Pearsons. What an incredible journey this has been. Thank you, Liz!

I always feel lucky to have the opportunity to work with Charlotte Herscher. Thank you for your skillful developmental editing and for your flexibility and kindness.

Shout out to Charlene Ragan for spending hours with me as we scribbled notes and somehow came up with the perfect ending for *BHOTB*!

Another person who has assisted me in so many ways over the years is my daughter and friend, Morgan Ragan. What a blessing you are! I had no idea you could brainstorm a novel and whip up amazing charts and lists and graphs to help me piece together so many quirky characters so I could see how this novel might just work after all.

Dillon Yuhasz, I am beyond grateful for your notable help with generating ideas and coming up with solutions on how I might thicken the plot and give my characters the motivation they needed! Thank you for providing me with the kind of intense and thorough brainstorming that made my head spin with possibilities. You are the reason I was able to finish this book. Thank you.

Much love and endless thanks to Joe Ragan, who is always ready to help me out with new scene ideas and/or finding the perfect bit of dialogue. You are my rock, my shoulder to lean on, my everything.

Lastly, to my readers: Thank you for choosing my novels to escape with. You're the best!